# MOTHER SHUCKER

## Sibby Series Book III

## SAMANTHA GARMAN

Tabula Rasa Publishing

*For Franklin B. Ashley*

## Disclaimer

No hormones were normal during the course of this pregnancy.

## Chapter 1

Lox: [laks]

    1. Smoked or cured salmon, usually thinly sliced.

    2. First comes the toasted bagel and a nice schmear. Add a hefty amount of lox, top it off with sliced onion, tomato, and capers. Squeeze a lemon over the top to bring out the salmon flavor. Take a *big* bite.

    3. Congrats, you just became an old Long Island Jew.

    "Okay, now let's talk about the perineal massage," Shana said, holding a plastic baby under her arm like a football.

"Let's not," I voiced. "Some things should stay in the bedroom…"

A couple of people in our birthing class sniggered.

Shana glared in my direction, expecting it to silence me.

I clamped my lips shut and Aidan put his hand on my thigh. I chanced a look at him. His eyes were trained on our class instructor, but I saw his ears turning red as he attempted to hold in his laughter.

"Sibby," Shana said with a lamenting sigh, "what did I say?"

"That I was supposed to keep my thoughts to myself," I repeated, like a kindergartener being chastised.

"And have you done that?"

"No."

She held up her index finger. "First, we watched a birthing video, and when the baby was coming out of its mother, *you* likened it to a scene in *Aliens.* Then, when you saw a baby in the video still in its amniotic sac, you made the cry of an orc from *Lord of the Rings*."

"Oh come on, it tore through the membrane like a Tolkien character!" I looked around, expecting someone to agree with me. But no one would meet my eyes.

"Sibby," Aidan whispered, "don't argue."

Clearly Shana wasn't done publicly listing my transgressions because she put her hand on her hip and went on. "When we broke up into groups, you were supposed to write down your biggest fears. And what did you do?"

"I might've drawn a pornographic sketch…" I looked at my lap. "Yeah, probably not one of my finer moments."

"And now I want to discuss perineal massage—something that will legitimately help you all as you go through labor—and *you* won't take it seriously. I'm sorry, Sibby, but I'm going to have to ask you to leave."

My head whipped up and my jaw dropped. "I'm being kicked out?"

"You're clearly not taking this seriously and the rest of the class is. You're disruptive and frankly, you're acting like a frat guy."

"Awesome!"

"It wasn't a compliment!" she snapped. She pointed to the door. "Go."

"But—"

"GO! You too, Aidan."

"Wha—what did I do?" he demanded, looking offended.

"You didn't keep your wife quiet."

"Keep his wife quiet?" I repeated.

"Oh boy," Aidan muttered.

I rose slowly. Not for any dramatic reason, but because I was physically struggling to get out of the chair.

"Fine. I'll leave," I said, tossing my hair over my shoulder. "I'll find another class with a sense of humor."

I stomped through the open doorway, belatedly realizing that I'd forgotten to grab my winter coat and bag. There was no way I was going back in there. I'd rather freeze.

The door opened and Aidan met me in the hallway. Thankfully, he'd gathered my belongings.

"You were ready to rumble," Aidan said, holding my coat out to me.

I slid my arms into it and zipped the coat closed. "She started it, but I ended it."

"She didn't start it. *You* started it. And you didn't end it. She did because she kicked us out."

"We don't need a birthing class."

"Do you know what's going to happen during labor?"

"Sure, I'm reading the baby books."

"Putting them on your face and joking that you'll learn by osmosis isn't reading," he said in dry amusement.

"Fine, I'll actually read them," I rolled my eyes and we headed for the elevator.

"We need a tribe, Sibby," he said. "These people were supposed to be our tribe."

"Those people are weird. They don't know how to laugh and I need laughter to get through this."

He wrapped his arm around me. "I know you miss Annie, but even if she were here, she wouldn't know what the hell to do with babies or birthing class or strange fluids that come out of—"

"Ack! Aidan! What did I say about mentioning fluids?"

"My bad."

I felt a pang in my chest at the mention of my best friend. My life hadn't been the same since she'd left the city for Montauk. We still talked all the time. Our text-message thread was a long list of memes and emojis. Still, it wasn't the same as having her living in the same neighborhood. We couldn't just grab dinner and chat about whatever.

The elevator arrived and we rode it to the first floor. "That was all Sibzilla back there. Let's blame her for my inability to keep my mouth shut."

"I don't think you can blame your alter ego for this one."

"Are you mad at me?" I asked when we got out onto the street. Brooklyn was bathed in darkness, the sun having set some time around five. December in New York was no joke. At least all the holiday lights were up in the neighborhood, so we had some cheerful light early in the evenings.

"I'm not mad," he said with a sigh. "But you've just made it harder. And it's already hard, you know?"

"I'm sorry. I know I can be—and I don't think—and my filter—" I sighed. "Can I buy you a drink?"

4

"Absolutely. I need beer and you need chicken nuggets."

"Another piece of pie?" Aidan asked in amusement.

I shook my head and blotted my mouth with a napkin. "Nope, three's my limit."

Aidan discreetly signaled for the check. A moment later, a cute waitress brought it over. She batted her eyelashes at my husband.

It ruffled my craw and stuck in my feathers, or something like that.

"Hi," I said to her. "I don't think we've met. I'm Sibby. This is my *husband,* Aidan. We're expecting twins. We have a dog, and we're happily married."

Aidan snorted into his beer.

The waitress looked at me in disbelief. "Okay…"

I tried to smile, but I was pretty sure it came across as a grimace because she backed up a few inches out of fear.

Aidan put his credit card in the check presenter. The waitress swiped it up and dashed away.

"I know I'm not supposed to encourage this kind of behavior, but I kind of like it."

I rolled my eyes. "You do not. You're just saying that for self-preservation. You're afraid I'm going to sit on you and crush your ribs."

He took my hand and smiled. "You're beautiful. You're

even more beautiful now that you're going to be the mother of my children."

I sighed. "I'd really like to have sex with you. Tonight."

"That can be arranged."

"We have to do it under the cover of darkness."

"Sibby…"

"No, Aidan. I don't want you to see my thighs rubbing together—it's awful."

"Your thighs have always rubbed together."

I gasped. "Um, how are we supposed to have a happy marriage if you don't learn to lie to me?"

"I don't care if your thighs rub together." He grinned and then leaned over the table and whispered something into my ear that made me want to get home, fast.

The waitress returned with his credit card. He quickly signed the slip and tipped her and then got up. He held his hand out to me and helped me slide out of the booth.

We walked north up Manhattan Avenue, the main drag in Greenpoint, and every now and again Aidan urged me ahead of him so we could walk single file and let others pass. People were boisterous and happy as they ducked into bars and restaurants, filling the city with life.

I shook my head. "Strange."

"What?"

"They're just getting their night started and we're already going home to our dog and footie pajamas."

"I don't have footie pajamas. *You* have footie pajamas."

"I can't zip up my adult onesie anymore. It's been retired."

"It'll come out of retirement."

"Yeah, in eighteen months."

"Why such a specific time frame?"

"I still have months before my due date. And then I need at least a year not to feel like an utter failure while I

6

try to squidge my body back into my regular clothes. I'm allowing a few extra months for wiggle room. No pun intended."

"If you want to get your figure back you might have to—"

"Don't say it."

"—join a gym."

"I hate your face."

"You love my face," he countered.

I nodded and sighed. "Yeah. Which is how I got knocked up with twins."

"My face had nothing to do with it. Do you need me to show you the pop-up book again?"

"Now I *really* hate your face."

After a slow climb to the second floor, we finally got to our apartment. "Whose idea was it to live in a walk-up? We should've moved to an elevator building," I huffed.

Prenatal yoga didn't do much for endurance training.

"I don't remember." He reached into his pocket for his keys. "It's going to be a bitch getting a double stroller down those stairs."

"Oh man, you had to remind me of that. Not that I'll be leaving the apartment for the first three months after the twins are born, anyway."

He pushed the front door open and let me step inside

first. Jasper was in the middle of the couch. He lifted his head and started to wag his tail.

A six-foot Christmas tree that Aidan had chopped down himself when he'd gone Upstate, rested in the corner of the living room. It was garnished with colored lights, candy canes, a little tinsel, and handmade ornaments from Aidan's childhood. A menorah rested on the fireplace mantle nearby.

"I think the tree covers the smell of charred turkey a little bit," Aidan said, his nose sniffing the air.

"Mostly, yeah a bit. I've got a super nose now though so I can still smell it." I shook my head. "We're never cooking Thanksgiving dinner again. From now on, it's turkey sandwiches all the way."

Aidan grinned.

The insurance claim had been a nightmare, but we got lucky and there was very little actual damage. Most of it had been cosmetic. With the insurance money that came through, we were able to repaint the kitchen slate gray to match all of our brushed-chrome appliances.

I sat down on the edge of the couch and patted my leg. Jasper came to me and jumped into my lap. I smushed his face between my hands and made a bunch of nonsense noises.

"Don't fall asleep," Aidan warned.

I rolled my eyes. "I'm not going to fall asleep."

"It's winter, it's dark out, and you're pregnant. The odds of me getting laid tonight shrink every minute you're on the couch."

"Wow. You must burn a lot of calories being so snarky."

He grinned. "I learned from the best."

"Flattery will get you nowhere."

"Flattery will get me into your pants."

Jasper let out a whine, which was dog speak for, "Take my ass outside or I'm going to poop on your floor."

"Once around the block," Aidan said. "And then I'll be back. Please be awake."

I saluted him and when he grabbed the leash, Jasper supermanned off the couch toward Aidan.

The door shut and I heard the patter of Jasper's paws as he scrambled down the stairs and then Aidan's hearty chuckle, laughing at something Jasper had done. I shucked out of my down coat and then moseyed to the bedroom. I turned on the lamps and then sat on the bed.

Leaning over, I attempted to reach my feet. It was a regular struggle between the frumpback whale and her boots. Unfortunately, the boots won.

I fell back against the pillows. My belly loomed before me. It was all I saw. Somehow in the last few weeks, I'd gone from sorta pregnant to when-are-you-due pregnant.

I closed my eyes.

I'd realized I first had the bump when I was getting dressed for my administrative hearing. I had to deal with the ticket I'd been given for peeing in a Folgers container on the subway. In public. I'd put on a black sweater dress that all of sudden had been a little too tight around my middle. I hadn't had anything else to wear, so I showed up to the courthouse feeling like I looked less than stellar. But breaking down in front of the woman who was handling my fine—who happened to be a mother of three—had turned out to be a saving grace.

Ticket and offense dismissed.

Something buzzed underneath my butt. I awkwardly rolled to the side and managed to get my cell phone out of my back pocket.

Grinning, I pressed answer. "Well, if I do declare…"

"Why does your Southern accent sound Polish?" Annie asked with a laugh.

"Yeah, about that…I think I've lived in Greenpoint too long. Mrs. Nowacki even left handmade pierogis in my refrigerator the other day. Tell me you want my life. Don't lie."

"I want your life," she said automatically.

"How's Montauk?"

"Boring. And exactly what I need. I can't get into any trouble up here. Because the only people below the age of fifty-five who live here are my cousins."

"So what do you *do*? I mean, when you're not working in your uncle's restaurant?"

"You mean when I'm not mediating my aunt and uncle's fights?"

"Yeah. That."

"I walk on the beach and contemplate life."

"See, I don't know if you're kidding, so I don't know whether or not to laugh."

"I'm serious, Sibby. I don't drink anymore and I run on the beach in the mornings. Still off all social media. It's been really good for me."

"When did you start doing that stuff?"

"Not too long ago. The healthy habits seem to be sticking, so I felt like I could finally tell you."

I heard the front door open. "Gotta go. Husband's home. I have to have sex with him before I fall asleep."

"Wow. You are really selling this marriage thing."

I hung up with her, tossed my phone aside, and struggled to sit up.

"Sibby?"

"Bedroom!"

I heard Jasper run to his food bowl and a moment later

he was chowing down. Aidan appeared in the doorway, his dark hair disheveled. "Whatcha doin'?"

"Trying to sit up."

I held out my hands. With a chuckle, he came forward and gave me a boost. "Anything else I can help you with?"

"Nope, I'm good."

"Really? Like maybe you want some help with your boots?" Before waiting for me to reply, he dropped to his knees. He unlaced my boots and pulled them off. He tweaked my big toe.

"Cute socks."

They were red-and-black plaid, and fuzzy.

I wiggled my toes. "My favorite pair."

"Who bought them for you?"

"Someone who loves me."

"You mean someone who doesn't want you sticking your ice-cold feet on his legs in the middle of the night."

"Yeah, he's the best," I said with a smile.

"A real *mensch*."

"Way to go on the Yiddish."

"I've been listening to a podcast on Yiddish since your mom told me I needed to know some of the lingo."

"Who would have thought that listening to three old Jewish men complaining in Yiddish would be so popular? They have thousands of subscribers. Like, how, just how?"

He grasped my right sock around the ankle and worked it off, flinging it into the corner of the room. Its mate followed suit.

Jasper's furry body appeared in the doorway, his tail wagging. He had that look like he was about to make himself at home on the bed.

"Go," I commanded, pointing in the direction of the living room.

Jasper whined, but dutifully turned and trotted away.

"There's nothing weirder than our dog watching us do it," I said.

Aidan laughed. "Are you going to continue cracking jokes or do you want to get down to business?"

I waggled my eyebrows. "Can't I do both?"

"No. And if you're cracking jokes it means I'm not doing a good enough job. Now be quiet and let me work my magic."

The next morning Aidan and I were both awakened by the buzzer. Aidan launched himself up, his hair askew, eyelids at half-mast. "Wha—what happened? Are you in labor?"

I sat up more slowly than he had, but I was more alert. "You're a few months too early, love. It's the buzzer."

"It's seven-thirty in the morning," he muttered. "Who the hell is here?"

I gently pushed him back down onto the bed. "UPS guy, most likely. Go back to bed; I'll get it."

Sure enough, it was the UPS guy.

"Package for you," he said abruptly.

Ha. Package.

I fake-signed his electronic thingy and took the box. "Thanks."

"Happy holidays," he said, and then left.

I closed the door and immediately took the box to the

kitchen table. I grabbed a knife from the knife block and was just about to slit the box's tape when Aidan trekked into the kitchen. He was walking around without a shirt and his flannel pants rode low enough on his hips that I could see his appendix scar.

That had been one terrifying experience. A call in the middle of the night… I'd thought the worst. Memories rushed to me.

"You're not allowed to die," I blurted out.

He raised dark eyebrows as best he could, still half-asleep. "You're the one holding the knife. You might want to stop gesturing with it in my direction. Then I have a chance at living."

I lowered the knife.

"Thank you." He took a deep breath and ran a hand through his hair. His cowlick stood straight up, making him look like a cartoon character. "I hadn't planned on dying."

"Good. In fact, we should do everything in our power to become vampires and then we can live forever."

"Sounds like a plan," he said, not at all taking me seriously.

And to think, he was putting up with my crazy all before a cup of coffee.

I nodded. "Glad that's settled."

He gestured with his chin to the box. "What did you order?"

"A bread maker."

"Why?"

"Because I want to learn how to make bread. Obviously."

"Obviously. Give me that," he said, reaching for the knife. "I don't trust you with that thing."

Couldn't say I blamed him.

While he cut open the box, I got the coffee going.

While it brewed, we oohed and aahed over the bread maker.

"This looks really high-tech," he said. "We have to read the manual."

"Whoa. Call the press. A *man* just admitted to needing to read directions."

"Har-har."

"Annie suggested this specific bread maker. She thinks even *I'll* be able to use it properly."

Aidan poured himself a cup of coffee while I flipped through the recipe book.

"Hey, look! We can make Jewish Rye!"

"Coffee?" he asked.

"Yes, please."

He fixed it the way I liked it and then set it down in front of me. While I was engrossed in my new bread maker, the buzzer sounded again. A few moments later there was a knock at the front door and Aidan let Caleb in. He was dressed in running clothes and the hair at his temples was dark with sweat.

"Did you jog here?" I asked.

"Yep."

My face torqued into a picture of confusion. "Why?"

"Why what?"

"Why do you jog, is what she wants to know," Aidan said.

"Because it's good for you. It's how I stay in shape."

I stared at him blankly. "I don't get it."

"Dude," Caleb said, conveniently ignoring me and looking at Aidan, "put on a shirt. You're making me feel inadequate."

"Why would you want to cover up a work of art?" I asked.

Aidan laughed as he started for the bedroom, and Caleb helped himself to a cup of coffee.

This was our morning routine. Caleb had grown needy since his split with Annie, but I didn't mind.

"Will you let me take Jasper for a jog one morning? I'd like a running buddy."

Aidan came back into the kitchen with his chest covered. "You can try, but you will fail."

"Huh?" Caleb asked, taking a sip of his coffee.

"I've tried running with Jasper. He's not a running dog. Every time I get going, he comes to a crashing halt. Then I come to a crashing halt. I might have fallen over into some trash cans once…"

"It's true. He came home with a banana peel stuck to his shirt. I think Jasper likes to make asses of us on purpose," I said. "The other day, I left the dog park with dog crap on my yoga pants."

Caleb chuckled. "Your dog is a menace."

"But we love him."

"So what did you get?" Caleb asked, touching the bread maker. "Looks like a time machine."

"Bread maker."

"Oh, yes! Can you make me a cinnamon loaf? Oh and banana bread?"

"Sure."

"Sweet."

Aidan smiled. "You might want to wait until Sibby works out all the kinks."

I glared at Aidan for alluding to my supervillain powers of appliance destruction.

"I'll be a guinea pig, no problem," Caleb said.

"Poached eggs okay for everyone?" I asked. They nodded in approval.

We spent the next hour devouring a dozen eggs and

two packages of bacon. I could eat like a six-foot man. No shame. I'd started wearing Aidan's sweats for big meals and I owned it.

"Thanks for breakfast," Caleb said as he loaded the last plate into the dishwasher. "Aidan, I'll see you at the bar later."

Caleb gave me a hug, rubbed Jasper's ears, and then left.

When the front door shut, Aidan said, "You don't have to feed him, you know."

I pressed the dishwasher start button. "I'm afraid if I don't feed him, he'll starve. Have you seen how much weight he's lost?"

"He'll gain it back. Caleb was fine before Annie came along. He'll be fine after. He just needs more time."

Hmm. I wasn't sure I believed that. Annie was a one-woman emotional wrecking ball.

"What do you have going on today?" Aidan asked, switching the direction of our conversation.

"Book-release stuff and coffee with Stacy."

"Say hi to the millennial for me," he said.

"Uh, Aidan? *You're* a millennial."

"Yeah, but she *acts* like a millennial. Who has pink hair nowadays unless you live in San Francisco?"

"Congratulations, you just became a seventy-five-year-old man. Let me grab you some ointment—"

He shuddered and cut me off. "You know how I feel about that word."

I hugged him. "I have to pick up all the bread-making stuff at the store. While I'm there, I can grab you some Metamucil and Grape Nuts…"

"You're thoughtful, Sibby. Really. By the way, let's ban the words Metamucil and ointment from our vocabularies."

"Hey, just thinking about the health of your plumbing."

"Let's also vow not to mention my plumbing. That's a conversation between me and my proctologist."

I blinked. "We're too young for this sort of talk."

Chapter 2

Matzah: [mah-tzah]

    1. Thin, crisp, unleavened bread eaten during Passover.

    2. It's like a bad cracker, except worse.

I lifted my first loaf of bread from the table and showed it to Stacy. "I don't know what I'm doing wrong."

She swept a lock of blond hair behind her ear. The tips were no longer pink, but Cookie Monster blue. "Did you follow the directions?"

"Yes."

"Exactly?"

"Yes, exactly."

I dropped the loaf of bread onto the floor of our pre-war apartment.

She leaned over and picked it up. "Man, that's dense."

"I've found another appliance to make me feel inferior. Wonderful."

"You just have to experiment. You'll get the hang of it."

I dumped the loaf in the trash and then gestured to the living room. She grabbed her mug of tea and followed me. She sat down on the couch and ran a hand across Jasper's back. His new favorite spot was on top of one of the couch cushions. It was a brand new couch that he seemed determined to smush, but he was so cute I gave him whatever he wanted.

"You're going to love me," she said.

"I already love you."

"No, I mean *really* love me."

I grinned. Who'd have thought that the young woman who'd accidentally outed my pregnancy to the entire world on social media would not only become one of my dearest friends, but also my unofficial PR rep? If it weren't for Stacy, I wasn't sure if I would have the balls to go through with releasing a book on my own. A book with an unlikable heroine. A book that was a complete and utter risk, but with a story I believed in.

"I'm waiting with bated breath," I said with a grin.

"Did you know that Letter has a romance-novel book club that meets once a month?"

"No! I had no idea!"

I'd been into the local bookstore in Greenpoint only a handful of times. It was cute and quaint, and had an eclectic selection which I loved.

"Well, the book club wants to read your book." She sat back, looking extremely satisfied.

"Really?"

"Yeah."

The nerves I'd already been feeling about releasing my book into the wild, intensified by a thousand. It felt like a ball of gas was swirling in my belly, ready to explode.

No, wait. That was *real* gas. I was getting heartburn.

"That's not all," Stacy said with a smug look.

"There's more?"

"They want you to come for a Q & A after they finish it."

Heartburn—and now the hand sweats.

Lovely.

"But what if they don't like it?" I asked.

"They'll like it."

"How do you know? What if I come to this thing and they've brought tomatoes and other rotten veggies to throw at me?"

"Um, this isn't the 1800s and it's not Vaudeville. So I'm pretty sure you're safe from vegetables flying at your face. I think this could be really good for your career. Especially since you're breaking out on your own."

I bit my lip.

"Besides, you're all over the internet."

"*You're* all over the internet," I reminded her. "And what does that have to do with anything?"

"Who we really are gets lost behind a screen. We have personas that aren't necessarily who we are in real life. It's good for us to set the phones and tablets down and get out there. Really connect in person. You're an author and people actually like you. They should get to meet you face-to-face."

"But then how will I stay an introvert if you're determined to drag me out of the house?"

She squealed. "So you'll do it?"

I nodded. "It's an amazing opportunity. Right now, my life is all about *yes*."

"Will you let me dye your hair purple?"

"That's a solid no."

Stacy laughed. "So not everything is a yes."

"Most things are."

"I noticed your office is still your office. Weren't you going to convert it into a nursery?"

"Yes. But we're waiting on custom-designed furniture. Aidan's uncle is making it. He's an expert craftsman."

"That's so cool! Custom furniture, a bread maker— what's next in the nesting lineup?"

"I don't know, but I have the urge to go to the Brooklyn flea market this weekend."

"Yeah? Is Aidan gonna go with you?"

"I don't know." I frowned. "He's been spending a lot of time at the bar. The holidays make people want to drink, so Veritas is doing really well, but that also means we have less time together."

"Well, if you need a buddy, keep me in mind."

"I will."

"Promise me we'll still be friends after you have the twins," she said suddenly.

"Of course we'll still be friends. Why wouldn't we be?"

"Because you're going to start doing parent-type stuff. Hanging out with other parents, you know? Your kids will play with their kids. Your whole life is gonna change."

I sighed. "Try not to remind me."

"Sorry." She smiled in sympathy. "I watched it happen with my sister. The bar was set real low for what constituted as a successful day."

"Meaning?"

"When she was able to leave the house without baby vomit or poop in her hair, she considered it a win."

"Yeah, maybe you don't tell me stuff like that." My hand went absently to my belly. I was still grappling with my new reality, but fighting it hadn't been a good plan of action. Pregnancy wasn't like a sweater that didn't fit. You couldn't return it to the department store where you'd bought it.

"I wonder if I'm going to be any good at this, you know?" I said softly. "I think that's what I struggle with the most. Aidan is so good at so many things. And I—well—if my underwear is on right side out, then I feel like I'm doing pretty well that day."

Stacy laughed. "Of course you're going to be good at this."

"How do you know? I'm not very maternal. I love the city. The kitchen exists only to hold appliances that I can't get to work correctly and sometimes destroy, and if it were up to me, I'd eat Thai takeout four nights a week."

"Well, at least the twins will learn to like ethnic cuisine. And, not maternal? Are you serious?" She pointed to Jasper. "You're already a mom. Puppies are good practice for babies. They go through a lot of the same stuff."

"First of all, Jasper was already an adult when we got him."

"He still went through the peeing everywhere phase. Little boys do that. They take their willies out and spray the walls."

"Ugh. Let me guess? Your knowledge comes from your sister?"

"Yep. Her kids are in between the peeing-on-stuff phase and the lets-talk-about-wrapping-it-up phase. She's not looking forward to that discussion."

I blinked. "This just veered off into a moment in time I'm not even close to ready for."

"And on that note…" Stacy stood up. "I have to meet Joe."

"Great. Run off to your boyfriend. You wind me up like a toy, and then leave while I'm self-destructing."

"You're capable. All you have to do right now is figure out how to use that bread maker properly."

I sighed. "I'm doomed."

"Sibby!" Aidan cried from the direction of the kitchen.

I shot up from a sound sleep, wondering where the fire was.

Oops. Bad form. Considering we'd already had one fire in this apartment.

"What is it?" I yelled back, somehow lifting my tired body out of the bed. I looked at the clock.

Yikes. I'd been asleep for two hours. I hadn't even heard Aidan come home.

"Sibby!" he called again.

Grumbling, I padded my way out of the bedroom and into the hallway. All I heard was Aidan cursing, so I sped up my steps and went into the kitchen.

And then I saw the bread maker overflowing. The lid of the bread maker had popped off and dough had slithered down the sides of the appliance to form a glob on the floor.

Jasper was currently licking it up and chewing as fast as he could.

"Oy! Cut it out." I waved the dog away from the mess. "What happened?"

"You tell me," Aidan said with a shake of his head. "I came home to find this thing bubbling like a volcano."

"I put all the ingredients in the bread maker and pressed start," I said in confusion.

"You followed the directions exactly as they said?"

"Yes."

"Sibby…"

"Yes, Aidan." I tried not to lose my cool. "Why don't you believe me? My first loaf this morning was total crap. So I decided to try again."

He picked up the recipe book. "Show me."

Rolling my eyes, I took the book and flipped it open to the recipe in question. My eyes travelled over the ingredients.

"Whoops," I said.

"Whoops?"

"Er—hi?"

"I missed you today." He leaned over and kissed me. "I should've led with that."

"That's nice. I missed you too." I looked back at the disaster of the bread maker. "This thing is determined to defeat me."

I started to clean up with Aidan's help.

"It can't be that hard."

"Pshhh. I'd like to see you try it."

Aidan wiped a section of the floor and said, "After we clean up, I'll put all the ingredients in this thing, hit the timer, and we'll have perfect bread in the morning."

"You know, if you weren't so cute, your arrogance would be really annoying."

He smiled like he knew better than to say anything, but really, he was already gloating. I wasn't lying to Stacy when I said Aidan was good at a lot of things. He just had skills.

And I was a master of spills.

"Good day today?" I asked him.

"Yeah, busy. So…I wanted to run an idea by you."

"Uh-oh. You're not gonna like, take me winter camping, are you? 'Cause that's not happening…"

He laughed. "Absolutely not. I want to stay married."

I smiled. "What's your idea?"

"I was thinking we could have a holiday party this year."

"Do we have the time?"

"You mean, do *I* have the time."

"Well, yeah. My book release isn't until after New Year's, thankfully. I've tackled what I can and that leaves my schedule wide open. Aside from all the sleeping I plan to do, I'm free."

"And nesting. Don't forget all the nesting."

"I'm not doing *that* much nesting."

"Are you kidding? It's a nesting-palooza in here. It started with the bread maker. What's next?"

"Nothing."

"You're getting packages from Amazon every day. What are you ordering?"

"Just some things. So we'll be ready," I said evasively. I prayed he would stop pushing for answers. I really didn't want to tell him what I'd been buying.

"Fine. You'll tell me when you're ready. Right?"

"Right. Just think of the credit card points and the cashback."

He shook his head and laughed. "So how about that holiday party? I feel like Caleb could really use the cheering up."

"So we're having a holiday party to make sure one of our best friends doesn't sit at home alone, in the dark, listening to Christmas carols, and clutching a bottle of Jack Daniels?"

"How very Charles Dickens."

I sighed. "It's a lot of work."

"Not really. The tree is already done."

"I have to bake."

"Maybe just a few things, but I'll help. And it will be a potluck so everyone is going to bring something. We can do a White Elephant, even."

"Hanukkah Harry."

"What?"

"I grew up calling a White Elephant a Hanukkah Harry."

"Right, well, okay."

I nodded. "But if we do this, we're doing it right."

"Meaning?"

"We're making ugly Christmas sweaters."

"Deal," he said with a grin. "I was thinking we could have it a few days before Christmas?"

I nodded. "Fine. Who will we invite aside from Caleb?" I asked.

"Terry and Zeb."

"Sure."

"Jess will be out of town with her husband."

"Stacy and Joe," I added. "Is that it?"

"I think so."

"Hmmm. Caleb and three couples? This sounds like a bad idea. Maybe instead of a holiday party, you guys should go winter camping Upstate."

"What's with the winter camping, Sibby?"

"I just know you like the woods and every time you

come back to civilization, you're frisky. So if you want to leave for a few days, I'm okay with it."

"I'm not going to leave you alone during the holidays," he stated, looking offended that I'd even suggest such a thing. "And for the record, I'm always frisky. You tell your friends that, right?"

I patted his arm. "Yes, honey. I tell them you're basically a nineteen-year-old boy and I'm very lucky."

He puffed out his chest, looking proud, and then he got back to the matter at hand. "We could invite a single girl to the party. He's not seeing Gemma anymore."

A few weeks ago, Caleb had found a month-to-month sublet in Greenpoint and ended his sleeping arrangement with Gemma Peters—the woman who'd dated both Caleb and Aidan. Not at the same time, clearly. I'd never met her, but I still didn't like the idea of her. For so many reasons.

My eyes narrowed. "Definitely no setup."

"Sibby…"

"No. He's not ready to date."

"You mean you're not ready for him to date."

"He just broke up with Annie. He's still licking his wounds."

"So, let him sow some wild oats."

"No oat-sowing. If he wants to do it, fine. But he doesn't need our help finding a woman. He's a sexy bartender who owns half of a very successful bar in Brooklyn."

Aidan's eyes narrowed. "You think he's sexy?"

"Figure of speech."

He paused a moment and then clearly decided to let it go as he asked, "What's for dinner?"

"Cornish game hens."

"That seems like a lofty aspiration."

"What, I cook."

"No, you burn. Soup. You burn soup."

"Do you want to sleep on the couch tonight?" I crossed my arms over my chest and glared at him.

"I don't like this. Can we be friends again?"

"Yes. Hug me!"

Aidan enveloped me in his arms and kissed the top of my head. "This is better."

The Cornish game hens were a bust, so we ordered pizza. I put away three quarters of a pie by myself and then fell into a blissful cheese coma.

The next morning, I rolled over and smelled something delicious. I went into the kitchen to find Aidan removing a perfectly made bread loaf from the bread maker.

He grinned. "You want some toast?"

Jerk.

Sighing, I went to the refrigerator. "I'll get the jam."

I scored big at the Brooklyn flea market and carried home what I could. The other stuff—the bigger stuff—would be delivered later that afternoon. Hopefully before Aidan got home from the bar, so I could have time to set up everything, and he couldn't tell me to return it.

"Where are you going to put all the loot?" Stacy asked.

I dropped the shopping bags in exhaustion. "I have no idea."

"Why did you need to buy a 1950s potato masher again?"

"I don't know the answer to that question, either," I said with a sigh. "It just looked cute. Like something I needed." Along with the potato masher, I'd bought a knitting bag, three types of knitting needles, knitting patterns, and ten balls of yarn.

My phone buzzed and I saw Annie's name on the screen.

"You mind?" I asked Stacy.

She shook her head as she peered at all the bags I'd carted home. She hadn't bought anything. Not even a pair of earrings.

"Hello?"

"You bought a sewing machine?" she inquired.

Yeah, I'd done that, too. My credit card had gotten quite the work out. Can those things sweat? Like seriously, it might need a headband.

"Yeah, I bought a sewing machine. What do you think of the picture I sent you?"

"I think it looks like a sewing machine. Did you take a cab home with it?"

"No, it's being delivered later today."

"Delivered?"

"Er—"

"Sibby?"

"When you spend a certain amount, they deliver the bigger items."

"Give the phone to Stacy."

"But—"

"Do it."

I handed the phone off to Stacy. "She wants to talk to you."

"Okay." Stacy put the cell to her ear. "Hey, Annie. What's up?"

I couldn't hear what Annie said, but it had Stacy blanching. "I tried. Believe me, I tried. Fine. Here's Sibby again." She gave me the phone. "I need a beer. Do you have any beer?"

"No, sorry." I held up my finger to quiet her and put the phone to my ear. "What did you say to Stacy? You crushed her spirit and now she wants to drink."

"I said that if she was going to be the Ethel to your Lucy then she needed to figure out how to talk you down when you get your crazy ideas."

"Ethel always got roped into Lucy's schemes," I reminded her. "So your example is subpar. Hold on." I put the phone on mute and went to hug Stacy.

"Thanks for today. You can leave my presence and go have a beer."

"You sure?" she asked.

"Yes. And for the record, no one has been able to talk me out of any idea I've ever had. Aidan couldn't even talk me into a baby. We had to wait for a condom failure for that to happen. Don't feel bad."

She smiled slowly. "All right. Don't forget, this weekend we have to stop into Letter to drop off the paperback proofs for the book club."

"I won't forget."

The door closed and I unmuted Annie.

"I think you said something way harsher than what you told me. Why aren't you nice to her?"

"Because I'm jealous. She's replacing me."

"No, she isn't, but you're not here. Do you want me not to have any social interaction?"

She sighed. "No. I just—you won't find a new best friend, will you?"

"You're a dingus."

Annie laughed in obvious relief. "Explain to me why you bought a sewing machine. You failed your theater-costume class. If I recall, you managed to sew fabric to your own shirt sleeve on a regular basis."

"The seam ripper did become my best friend that semester. I don't know. I just thought it would be cute to make baby onesies and bibs out of Aidan's old shirts. There will be two of them. These kids will need lots of bibs."

She paused. "I'm sorry, but can you please put my best friend on the phone?"

"The Sibby you know has left the building. In her place has become this nesting, bread-destroying homebody monster."

"Well, I guess we're all going through some changes," she said quietly.

"How are you? Are you okay?"

"I'm...fine." She paused again. "How is he?"

I bit my lip, unsure if I was supposed to tell her he'd "broken up" with Gemma Peters. She was the villain, and all villains had to be referred to by their full names.

"He's hanging in there," I said finally, deciding it wise not to mention Gemma to Annie. No one needed any reason to lose their shit, not when they were both already so close to doing it anyway.

"He usually comes by for breakfast and coffee. So we're taking care of him."

"Good. That's good." She sounded relieved. Like she wanted to know that he was being cared for, but didn't have to be the one to do it.

"How's the anonymous pregnancy blogging going?" she asked. "Have you told Aidan about it yet?"

"There's nothing to tell. It's just a place for me to share

my thoughts and fears with strangers. Aidan doesn't need to know."

"Uh huh. I thought the definition of true intimacy was being able to talk to your partner about anything."

"Okay, which self-help book are you reading?"

"*How to Love Yourself after Another Breakup.*"

"That's the name of the book? Really?"

"Did pregnancy turn off your sarcasm detector?"

"It's not turned off, but it's definitely been rerouted."

She chuckled. "So the blog?"

"Still finding its rhythm. But I have to say, there's something oddly comforting about telling your fears to a bunch of strangers who don't know who you are."

"I'll take your word for it."

There was a knock on the door.

"Annie, I've gotta go. Mrs. Nowacki is returning Jasper."

"You found a doggie babysitter right across the hall. You live a charmed life."

"I got pregnant even though I was using birth control. Not charmed."

"You should've kept your knees closed, you dirty camping hussy."

I laughed. "If you can't be a hussy with your own husband who can you be a hussy with?"

"Valid point. Okay. Talk to you later."

We hung up and I went to the door. Mrs. Nowacki stood in the hallway, holding Jasper's leash. Her gray hair was pulled back into a bun, and she was wearing a Mr. Rogers red sweater and a black skirt with tights.

I'd never seen the woman in pants. Not even when it was ten degrees outside.

"How was he?" I asked, bending over to brush my fingers through his wiry hair.

"He good boy. Though he like to sleep on his back to show everyone his—"

"Yes, he does. Thank you for watching him. Aiko didn't have a problem?"

She shook her head. "Cat and dog get along now. They cuddle. I took him for walk one hour ago."

I let Jasper off the leash and he bounded into the apartment, making a beeline right for his empty food bowl.

As Mrs. Nowacki and I chatted, Aidan came up the staircase, carrying a box.

"Oh, another delivery for you?" Mrs. Nowacki asked. "From the jungle?"

"Jungle?" Aidan asked with a puzzled look.

I grinned. "She means Amazon."

"Ah. No. This is from the Brooklyn flea market. I took it from the delivery guy."

"Crap," I muttered.

Mrs. Nowacki raised an eyebrow. "I better go." She darted behind her apartment door and then shut it firmly. For an older woman, she was fairly quick on her feet.

Aidan came inside and set the box down on the coffee table. When he stood back up, he looked around and saw all the flea-market bags I hadn't yet been able to hide.

"Sibby?"

"Yeah?"

"Want to tell me what's in the box?"

"Not really."

"Sibby…"

"Why don't you feed Jasper?" I suggested, trying to move him away from the box.

Jasper let out a pathetic whine.

"He's in cahoots with you," Aidan muttered, but he was momentarily distracted by our dog. He gestured to the bags. "Did you buy the entire flea market?"

"Remember that you love me."

"Yeah, that's true."

I got into the box and pulled out a sewing machine.

He stared at me for a moment. "Why did you—you know what? Never mind. Come on, let's make dinner."

# Chapter 3

Gefilte Fish [ga-fill-tah fiSH]

    1. A dish of stewed or baked stuffed fish, or fish cakes boiled in a fish or vegetable broth and usually served chilled.

    2. As vile as it sounds.

    The holiday season in New York was weird. True New Yorkers didn't feel about the holidays the way normal people did. Our city filled up with tourists and visitors from around the globe, all wanting to have a magical holiday experience in our city. The Macy's holiday window, the tree in Rockefeller Center, ice-skating in Central Park.

New York was congested on a good day, but from the month of December to the first week into January, the city was so full of people it was almost unbearable.

Aidan and I had decided to throw our holiday party, but because it was a fairly last-minute idea, we hadn't counted on the fact that *all* of our friends had decided to escape the holiday fray.

Zeb only had a few days off from the West Village restaurant he managed, so he and Terry went for a quick romantic getaway to Vermont. Stacy's boyfriend Joe was in a band that had been getting some attention lately, and they'd booked a gig in Vegas. So off they went to Sin City. Annie, of course, was MIA in Montauk. Nat had moved to Houston with her toddler and husband, so she wasn't around. Mrs. Nowacki had fled the cold and gone to Florida to spend the holidays with her son. Even Caleb, our lonely little Caleb, had plans to visit his parents Upstate.

Our party never happened, but Aidan had found a couple of young bartenders, who weren't leaving town to cover for him at Veritas on Christmas Eve. So it was just Aidan, Jasper, and I, in our ugly holiday sweaters, alone in the apartment, watching *Love Actually* and drinking hot chocolate all night.

Christmas Day we ordered Chinese food and I attempted to knit.

"What do you think?" I asked, holding up the lumpy, hole-filled red scarf.

"I think it's a really nice color," Aidan said diplomatically.

"Rats. I thought I was getting better at this." I hadn't actually finished a knitting project. If I wanted someone to actually wear the scarf, I had to make it presentable.

Aidan stretched out his long legs and leaned back

against the couch. "When are you going to tackle the sewing machine?"

I looked at the sewing machine that now took up the entire corner of our living room. At the time, it had seemed like a justifiable purchase. Now, its lack of use felt like a mockery of my idea.

"Aidan, I can't even knit. How am I supposed to think about mastering a sewing machine?"

My phone buzzed on the coffee table and I struggled to grab it. Jasper, who was resting half his body across my lap, didn't even move. Aidan came to my rescue.

He grasped my phone and handed it to me. "Annie," he said.

I put the phone to my ear. "Hello?"

"How much Chinese food have you had?" she asked as a way of greeting.

"Um. Hard to know. I ate an entire order of egg rolls by myself."

"Well done."

There was yelling and then singing in the background. "What's going on?"

"My aunt and uncle are drunk. Christmas Day mimosas. When they're not singing, they're fighting."

"Fighting about what?"

"My uncle wants to make T-shirts for the restaurant. Which isn't the issue. The issue is he wants to put fish puns on them."

"Oh no." I laughed. "Like what?"

"*Just for the halibut. Oh my cod*—"

"Stop, just stop."

"So my aunt is trying to talk him out of it. Thus all the yelling."

"Aside from that, how's your Christmas going? Are you imbibing?"

"Nope. I've remained strong."

"Good for you! Are you coming to visit any time soon? You know the city clears out in January…"

"The earliest I'll get down there is February for your baby shower."

"That's still over a month away."

"Sibby, don't guilt me. I need to stay close to Montauk for a while. It's better for me."

I bit my tongue, literally, because I was about to ask her if she was hiding in Montauk. "Okay, sure. I just miss you."

"We good?"

"We're great," I said with genuine enthusiasm. I really didn't want her to feel guilty about needing to put herself first. "I'll call you on New Year's Eve."

"Do you think you'll even be awake when the ball drops?" she teased.

"Definitely, because I'm going to take a nap. I'll be fresh."

"If I don't answer, it's because I'm working."

"Roger that."

We hung up and I snuggled up against Aidan's chest. He put his arm around me and kissed my forehead.

"Thank you," I said to him.

"For?"

"Loving me always."

"Ditto."

We settled in to finish watching *Love Actually* while our dog snored and chased rabbits in his dreams.

## Chapter 4

Knish: [ke-niSH]

1. A baked or fried dumpling of dough that is usually stuffed with potatoes and onion.

2. The knish is delish.

"I'm going to vomit," I said to Stacy.

"Nerves or pregnancy?" she asked.

"Nerves. Definitely nerves."

"Why are you nervous?"

I blinked. "Seriously?" I grabbed my to-go tea from the counter and we headed out of the coffee shop into the dreary January day. I made sure my scarf—the one I had knitted with moderate success—was firmly tucked around my neck so I wouldn't catch a draft.

"Yeah, seriously. What's the worst thing that could happen?"

"They could all hate it," I reminded her.

"And that will do what exactly? Make you change the entire book before it launches?"

I moaned dramatically. "It's one thing for faceless strangers to hate your book and then troll you online. It's very different to sit in a room with your readers and have no idea what they're going to say. I'm a delicate flower. I can't handle this."

"Why did you say yes then?" she asked in curiosity. Not to be mean or harsh, but because she genuinely seemed like she wanted to know.

"Because you have to put yourself out there. It's very easy for me to become agoraphobic and I'm trying to fight that."

"Jeez, Sibby. How much caffeine have you had today?"

"None. I've switched to decaf."

"So you're like this normally? All chipper and stuff? Without any additives?"

"Since when did you become such a ball-buster?"

"I'm trying to channel Annie for you. I feel like she'd know how to handle…this."

"Handle *me*, you mean," I said in amusement. "I need a handler now?"

"Maybe?"

"You know I like you for who you are, right? Not because of your social-media following or because you knew people at Letter to get my book in front of their romance book club."

"I do know that, yes."

"You sure? I don't want you to be anyone but who you

are. You're not Annie. You don't want to be Annie. The world is good with one Annie."

She grinned. "I'm so telling her you said that." Her smile slipped. "She's not gonna like, come after me, is she?"

"Come after you? For what exactly?"

"I don't know. I don't want her to think that I'm trying to take her place because I'm not," she hastily explained. "But it's been really wonderful getting to know you these past few months. I feel like—well—it's really hard, you know? To find people who are genuine and say what they mean, who you can really count on as a part of your tribe."

"Say what they mean, huh? After accidentally telling everyone to stuff it where the sun don't shine, on that Instagram video, it's been a lot easier to just come out and say stuff."

"They loved you for it, you know."

I thought about what she said. Lately, it had felt like my tribe had abandoned me. Which wasn't really true. But everyone had their own lives and worked weird hours. Plus, when people coupled up, it was inevitable that you saw less of them. Friends became about proximity, or you didn't really have any.

We arrived at Letter. I had no idea what awaited me inside.

"You can do this," she said.

"This is either the best idea in the world, or the worst."

"Can I put something into perspective?"

"Yeah."

"How many readers are out there?"

"I dunno. Millions. Billions."

"Right. There are fifteen of them in this room. Let's

say they all hate your book. Let's say they think you're the worst writer since—"

"Get to the point," I gritted out.

She grinned. "My point? There are so many readers out there that haven't even heard of you. And if this book club hates your book, that's just one small percentage. It just means they weren't *your* readers."

"Pretty valid point."

"Also remember that most people are hardly ever mean to your face."

"Thanks," I muttered darkly.

"That's the spirit!" She grasped the door and held it open for me.

It was warm in the small bookshop. There were only a few customers milling about, perusing the shelves for their next read.

We went to greet the young woman behind the counter. She was a quintessential Brooklynite. Skinny-leg jeans, slouchy beanie, plaid shirt more for style than for warmth. It was rolled up to the elbows and I could see a small tattoo on her wrist.

Hipster queen.

A book, open and facedown, was on the counter in front of her. Some sort of epic fantasy novel.

"They're all down there waiting for you," she said to me with a smile.

"Thank you." I took a deep breath and looked at Stacy. We headed toward the back of the bookstore. There was a staircase that led down into the basement where the romance group held their gathering.

I put a hand on Stacy's arm to stop her descent down the stairs. "Promise me something," I said, my voice pitched lower so I wouldn't be overheard.

"Sure thing. What?"

"Whatever happens down there, however this goes, remind me that I'm not an imposter. That this won't make or break my career. Either way."

She smiled. "Sibby, you told the internet to fuck off when you got a summons for peeing on the subway. If you can recover from that blunder, then whatever happens down there won't matter. And further more, my YouTube following grew by ten percent after you aired that video. Your blunder actually helped my career."

"You're becoming more and more like Annie every day."

She grinned. "Really? Awesome!"

"That wasn't a compliment," I said with a chuckle. "Let's get the show on the road."

Stacy waved a hand in front of my face. "Sibby? Sibby can you hear me?"

I gently grasped it and moved it down to her side so I could stare at the shelf of popcorn, chips, Funyuns, pork rinds, corn nuts, and every other terrible food choice waiting for me.

"Don't do it," she said. "You'll regret it."

"I'm in mourning," I told her. "I need comfort. I can't drink. Junk food is the next best thing."

"Think of the twins."

"You're right. They need to cultivate taste. Entenmann's chocolate donuts would be better… No." I shook my head. "I need to be strong." I sighed and reluctantly turned away from the junk-food aisle.

"What aisle is the dried fruit in?" I asked her.

She exhaled in relief. "Aisle twelve, I think."

I turned down aisle twelve and came to a stop in front of the bags of prunes. Without thinking I just started grabbing them. I hadn't thought to get a cart, so I could only carry six bags.

"Load up. Get as many as you can." I said.

"Uh—don't you think you have enough already?"

I glared at her. "Really? You want to rumble with a depressed pregnant woman?"

She quickly picked up as many bags as she could. "Am I allowed to ask…why so many prunes?"

"I feel bad for prunes. You know, they have a reputation in the fruit world."

"All right." She nodded like she understood. "So you think eating your weight in prunes and shitting your brains out later is a great way to deal with all that just happened?"

"Junk food is a bad idea and I'm trying to be a thoughtful adult."

She wisely closed her mouth and followed me to a checkout lane. The cashier took one look at me, then at the merchandise and didn't even blink as she rang up twelve bags of prunes. I carried my stash out of the store, Stacy trailing behind me in silence.

"I know this is a weird question," I told her, "but can we go to a bar? I want to buy you a drink and then watch you drink it."

"You want me to get drunk for you? That's a neurosis I've never encountered before."

"I'm from the school of Woody Allen—I'm neurotic

44

and quirky, and you love me for it."

She raised an eyebrow. "I'll let you choose the bar."

Gotta love that about Greenpoint: there was a bar or restaurant every three feet. We ducked into a dimly lit dive. It was the kind of place that wouldn't judge you for having a drink before the sun actually set.

"Shot and a beer," I said to the bartender. He twirled his handlebar mustache like a melodramatic villain. My coat was open, and it was clear that I was pregnant. His eyes were trained on my belly.

"Not for me, for her." I gestured to Stacy. "I'll have a club soda."

"What kind of shot do you want?" the bartender asked after a moment, directing his question to Stacy.

"Oh, vodka. Please."

I slapped a twenty down on the bar and we took our drinks to the corner table.

"Did he have the right to be that judgy? The bar is empty," Stacy said.

"I chalk it up to the time of day. And when a pregnant woman walks into a bar while it's still daylight out, asks for booze, then yeah, I'd say it's okay to judge."

I set aside the grocery bags and riffled through one of them. I tore into the prunes. I'd put away two in the time it took Stacy to take her shot.

She shuddered. "Gah, that was awful. I know for a fact that came from a plastic bottle. Yuck."

I chewed on another prune.

"So, are you going to lament, or just watch me drink in morose silence?"

"I got arrogant," I said. "Oh sure, before we met with the book-club gals, a part of me was worried that they would hate my book, but mostly I was just saying that so you'd think I was being humble. I didn't actually think they'd hate it."

"Not all of them hated it," she pointed out.

"No. Just most of them."

"Then they're not your target audience."

"You're missing the point."

"What's the point?"

"What if all I can do is write dirty rom-com? What if I'll never be able to write anything else? There are so many authors out there that try to write in different genres and they flop. What if that's me? What if I flop? What if I release this book and it just kerplunks?"

"Sibby—"

"I haven't gotten any early reviews. That's bad. That means bloggers and reviewers have read it and hated it."

"Or," she interjected, "they haven't read it yet."

I moaned. "That makes me feel even worse. Like they couldn't bother to read it, and then when they do they'll hate it."

"You kinda wrote a villain," she said. "I love her. Personally. You know how much I love her. She's prickly and tough. You don't even like her all the time. But damn if she doesn't own her shit and go after what she wants."

"Modern day Scarlett O'Hara," I muttered. "Unlikable, takes no shit, and does whatever she has to do in order to survive."

"Sibby, that's it!" she exclaimed. Her cheeks were flooded with liquor and excitement.

I frowned at her. "What's it?"

"Do you trust me?"

"To operate heavy machinery? Not right now."

She rolled her eyes. "I'm talking about your book release. I think I know a way to spin this!"

My eyes were glued to the computer screen. I kept hitting refresh.

Click. Click. Click. Pause. Click.

"Sibby," Aidan whispered as he stood over my shoulder.

"Huh?"

"Sibby, come to bed."

"Just a few more minutes."

"You've already hit publish. You have to wait for it to go live now."

"No, just—"

"I'm cutting you off," he said, gently clam-shelling my computer.

I looked up at him from my office chair. "You know you're in the danger zone, right?"

"This stress isn't good for you. It's not good for the twins." He took my hand and pulled me up from the chair. The office would soon be a nursery, as soon as our furniture was complete and delivered.

"I'm too wired to sleep," I said.

"Let me make you some tea." He took me into the kitchen, gestured for me to sit down, and put the kettle on to boil. "I don't know what it's like."

"What?"

"To be consumed. Like you are with your books."

"That's not true. You've poured your heart and soul into Veritas."

He grinned. "Oh, so you have noticed."

"The design of Veritas is all you. I remember the hours you spent trying to decide between which wood you wanted to use to build. I remember the paint samples painted on our walls. You agonized for weeks about the drink menu, and which wines you wanted to carry. You live and breathe Veritas. And you're successful because of it."

Jasper jumped down from the couch and came into the kitchen to rest his head in my lap. It was like he knew I was stressed. Pets had a funny way of knowing when you needed more love, more comfort.

"You can't turn it off, can you?" he said thoughtfully. "Just like I can't turn it off."

I shook my head. "No. I can't. This book is different though. It's all me. From conception to release."

"You won't sleep tonight, will you?"

"Probably not."

"I'm proud of you, you know. For going out on a limb and doing this. You could've played it safe, kept this book in a drawer."

"In about a week I'll know if I should've done that," I muttered darkly.

My phone chimed with a text.

Annie: Your book just went live and I bought the first copy. Congratulations, you badass mother shucker. You got this!

Me: Mother shucker? What's that about?

Annie: I'm starting to dig the fish puns.

Me: Oysters aren't fish. They're shellfish.

Annie: Go away, I'm reading.

"Annie says the book just went live," I said, setting my phone aside.

"Funny. The moment you step away from your computer it goes live." He brought me a cup of tea. "Maybe you should take the train up to Montauk tomorrow, get out of the city. Visit Annie."

"No point in going anywhere there's internet; I'll be way too plugged in."

"I could always take you camping outside of cell coverage…"

"Wow, you like to live dangerously."

Aidan laughed, but then quickly sobered. "I'm sorry they hurt your feelings. The girls at the book club. The ones who didn't like your book, I mean."

"They didn't hold back, that's for sure. It was really tough to hear." I stared down into my mug. "It feels personal, you know? I poured everything I had into it— and when someone doesn't like it, it feels…it feels like they don't like *me*."

"Because your book is an extension of you."

I nodded. "Yeah. It's weird."

"It's not that weird. I imagine it's how all artists feel. You make art and once you show it to the world, it's out there being judged. But you know the amazing thing about opinions?"

"What?"

"They're subjective."

"True, but why is it easier to believe all the negative ones? My agent didn't like it. She couldn't even sell it to a publishing house. My usual editor passed on it. What does that say?"

"It says you took a chance because *you* believe in it. You told the story you wanted to tell. Whatever happens now happens. I know whatever I say won't make the sick feeling in your stomach go away, but I wanted to say it anyway."

"Thank you," I said. "For supporting me." I took his hand and squeezed it.

He paused for a moment and said, "You could quit, you know."

"Quit what? Writing? Never."

"Didn't think so. Just seeing how you really felt."

I looked down at Jasper and stroked his head with my free hand.

"We've been talking a lot about me. Why don't you tell me how you are, Aidan?"

"Let's move to the couch and get comfortable."

"If I do that I'll fall asleep."

"Yes, but I think you need that. Come on, Sibby."

We settled down onto the couch, Jasper finding his own sliver of comfort on the cushions. I grasped one of Aidan's feet and pulled off his sock.

"What are you doing?" he asked.

"Giving you a foot rub. Hand me the coconut oil over there."

He reached behind him, grabbed the jar on the end table, and handed it to me. While I massaged his foot, he leaned his head back and closed his eyes.

He'd been working seventy, sometimes eighty-hour work weeks, leading up to the holidays. Even now that holidays were over, it didn't look like he'd be able to cut back anytime soon. Growing pains of a young business, but totally worth it. Things were going well and Veritas had been written about in a few New York magazines. We knew he couldn't ease up. He couldn't lose this momentum. It was do or die for Veritas and the time was now.

"You look tired, love," I told him.

When he didn't answer, I realized he'd already fallen asleep. I didn't feel like waking him, so I gently removed his leg from my lap. After I scooted off the couch, I covered him with a blanket. Jasper stayed with Aidan and soon the both of them were snoring in unison.

I headed to bed, knowing Aidan would find his way there later. It took me forever to fall asleep and when I did, I dreamed of book critics throwing my book at me as I walked down the street.

I woke up suddenly. The alarm clock told me it was just past six in the morning. Both Aidan and Jasper had come to bed, and despite having author nightmares, I hadn't heard them enter the room.

Knowing I wouldn't be able to get back to sleep because my mind had turned on, I hauled myself out of bed. I shut the bedroom door and then trod over to my cell phone—which I'd purposefully left in the living room. I looked at the screen. Stacy had texted not five minutes prior.

Stacy: Don't look at the internet.

I called her immediately and she answered on the first ring.

"How bad is it?" I asked, my stomach sinking.

"I'm sorry, Sibby. The reviews coming in are ugly. Like *ugly*."

I pinched the bridge of my nose and tried not to cry.

"I feel like this is my fault," she said quietly.

"Your fault? Why would it be your fault?"

"Because I loved this book. I love all your books, but this one, I don't know. This one really spoke to me. I believed in this book." She paused. "I *believe*."

"Me too."

We fell silent for a moment.

"What would you do? If this were you?" I asked.

"Honestly?"

"Yeah."

"Stand behind it. Don't back down."

"Really?"

"Absolutely," she said. "Own it. You've always done that. You fuck up sometimes, but you tough it out and people love you for it. They recognize you for it. It's who you are."

"Thanks, Stacy."

Aidan came out of the bedroom, yawning, with Jasper in tow.

"Gotta go. Husband is awake and the dog needs to go outside. I'll catch you later." I hung up.

Aidan came over to me and pulled me into a loose hug. When I leaned back, I took a moment to study him. He looked more tired than he had when he'd gone to bed the night before. The bags under his eyes were more pronounced. It didn't look like he'd slept well and I knew he was burning the candle at both ends.

"Have you been awake long?" Aidan asked.

"No, I woke up a little while ago."

"Who were you talking to so early in the morning? Annie?"

"Stacy."

"Oh." He paused. "The book?"

"Bad."

"Ah, I'm sorry, Sib."

I shrugged and then pulled away, mashing down my tears. "It is what it is."

"It's only the first day the book is out there. It could turn around."

Ever the optimist. Loved that about him.

"It could. And someone could finally find Bigfoot."

I greeted Jasper with a smile. He looked up at me with wide, brown eyes, begging me to take him for a walk. I went to the front door and slid into my coat, boots, hat, and gloves. Jasper stretched in excitement when I reached for the leash, and his tail began to wag furiously.

"I'll be back in a few minutes," I said.

"I can take him out."

I shook my head. "I need some air. To clear my head."

Aidan yawned and nodded.

Jasper and I got down to the sidewalk and he did his business quickly. We set off for the park. My phone rang and I answered it.

"You bitch," Annie stated.

"What? What did I do?"

"You kept me awake the entire night reading."

"Why? You read the early drafts. Was this one that different?"

"Yes, smart-ass. This one had polish, and it felt like I was reading it for the first time."

I smiled even though she couldn't see me, but the smile quickly gave way to tears. I'd walked with Jasper to a park that was nestled against the East River, overlooking the skyline of Manhattan. I sat on a bench and watched as water taxis crossed the sunlit river, back and forth, from Brooklyn to stops in the city.

"The book is a flop," I wailed.

"It's day one. You *can't* know that on day one."

"Yes, you can."

"Tell me why you think your book is a flop."

So I told her.

"Have you looked at your actual sales?" she wondered. "You can do that, you know."

"I don't need to check my sales to know what I know."

"Or, you only think you know what you know. But how do you *know?*"

"Huh?"

"Just check the sales. Sales don't lie. You had a strong

release plan—at least, that's what you told me and I'm taking your word for it. You had Stacy behind you. She's great with social media and you were running ads, right? You're getting negative reviews, but that at least means people have read the book. Any new reader will be insanely curious if the negative reviews are right or wrong. This book is your dark horse."

"You really think I should check the sales?" I asked, a seed of hope taking root.

"Sales put food on the table. Reviews don't."

"That's the clarity I needed. I'm just scared."

"Where's Aidan for this clarity?"

"Exhausted," I told her. "He's utterly exhausted. He can barely function, Annie. I'm afraid he's going to work himself into the ground."

"Have an intervention."

"Yeah, he needs to take a breather," I said.

"You both do. Slow down. Smell the roses."

"I can't just turn off this stress."

"Of course not, but before you worry yourself sick, check your sales. I'll hold."

"I'll look at my sales with Aidan and then I'll text you. Might need you to drink a bottle of tequila for me."

"I'm off the sauce, remember?"

"Damn. So if my fears are warranted, I guess I'll just have to shoot orange juice that's way past its expiration date."

"Life on the edge. Later, mother shucker."

"Stop calling me that. It's not cool."

"Getting it on a shirt and sending it to you."

"Won't wear it."

"Getting you a mug, too! K, thanks, bye!" She hung up.

I looked at Jasper. "Your Aunt Annie is off her rocker."

He wagged his tail in agreement and I rubbed his head. "I really miss her."

Sighing, I stood up from the bench. "Let's go home, mutt."

Aidan was in the shower when I got home. I took my laptop into the bathroom and sat down on the closed toilet.

"Are you coming to shower?" Aidan asked, peeking his lathered head out from behind the shower curtain.

"In a second. I want to check—"

"Oh God, please don't stress yourself out by reading the reviews."

"I'm not. I'm checking sales."

"Okay. I'm here for you, Sibby." A lump of suds dropped onto the floor as his head disappeared back into the shower.

I held my breath as the browser loaded and the screen went cloudy with steam. After a moment, I wiped away a clean spot to see and then exhaled deeply. "Okay then."

"What's that mean?" Aidan asked, raising his voice so he could be heard over the sound of running water.

"It means it's selling, but definitely not like my dirty rom-com." I rubbed my screen again and then clamshelled my computer and set it down on the floor outside the bathroom. With the door open, it gave Jasper time to slip in and lay down on Aidan's pajama pants piled on the floor.

I quickly got out of my clothes and climbed in behind Aidan. There was something to be said for conserving resources. Plus Aidan was naked and that always cheered me up.

"You're not yelling or crying right now. I'm kind of worried about you."

"I went out on a limb, right? I went rogue. This isn't another rom-com. I have to own everything that happens from here on out."

He pulled me into his arms and I closed my eyes against his chest as hot water steamed down on us.

"I'm proud of you," he said.

"Thanks." I sighed and stepped back as his arms dropped from around me. "What time are you out of here today?"

"You're kidding, right?"

I frowned as I reached for the shampoo bottle. "What do you mean?"

"I was with you for every one of your release days. I stayed with you to celebrate then, and we're going to celebrate now."

"With waffles at the diner?"

"Is that what you want?"

"Yeah."

"You're easy to please."

"Sometimes," I said. I needed to change the subject and talk about something else. "We've got an ultrasound next week." I'd never been so organized in my entire life— sending Aidan invites to our shared calendar, reminding him of everything we needed to do to prepare for the twins.

"Right. And we're definitely finding out the sexes."

"Yes. I've had enough surprises to last me a lifetime," I muttered, causing him to laugh.

"Careful," he said, holding onto my elbows and maneuvering me underneath the shower head.

"You ever feel like there's not enough time?" I asked him as I washed the shampoo out of my hair.

"You mean before the twins arrive?"

"Yeah, that. But I mean in general. Like there isn't enough time to become an amazing cook, an expert knitter, and not completely terrified of the sewing machine. There's not enough time to…"

"Go on," he said.

"To become an adult."

"Ah, are you suffering from the same thing I'm suffering from? Extreme inadequacy-itus?"

We rinsed off and I turned off the shower. "You're feeling that too?"

"Why do you think I work all the time?"

"Because you have a strong work ethic?"

"Thanks," he said with a smile. He pushed back the shower curtain, releasing a cloud of steam that fogged up the bathroom mirror. He grabbed a towel and handed it to me, then one for himself, and began to dry off.

"But no. I work all the time because if I'm exhausted then I don't have time to think about all the ways I'm going to fuck up our children."

"Wait a second," I said, rubbing the towel across my wet hair. "Are you telling me that we've been feeling the exact same way?"

"Yes. And coping with it differently. Why do you think I didn't lose my shit when I saw the sewing machine we don't have room for?"

"I thought it was because you love me and want me to be happy."

Aidan laughed. "There's an element of that. But mostly, I knew it was your way of preparing, of nesting."

I was guessing that he hadn't discovered the hoard of diapers underneath our bed and on the top shelf of our bedroom closet. One of my recent nightmares had been running out of clean diapers for the twins and having to carry them around while they continued to pee and poop all over me.

Yeah. My dreams were terrifying.

I leaned over and kissed his lips. "But you're right. Let's try not to freak the hell out all the time. It will be hard, but maybe we can be each other's check-and-balance system."

He helped me out of the tub, making sure I didn't slip and then he hugged me. "I love you, Sibby."

## Chapter 5

Tzimmes: [tsmis]

    1. A stew of sweetened vegetables served on Rosh Hashanah to celebrate a sweet new year.

    2. I'm guessing you still can't pronounce this one. Me either.

    "You know you're going to have to handle most of the parenting, right?" I told Aidan on our Uber ride home from the Manhattan doctor's office. We had just learned that we were going to have twin boys. When we saw the sonogram, I'd started to cry. Equal parts fear and joy. And then Aidan had gotten misty-eyed, and that had made me blubber.

"I can't teach them to pee standing up, or how to shave, or any of that stuff. I'm basically going to feed them and try to keep them alive, and you get to do the rest."

He lightly rubbed a finger across my upper lip and said, "Yeah, you *definitely* can't teach them how to shave."

I not so gently elbowed him in the side and then turned my head to the window and discreetly ran a finger over the top of my lip. It was time to take care of that again.

Thanks, prenatal vitamins. They apparently made hair grow *everywhere*.

That night, I lay awake, my mind bouncing around from thoughts of raising two boys to my book, grocery bills, and everything in between.

Aidan was tall. The men in his family were giants. Beautiful, Irish giants, but giants nonetheless. How much was it going to cost to feed two growing Irish giants?

That thought led me to thinking about my flop of a book. How was I going to feed my children and my husband if I wrote books that flopped? Had I peaked? Should I have stuck to dirty rom-com? That was a sure thing. We could eat if I kept writing rom-coms.

Round and round my mind went. I fell into an exhausted sleep, sometime around five in the morning, and barely registered Aidan kissing me goodbye.

Jasper nudged me with a wet nose a few hours later. I woke up, still feeling emotionally hungover.

I came out of the bedroom and found Mrs. Nowacki sitting on our couch. It wasn't weird that she was there. We trusted her to have a key, use it sparingly, and not freak out if she saw one of us naked in the kitchen by accident.

"You sleep late," she commented.

"I'm pregnant."

"Hmm. When I was pregnant, I was up at dawn making the borscht and bread."

"I need coffee," I muttered.

"I make us tea. It is green tea and has caffeine to get your motor running." She gestured to the plate of cookies on the table. "Eat. Eat."

I took a cookie and sat down on the couch. Jasper hopped up and settled between us, resting his head in Mrs. Nowacki's lap.

"How is life? Good, yes?" Her shrewd eyes pinned me to the couch.

"Life is good."

"And book?"

"What book? The book I just released? It's—well—out there."

She shook her head. "Not that book. New book."

"What new book? I just said—"

"Your new book. The one you *should* be writing."

I finished the cookie in two bites. Damn, it was good. Polish baked goods were drool-worthy. I took a sip of tea to wash the cookie down.

"I'm taking a break."

"You cannot take break. In my village, when we take break, we didn't eat for days."

"That sounds awful."

She shrugged. "Sibby, it will only become harder. Your time won't be your own soon."

"But—"

"When *dzieci* come, they scream all the time. You will lose mind. My four were each a year apart. Trust me, I know what I am saying."

My mind rebelled at the thought of that many children, spaced so closely together. Though I was doing a fairly adequate job of raising a full-grown dog, I still wasn't convinced I'd do a decent job being a parent to humans.

Two tiny humans who would spit up, cry, poop, sneeze, and sometimes vomit all over me.

I quickly devoured three more cookies.

"This has been fun," I said darkly. "But I have to make a call. It's kind of time-sensitive."

I had to find us a new birthing class. I owed it to Aidan and myself to be armed with as much knowledge as possible, and Mrs. Nowacki was reminding me I really didn't know what I was doing.

At all.

"Jasper will need his walk in a little bit. Want to go with me?"

She shook her head in a definitive no. "I have appointment this afternoon. I get ready to leave now." Mrs. Nowacki got up and patted Jasper's head. His tail thumped and then he closed his eyes again.

When the front door shut, I picked up my phone and called the birthing center and signed us up for a new class.

Aidan came home mid-afternoon. Jasper sat up on the couch, his tail walloping the couch cushions.

"I have good news," I said, taking Aidan's coat and hanging it up for him, and giving him a quick kiss.

"So do I. You go first."

"I found us another birthing class."

"Good," he said.

"And I promise to keep the snark to myself."

Grinning, he took off his beanie and set it in the basket by the door. Jasper nosed his leash.

Subtle, dog. Real subtle.

"What's your news?" I asked.

"Was Mrs. Nowacki here? Did she bring cookies?"

"How did you know?" I demanded.

"There are crumbs on the couch and there's chocolate on your face."

"Yeah, sounds about right." I swiped at my cheek, but apparently I missed a spot because Aidan reached out and cleaned me up. "Thank you. Now, what's your news?"

"Right. Sorry. I'm reeling." He paused for a moment. "The space next to Veritas is vacant."

"When did that happen?"

"Today."

"So the overpriced, poorly run, hobo-chic boutique finally went under, huh?"

"Yeah, she's out of business."

"Poor thing. Daddy must have cut off the money spigot."

"Say what you will, but she gave me a head's up. That was nice of her."

I arched an eyebrow. "She couldn't give Caleb a head's up, huh? Had to tell *you*…"

"Is someone jealous?" he teased.

"Of the hot, skinny, not pregnant girl who doesn't have to wax her lip every two freakin' weeks due to sudden hair growth? Of the girl whose dad paid for her to open a business and got to sit around for months, flirting with two hot guys next door, one of which is married to *me*. Yeah. Little bit jealous, Aidan. Little bit." I pinched my fingers together and held them in front of my face for dramatic effect.

"I think you're hot. Mustache and all."

I laughed, but it suddenly turned to irrational tears. "I had to stop shaving my legs. I don't want to bend over and lose my balance."

"Sibby, it's okay—"

"No, it's not!"

"You never shaved your legs to begin with. Even when we first starting dating."

"Oh my God, why are you reminding me of my utter failure as a woman? That is not the way to win."

Jasper trotted over to me and bumped my leg with his nose. Aidan pulled me into his side. When I'd finally gotten myself under control and dried the tears from my cheeks, I looked at him.

"I freak out on you at least three times a day now. How do you never lose your cool with me?"

He grinned and kissed the end of my nose. "I constantly remind myself that you're the one that has to do the labor thing. If you can handle that, I can handle anything you throw at me."

"So I basically get brownie points for life."

"Pretty much, yeah."

I kissed him. "We were just about to go for our walk." As half-owner of Veritas, Aidan was able to have a little more of a flexible schedule. Something I greatly appreciated.

"You and Mrs. Nowacki?"

"She can't come today. She had an appointment."

"For?"

"I didn't ask. Boundaries."

"She has no boundaries and you have no filter. It's a match made in heaven."

I pushed against his arm.

"I like that you guys take care of each other. And Jasper. But I do think it might be time to hire a dog walker."

"Why?"

"It's winter. It's icy. She's...ya know."

"Old?"

"And you're...ya know."

"Resembling a large mammal that gestates its young for twenty-two months?"

"What mammal does that?" he asked, feigning innocence.

"You know. You got that answer right on *Jeopardy!*"

"This conversation is getting weird," Aidan muttered. "I just worry about you both, okay? Jasper likes squirrels and pigeons. I'm afraid he's going to take off and pull you both to the ground. I can see it now: you two tumbling on the ice, falling down like bowling pins."

"That's a nice visual, honey. But we're okay. Mrs. Nowacki and I have a system."

"Sibby…"

"Listen, when I get too big to bend over to pick up dog poo, we can hire a dog walker."

"You just said—you know what? I'll let you have this one."

Jasper woofed, eager to get out of the apartment. Though he was really good at napping, when it was time for his walk, he knew it. And let us know it.

"He really needs to go," I said.

"I still have to talk to you about the empty space next to Veritas."

"Oh right. That was a thing we were discussing. Well, tell it to me fast."

"This isn't a tell-you-fast sort of thing. It's more of a take-you-out-to-a-nice-dinner-and-butter-you-up-with-jewelry sort of thing. But you're more into hibernating lately. Maybe I should cook you dinner and then—"

I zipped up my coat and sighed. "You and Caleb want to expand the bar."

"How did—"

"Please." I rolled my eyes. "I knew the moment you mentioned the empty space next to Veritas."

He sighed. "Yes, we want to expand. Only, we don't want to make the bar bigger, we want to make it a small liquor/wine store unique to Veritas. Customers can have a glass of wine or cocktail in the bar and then come over to the store and buy the stuff they need to make the drinks at home. Eventually we want to do wine and liquor tastings and have the best of both worlds. People want to come out and drink, they drink, but if they are having a party or something, we just sell them the bottle and get that business too." His blue eyes were steady. "What do you think?"

"You know I support you guys. But the timing…" My shoulders slumped in defeat. Was I really going to be the one to rain on his parade? I needed him, bad. And Veritas growing would be amazing for our future; but I was so, so pregnant and my emotions were running amok.

"Can we press pause on this conversation? I have to pee," I asked, stalling for time.

"Can't I just talk to you through the closed door?"

"Let's leave some romance in our marriage, okay? It's all going to die when you see your children come out of my body anyway, so let's hold onto these last few months."

"And this year's Academy Award goes to—"

"I'll meet you both downstairs, okay?"

I shuffled to the bathroom and breathed a sigh of relief when I heard the front door close. I really needed a moment to myself. I thought about the bar expansion and realized that, like my book release, sometimes you just had to go for it.

I met Aidan downstairs. "Dog park? He needs a good run."

"Let's go."

The day was bright and clear, and most of the ice had melted off the sidewalk. The park wasn't busy since it was the middle of the day. We let Jasper off and he immediately began to wrestle with a Boston terrier in the mud.

Fantastic.

Everyone looked like they were having fun and then I heard laughter. I looked up to see the Boston terrier face-humping Jasper.

"Aidan!" I gasped.

"On it!" Aidan ran toward the dogs, clapping his hands and yelling *no*. But the Boston terrier had no shame and kept pumping away.

"Trevor!" a woman called. "Ohmygodstophumpingeverydogyoulike!" She quickly clipped his leash onto his collar and tugged him away as he continued to thrust in the air.

"I'm so sorry," she breathed. "He's been doing that a lot recently. I don't know why. We're seeing someone about that."

Aidan looked down at Jasper, but he didn't look any worse for wear. He even leaned over and started licking Trevor's ear.

Guess he wasn't scarred for life.

My husband looked down and rubbed Jasper's ears. "I think everyone's good, so no worries. When you say you're seeing someone—"

"Dog trainer," she clarified with a wide, flirtatious smile. She tossed her blond hair over her shoulder. How she stayed warm in a thin peacoat and no hat, I'd never know. I looked like Chilly Willy the Penguin, complete with the pom-pom hat and bright red mittens.

"I haven't seen you here before," she said to Aidan, without so much as a look in my direction. "I'm Bonnie Jo."

Her initials were BJ?

That was some clever advertising.

"Aidan." He turned and smiled at me. "And my wife, Sibby."

I swore I could hear her sigh internally.

"Nice to meet you, BJ!" I called out.

"Bonnie Jo," she mumbled, quickly tugging on her humping dog and leaving the park.

Aidan came back to my side and wrapped his arm around me.

"Un-frickin'-believable. It's like the bigger I grow, the more invisible I become. Like, I'm standing *right here*."

"That's not true."

"You're not allowed to leave the house without me when the twins are born. I'm convinced it will make you irresistible to the entire female population of Brooklyn."

"What about Manhattan?"

"Don't," I seethed.

"Is there anything I can say that will make you feel better?"

"Nope." I turned to look at him. "We didn't finish our conversation from earlier."

"Which conversation would that be?"

"You know."

He sighed, clearly expecting the discussion to turn sour.

"I think you need to go for it. Who knows when this space will be vacant again, if ever. Greenpoint is growing like mad; no one can keep up. Open the liquor and wine store. Do it."

His blue eyes delved into mine. "You sure?"

"I'm sure. I'm not going to be the reason you don't go for the big dreams."

His smile was wide and genuine. "This. Right here."

"What?"

"This is why you never have to worry about me looking for anyone else. There is no one else for me, Sibby. You're it."

I sighed. "You're really good at this marriage stuff."

Aidan left the apartment early the next morning to meet with a wine distributor in the city. I sipped decaf coffee and replied to emails from readers who'd read the book and actually enjoyed it.

It turned out that a lot of people had been curious enough to pick up the book despite the negative reviews. They even went as far as to leave their positive thoughts in the form of reviews. Things were slowly starting to look up.

As for the few emails from people who felt like they had to tell me everything wrong with my book, I sent those to the junk-mail folder and decided it was best to pretend they didn't exist.

I was done burying my feelings in a container of ice cream flavored with tears. Time to deal and move on.

I finished my work, and my mind began to race with other thoughts—like the looming baby shower and the unfinished nursery. My mother was flying up for the shower and I needed an extra dose of serenity to prepare for her.

My phone vibrated with a FaceTime incoming call. It was like she could sense my anxiety and knew to call me, even though she was in another state. I took a deep breath, girded my loins, and answered.

The screen filled with my mother's cleavage.

"Ma!" I called. "Change the angle of the camera!"

"Oops." The phone shook and then suddenly my mother's face appeared. She smiled. "I never can get this FaceTime thing down."

I rolled my eyes. "Yes. I know."

"Show me your belly."

I dutifully angled the phone downward.

"You look bigger!"

"I *am* bigger," I grumbled.

"Sibby, it's a good thing," she reminded me. "You want to get bigger. It means the twins are growing."

I loved my mother, I really did. But sometimes I wanted to slip her a sedative.

"How's Dad?" I asked, changing the subject. I didn't want to discuss bodily functions and the like and I knew she was t-minus ten seconds from that. "Is he there?"

"No, he's in the hospital."

My veins went cold. "What? Why? What happened? Is he okay?"

She waved her hand at the camera. "Of course he's okay. He's just getting his routine colonoscopy."

I pinched the bridge of my nose.

For someone who claimed to be an expert communicator, she certainly had a way of relaying ultra-personal information without thought.

"He's getting a colonoscopy right before you guys are scheduled to fly up here? Is that a good idea?"

"Monitoring the prostate is always a good idea, Sibby. Erectile dysfunction can—"

"Ma! Stop!"

She shrugged and then examined her manicure.

"Did you call to tell me about Dad's colonoscopy, or is there some other reason?"

"I wanted to ask you about Snapbook."

I frowned. "You mean Snapchat? Or Facebook?"

She blinked. "They're not the same thing?"

Moses, help me.

"What's the one where you take a selfie and then it disappears after a few seconds?"

"Snapchat."

"Yeah, I don't want that one."

"So Facebook?"

She nodded. "Yes. Facebook. I want to get on the Facebook."

"Why? You're on Instagram. Isn't that enough social media for you?"

Please God, let that be enough social media for her.

"I'm on Instagram to follow you and your life. You post a lot of pictures of Jasper sleeping with his legs—"

"Yeah, that's his thing."

"I like when you do videos of you walking around the city and pointing out real places that you've included in your books. You're so talented, Sibby."

"You're my mother. You're supposed to say that."

"Not true. You know I enjoyed *Flicking the Fava* and your other books in that series, but your new book had a little more meat to it."

Yes. My mother had read my dirty rom-coms. Which apparently had inspired my parents to try the reverse cowgirl.

Yeehaw!

"I appreciate you saying that," I said. "So, why Facebook?"

"This nice young man at the Temple recommended it. He said it's a great way for people to find my business."

"You have a business?"

News to me. And probably my father.

"Yes, Sibby. I started a business."

"Um. When?"

"Last week." She cocked her head to one side. "Didn't I tell you?"

I held in a sigh. "No. No you didn't."

She grinned. "Well, I'm excited about it and I want your help getting on the FaceChat thing."

"Facebook, Ma. Facebook."

"Right. Facebook."

I paused.

She waited.

"Are you going to tell me what this business is?" I prodded.

"I started a matchmaking service."

"You're kidding?"

"No. I'm completely serious. Sibby, do you know how many people got married last year because of me?"

"Um. No?"

"I set up four couples. Four, Sibby. That's eight lonely people who found love because of me. All from my age bracket."

"That's great, Mom. Really. Super awesome."

"They all started recommending me to their lonely friends and before I knew it I had more people coming to me, begging me for help."

"Well, it makes sense. You know pretty much everyone there is to know."

"Exactly! So when I'm up there in a few days for the baby shower, will you show me how to set up my account?"

"Sure. I'll help."

"Great! You're my favorite daughter."

"I'm your only daughter. I win by default."

"Can I tell you the best part?"

"The best part of what?"

"My business!"

"I thought the best part of your business was finding second chances for the sixty-plus crowd…"

"Don't be snarky."

"I'm awake, Mother. I'm snark-free only when I sleep. And even then I'm not so sure."

"I'm choosing to ignore that."

"Okay." I arched a brow. "So the best part of your business?"

"The name." She paused dramatically. "Rent-a-Yenta."

"Rent-a-Yenta? So you're basically a professional meddler?"

"I'm hanging up now."

The screen went black.

I'd been on the planet nearly thirty years and my mother was still surprised by my personality.

## Chapter 6

Manischewitz: [man-ah-she-vitz]
1. An extremely sweet, kosher concord wine.
2. Worst hangover ever.
3. EVER.

"Your boobs are *huge*," Annie blurted out.

"I know. Can you stop staring at them—you're making me feel like a hooker."

"Sorry. But they're like, right there."

I stepped aside and let her into the apartment. She wheeled her suitcase into the corner, collapsed the handle, and then turned to face me.

"You're a thin bitch and I hate you," I said with a grin. "I missed you too."

I shut the door and we hugged. She pulled back and looked around. "Holy crap, what happened to your living room?"

Aidan and I had moved my office desk into the only available corner of the room, opposite the card table with the sewing machine and knitting station. The room was beyond cluttered. I belonged on one of those TV shows about hoarding.

"I told you I was nesting."

"Did you finish my scarf?"

"It's still a work in progress. I should be proficient at knitting in about a hundred years."

Bending down, she stroked Jasper's head. "Hiya, mutt." When she'd had her dog-love fill, she stood up. "Where's the sperm donor?"

"At the bar."

Her good humor fled and she paled. She cleared her throat. "Is Aidan meeting us for dinner?"

"No. He and Caleb are grabbing a bite. To discuss some stuff." I paused. "They're going to expand the bar."

"Wow. Really?"

"Yeah. The place next door finally became available."

"Caleb mentioned it a few times when we were…"

We fell into a silence that I wasn't sure how to navigate. Finally, I snapped out of it.

"Get you something to drink?" I asked. "I picked up some beer. I've got wine——"

"Water is fine. And I can grab it. You sit."

She didn't need to tell me twice. I plopped down on the couch and put my feet up. Good thing it was winter and I was constantly wearing socks, so I didn't have to see my kielbasa-sized toes.

"How was your trip?" I asked as she came back into the living room. Her blond hair was pulled back into a sleek ponytail and she was dressed for the city. Skinny-leg jeans, sexy boots, stylish jacket.

I wondered if she was secretly hoping to run into Caleb. But I wouldn't dare ask. Caleb was a touchy subject. Just the mention of the bar had made her squirrelly.

"Trip was fine," she said.

"And how's Montauk? Still boring?"

"Yup."

"Still not drinking?"

"Yup."

"Still happy about that?"

She looked amused. "Yup."

For as long as I'd known Annie, she'd been a partier. Lived life in the fast lane. Caleb had been the first guy she'd really loved, but she'd blown up that relationship by refusing his proposals and then flirting with another guy.

Caleb had had enough. It had not been a good breakup. It had been messy and we all still felt the after-effects.

But apparently, the implosion of her life in New York City and driving away the only guy she'd ever been serious about had caused her to do a dramatic one-eighty. It was an I-fucked-up-and-need-a-total-behavior-change moment, and it seemed to be sticking.

"Can I ask you something? Like *really* ask you something?"

"I guess." She looked at me warily. "If you must."

"Did you really want to be in a relationship with Caleb or did you think we were at that age where you think you're supposed to do all those things?"

"Right in the gut," she muttered. "That was a sucker punch."

"Sorry," I said with a winsome smile and raised eyebrows.

"I wanted to be with him. And that didn't have anything to do with getting older."

"Do you still love him?"

"Shouldn't we be going to dinner?" She stood up, holding onto her nearly empty water glass.

"We're three blocks away," I said. "And isn't it a little too early for you to be eating?"

"Don't you need to feed the growing beasts or something?"

"Oh, no you're not deflecting. Not tonight."

Recently my attention could often be diverted with food—and always with the promise of chicken tenders—but this was not one of those moments.

"You can tell me," I said. "I won't tell Aidan."

"Yes, you will. Because you're married and you have that rule where you don't have secrets between you."

"He doesn't know about that time we gave ourselves at-home Brazilian waxes…"

She smiled in genuine mirth. "My God, I had wax on my crotch for, like, two weeks." She paused for a bit and then said, "But that's not a real secret, Sibby. That's just an embarrassing anecdote that we'd prefer not to share."

"Annie, if you want me to keep anything on lock down, you just invoke the best-friend clause. I won't say anything to Aidan about anything. I swear."

She sighed. "Yes, I still love him—and before you ask, no, I'm not going to try and win him back."

"Why not?"

"Because."

"Oh, that's a good reason. Why not, Annie?"

"You're driving me to drink," she warned.

I fell silent.

"Is he still dating that girl?" she asked.

"You don't know?"

She shook her head.

"They stopped seeing each other a few weeks ago. You really didn't know? Because you've been off social?"

"I looked him up one night," she admitted. "Right when I first got to Montauk. I'd had too much to drink, went onto his Instagram, and then wanted to throw up when I saw his photos with her."

"Let me guess, that was the turning point for you in this no-drinking thing."

"Bingo! I haven't looked at social media since that night."

"I admire the willpower."

"It's not willpower." She smiled sadly. "It's self-preservation."

The door to the nursery opened and Annie strolled out, covering her mouth as she yawned. She was wearing a pair of blue-and-white striped pajama bottoms, puffy, pink socks, a huge T-shirt with a unicorn on it, and her blond hair was in a messy bun on top of her head. She somehow managed to stay smoking hot first thing in the morning, and it seemed like no matter what she did, she still looked like she was in college, body and all.

Wench.

"Morning," I said, sipping my cup of coffee.

She waved at me and grunted as she trod toward the coffee maker. Annie stared at it for a moment before looking at me over her shoulder. "Should I even bother?"

"Nope. Decaf."

"The only thing worse than decaf coffee is light mayonnaise. Why do you even drink this stuff?"

"Ritual. So I feel like some things will never change."

I grinned into my mug and set my phone down on the kitchen table. Remnants of my breakfast littered the plate. In true best-friend fashion, Annie sauntered over, plucked the crust of my toast off my plate, and ate it.

"I was going to eat that."

"No you weren't." She chewed and then swallowed. "Damn it. If I want lukewarm, watery, caffeinated coffee from the bodega I have to put on real pants."

"Welcome to my life," I muttered. "You haven't known real struggle until you're pregnant and fighting your way into denim."

"How much longer should I expect to hear your snarky my-life-is-harder-than-your-life comments? When do I get to play that card?"

"When you get pregnant. Then you get a free pass to complain about all the things."

"Pass." She saluted and then looked longingly at the coffee maker. "Fuck it. I'll drink a cup and then get the real stuff in a bit."

"Was the air mattress okay?" I asked.

"Yep. It was pretty comfortable actually. Thanks for letting me crash in your spare room. You know it's supposed to be a nursery, right? Shouldn't you start decorating?" She spooned sugar into her mug, stirred it, and then brought it back to the table.

"Yes. I have plans."

"Are they going to happen before the twins come? Because right now you don't have any baby furniture. Where are they going to sleep? Not in the bed with you and Aidan, right? Because I have some thoughts on that…"

"Yeah, no." I laughed and reached for my phone. "Didn't I show you the furniture in progress?"

"No."

"Oh. Well, hold on." I swiped at my screen and then gave her the phone.

"Wow. This is beautiful stuff. Aidan's uncle, right?"

"Yeah. He's nearly finished. We should get it in the next month or so."

"Not that this stuff isn't beautiful, but why not Ikea or Amazon?"

I frowned as my hand rested on my belly. "It's not a secret that I was…less than ecstatic when I discovered I was pregnant."

"That's putting it mildly."

I mock-glared at her as I went on, "I was in shock for the first trimester. Cut me some slack." I rolled my eyes. "I just—I don't know. It all came out of nowhere, ya know? But one day, I woke up and I was excited—really excited that we were going to have children. I wanted furniture that would last. I wanted, I don't know, something tangible to remember this time. I know when I look at that furniture a few years from now I'm going to remember the sleepless nights, the crying, the hardships, but I'm also going to remember the beautiful things too."

Annie's eyes were watering. "Mother shucker, you just made me cry. And I'm dead inside."

"You're not dead. A little stunted maybe," I teased. "Still hell-bent on calling me mother shucker, huh?"

She wiped underneath her eyes. "I'm trying to get

myself in the habit of not swearing. I don't want your kids' first word to be an expletive." She peered at me. "You know you lost yourself to the baby cause, don't you?"

"Yes."

"Is this our new normal?"

"Is it bad?"

She shook her head. "No. Just different. I can do different."

"I'm afraid once Aidan sees his children come out of my body, he won't want to have sex with me ever again," I blurted out.

"Maybe you should talk about these concerns with the other women in your birthing class? I have no idea what you're going through. I once ate a burrito and had a burrito baby belly, but that isn't the same thing."

"Definitely not the same thing. And I can't talk to those women in my birthing class."

"Why not?"

"Because, they're all like five foot nine, and retired models and, *Oh, but we don't have all the problems you have.* Look at my nose."

She peered closer. "What's wrong with your nose?"

"It grew."

"It didn't."

I nodded vigorously. "It so did. Because *everything* grows… Listen, I think I cracked jokes in my first birthing class to deflect what was really going on."

"Gee, ya think?"

"Can we talk about you now?"

"I'd really rather not."

"Are you ever going to move back to Manhattan?" I asked, clearly not listening to her.

"Probably."

"Do you really hate Montauk as much as you claim?"

"Yes."

"Do your aunt and uncle really fight that much? Or are you exaggerating?"

"Oh, no, they definitely fight all the time. I think it's their version of foreplay."

"Yuck."

Annie got up and began to pace. "My uncle's restaurant isn't doing well, Sibby. And he refuses to listen to me. He won't let me change the menu or modernize the decor. It's frustrating because I know I can do something to help. If only he'd let me." She sighed. "If he doesn't start listening to me he's going to lose the restaurant, and I just can't fail at one more thing in life, ya know?"

"I know. Believe me, I know. So what are you going to do?"

"Right now? Put on pants and get a real cup of coffee. This decaf crap will be the death of me."

"I'm so confused about what's going on in here," Aidan said from the doorway of the nursery.

"What's it look like?" I asked, tracing a stencil onto the wall.

"It looks like you're decorating…"

I grinned. "You're smart. I'm glad our children have half your DNA."

"Someone is in an extra snarky mood today," he said with amusement.

"I took a lot of Vitamin C." I gestured to the wall. "Give me two seconds and I'll be done tracing this thing."

"Did you measure?"

"Measure? Measure what?"

"Oy."

"Aidan. Don't *oy* me. Tell me what you meant about measuring."

"From the top of the ceiling to the middle of the wall. And then the distance between each stencil."

"Yes, I measured."

"Did you have to use a step ladder?"

I sighed. "Yes, I had to use a step ladder. But before you start worrying about my safety and the safety of your unborn children, you should know that I had Annie stand on it. Happy?"

"Incredibly." Aidan grinned. "So where did she go? Abandon you mid-project?"

"She had a genius idea and had to see it through. She went to meet with someone but wouldn't tell me who."

"That's weird."

"Very." I shrugged. "What are you doing home? Didn't you have a meeting with the landlord of the bar?"

"We had the meeting. It was short." He raked a hand through his hair. "He wants to sell the building."

"I'm not going to like this next part of the conversation, am I?"

"Probably not. You remember the money my grandmother left me? I want to use it—to buy the building."

I let out a slow breath. "We were saving that for a down payment on a house Upstate…"

"I know."

"I can't really say no. You know that, right? I already

said I supported the decision to go ahead with the expansion, so—"

"Really?" His eyes were wide, hopeful. "You mean it?"

"Make no small plans. It's all or nothing."

He wrapped me in an exuberant hug. "Thank you," he whispered against my hair. "I know this isn't—"

"We're good. I promise. But on one condition."

"Name it."

"You help me with these stencils."

He laughed and released me. We spent the rest of the afternoon turning the office into the nursery. We hung pictures on the walls. We painted the stencils and they looked uniform.

Win.

Jasper sat idly by, supervising. When we were finished, we moved to the living room and collapsed onto the couch. We were zoning out to bad TV when the front door opened and Annie burst inside.

"Guys! I figured out a plan to save my uncle's restaurant!"

We both waited with heightened expectation. When it was clear she wasn't going to say anything more, I prompted, "Well?"

"Oh, I can't share the plan yet. If I do I'll jinx it."

"Then why did you say anything at all?" I demanded. "You know I hate being kept out of the loop."

"You'll be in the loop soon. I just have to get some stuff in order first."

"You make me tired," I said to her.

She grinned and then looked at Aidan. "What are you doing here?"

"Uh, I live here?"

"No, I mean, didn't you have a meeting?"

"We're buying the building," Aidan stated.

"You're going to have a mortgage?" she asked.

"Yup."

"Wow. Totally adult of you. Babies, sewing machines, and mortgages…"

Aidan laughed. "I know, right?"

"How do you feel about it, Sibby?"

"It's terrifying," I admitted. "I kind of want to throw up over the idea, but it's inevitable. It just needs to happen, and I support him."

Aidan took my hand and brought it to his lips for a kiss.

"Ugh. You guys are so healthy and cutesy and gross. It's horrible." She smiled, letting me know she was teasing and that she was actually happy for us.

"We finished the stencils," I stated. "Come see."

I showed her the nursery and she nodded. "They look great, Sib."

"Thanks. Now my mom won't lecture me."

"I think that's wishful thinking on your part," Aidan said from the doorway of the nursery. "She likes to have an opinion on things. Did you tell Annie about your mother's newest adventure?"

Annie raised an eyebrow. "I'm waiting with bated breath."

"Mom started a matchmaking business. She's servicing all of Atlanta."

"Serving. Serving all of Atlanta," Aidan corrected.

I shrugged. "Same thing."

"Eh, not really. Aren't you supposed to be a writer?"

"That's why God invented editors."

"I feel like I'm living in a sitcom," Annie said to both and neither of us.

"Too bad you gave up drinking," I commented. "We're funnier when you've been drinking."

"You gave up drinking?" Aidan asked in surprise.

"Yeah. For a few months now."

"Why?"

"Long story." Annie's phone buzzed and she pulled it out of her back pocket. Her face lit up. "Excuse me just a minute."

"It's not that long of a story," I whispered to Aidan when Annie left the apartment for a moment of privacy. "When she gets drunk she social-media stalks Caleb."

"Ah. Been there."

I frowned. "Who do you stalk when you drink?"

"You."

"You can't stalk your own wife on social media."

"Yes, you can. And it's not so much stalking you as it is wondering what you're saying about our life to thousands of strangers."

I made a face. "I'll try to get better about that."

"No, you won't."

"No, I won't," I repeated.

# Chapter 7

Pastrami on Rye: [pah-stramee on rye]

    1. A hot sandwich, comprised of thinly sliced pastrami, sometimes topped with chopped liver or Russian dressing on rye bread.

    2. You'll have leftovers for a week.

"Sibby?" Annie asked.

"Hmm?"

"Why is the coffee table baby-proofed already?"

I currently had a sewing tape measure around my waist and was documenting the inches my belly had grown, so I could post the results on my anonymous pregnancy blog.

"Sibby?" Annie pressed.

"What was the question?"

"You know, if I wanted to be ignored, I could just start dating someone."

I looked up. "Wow, your anger at the male species is really coming out. You know that, right? *Bitter and hostile, party of one, your table is ready…*"

She rolled her eyes and pointed to the coffee table. "Why is this baby-proofed?"

"Oh, that's not baby-proofed." I lifted up my yoga pant leg to show her the massive purple-and-yellow bruise on my patella. "It's Sibby-proofed."

Her shoulders shook with laughter. "You're ridiculous."

"I think I'm getting clumsier as time goes on."

"I didn't think that was possible."

"Right?" I paused. "You know that scene in Jurassic Park, where the water in the glass shakes?"

"Yeah."

"That's me. I'm the T-Rex. Angry and hungry, and all I want to do is stomp on humans and eat goats."

"Are you sure going to the mall today and shopping for a dress to wear to the baby shower is a good idea?"

I glared at her. "What are you saying?"

She backtracked immediately. "Nothing. I'm saying nothing. In fact, we should probably get going."

"I need to eat first. My blood sugar is dropping."

"No kidding," she muttered with a shake of her head. "How does Aidan handle you?"

"Handle me? What do you mean *handle* me?"

"I just mean, that sometimes, it feels like we all have to watch what we're going to say for fear of—well—for fear of upsetting you."

"You're not being very tender with my feelings."

"Let's just not talk about this, okay?"

"No, come on. Get it off your chest."

"No. Because whatever I say will make me unlikable and I'm already unlikable."

"Unlikable? To whom? Me? I like you even though your honesty sometimes hurts my feelings. So just say it," I demanded.

Annie huffed. "Fine. Sometimes you're irrationally unreasonable. Like hormonally unreasonable."

"You don't think I know that? I can't freakin' help it and even knowing that I can't help it pisses me off."

"Telling a pregnant woman she's unreasonable is like punching a nun. You just don't do it. I shouldn't have said anything. I should've just let it go. I just—I'm not good at all of this, okay? I'm not good with all these emotions."

"Maybe that's your problem."

It was her turn to cross her arms.

"You've done all these things to change your life, right? Cut out booze, got rid of social. You moved and now you run on the beach like some retired Zen guru. But have you *dealt* with everything that happened? I mean with your parents? With Caleb?"

"Yes, I've dealt with it."

"I don't believe you. For what it's worth, I think you ran away."

"I didn't run away. I needed a change of scene."

I nodded. "Okay. You needed a change of scene. And you are making changes to your life. But what about your coping skills? When does your life get normal again?"

"You're starting to sound like an audio self-help book."

"Thank you."

"That wasn't a compliment."

"I know, but I chose to take it that way."

"What do you want me to say?" she asked, sounding defeated instead of defensive. "I'm not a sensitive person. I didn't grow up in a house where people showed open affection. We didn't talk about our feelings. My mother popped pills with martinis and her idea of connecting was giving me her credit card, and telling me to buy something I wanted, and dropping me off at the mall. My father was weak and miserable, and he let her treat him like crap. How was I supposed to have a good model for a relationship? Everyone I know is dysfunctional. Well, except you and Aidan."

"Oh, we're plenty dysfunctional, trust me."

"You're just saying that to make me feel better," she said glumly.

"No, we really are," I promised her. "We're happily married, but that doesn't mean we don't have problems."

"Name one problem. Name something you fight about?"

"Um…"

"Yeah, that's my point. If you can't say something right off the bat, then I don't really believe you when you say you're dysfunctional."

"Okay, so maybe we're not overtly dysfunctional and maybe I shouldn't be so cavalier about it. We do have a really good relationship. Do we get along all the time? No. Am I overjoyed that this bar expansion is happening while I'm super-fucking-pregnant? Absolutely not. Aidan's dreams are changing, like pretty much overnight. A few months ago, he wanted to buy a house Upstate. Now he wants to tie up our savings into this expansion."

"Well, did you ever really want to move Upstate?" she asked. "You're not like, nature girl, you know?"

"I think eventually I'd be happy to get out of the city, but for now, I like my life here. But that's not the point. The point is Aidan is making these huge changes to our life. It wouldn't be such an issue, except now we're about to have not one, but *two* babies. It's not just us anymore. We have to actually think about long-term goals and stuff. It's just weird. Like, we can't put ourselves first anymore."

"Yeah, that's a trippy mindset. But you're good, right? With Aidan and the bar expansion?"

"Definitely. There's no resentment there."

"That's good." She nodded thoughtfully and then fell silent.

"Have you thought of going to therapy?" I asked.

"Where I sit and whine about my childhood? No thanks."

"Okay. Fine."

"Besides, if I'm going to talk to anyone, it's going to be you. Because you don't take no for an answer and you like to open the hamper, pull out my dirty laundry, and then make me smell it."

"That's gross."

"You poke and prod. Sometimes I hate it—in the moment. No one likes to self-reflect."

"Well, from best friend to best friend—though you look like you're doing better, I still know what's going on underneath."

"And what's that Mistress Self-Help?"

"You're holding it together, but just barely. And I know, with just the right tap, you'll shatter. "

Her expression sobered. "Got me all figured out, do you?"

"I'll be there," I said. "When you fall apart. And I'll help you pick up the pieces."

"Why do you put up with me?" she asked in genuine curiosity.

"Because you're my best friend. And you're really good at being my best friend. You don't leave your men behind."

"This isn't war, Sibby."

"You're right. This is life. But I'm here for you, Annie. You can't get rid of me."

She grinned suddenly. "I'm super glad to hear that."

"You've got to be kidding me," I muttered as I turned from side to side and looked at myself in the dressing-room mirror.

"Did you say something?" came Annie's voice from the dressing room next to me.

"No."

"How are the dresses looking?"

"I look like a bottle of Pepto-Bismol and a holiday parade float had a drunken one-night stand."

"I have no idea what any of that means." She knocked on the dressing-room door.

With a labored sigh, I opened it, and let her inside before steadfastly closing the door and locking it.

She looked me up and down. Her lips twitched like she was desperately attempting to hold in her laughter and was seconds away from failing.

I sighed. "It's okay. You can let it out."

"Thank God! Oh, it's so, so bad," she wheezed before bracing her hand on the wall and laughing until tears streamed down her cheeks.

"Any chance these are circus fun-house mirrors and I

don't actually look like that?" I asked as I stared at my gargantuan reflection.

While Annie suffered from random bouts of laughter, I got a quick look at the outfit she had chosen. It was a little black dress that clung to her curves and hid any flaws she —oh, who was I kidding? The girl had none.

That body was smokin'.

"Will you stop laughing at me?" I demanded. "It's not my fault that every single maternity dress ever made comes exclusively in marshmallow Peeps colors."

That only made her laugh harder.

There was another knock on the door. "Miss? How is everything fitting?" the dressing-room attendant asked. "Can I get you anything in a different size?"

"Back off," I growled.

Annie wiped the tears from her cheeks. "We're okay, thank you!"

I swore I could hear the sounds of sniffling.

"Dude, I think you made her cry," Annie stage-whispered. "As if working retail isn't hard enough…"

"And I should know better, considering I used to be a server."

"For like a minute."

"Long enough." I shuddered at the memory of working at Antonio's. I remembered all the times I had wanted to cry. "I'll go apologize when we get out of here."

"I'm sure she'd appreciate that."

I looked her up and down. "What's it like?"

"What?"

"Everything you put on makes you look like a rock star."

"You'll look like that again one day, don't worry."

"Not only are you bad at comforting me, but you're a shitty liar."

"I'm afraid to say what I'm about to say—but I'm trying to do the feelings thing."

"Say it."

"Didn't you know—well—how much your body was going to change?"

"I'm proud of your diplomacy."

"Hardest thing I've done in my life."

"I avoid mirrors, put it that way."

"Really?"

I nodded.

"You can't avoid mirrors today if you want to find a dress that looks great on you for the baby shower."

"They all have empire waists."

"So? We'll get you a tiara and call you *Your Royal Highness.*"

"It feels like I'm giving in."

"To what, exactly?"

"To bad maternity clothes. We're in New York City. This is the epicenter of fashion. I should still be able to look trendy, not like I belong in an Easter basket."

"Oy." Annie ran a hand across her face. "And for the record, you just made an Episcopalian say *oy.* How'd I do?"

"Eight out of ten. Great inflection, but it needed a lot more guilt to be authentic."

She shook her head. "You also weren't trendy when you were skinny…"

"You. Bitch. If you're not nice to me, I'm going to demote you to sorta best friend. I'll give the title of real best friend to Stacy."

"You wouldn't dare."

I shrugged. "Try me."

"I love that you dress like a hipster," she lied poorly. "And from the back no one can tell you're pregnant."

"You ever think we should do a podcast together?"

"What would we call it?"

"*Two Snarky Bitches*. All we have to do is record our banter. I think we can sell this."

"I'm in." She grinned. "We have one department store left. If you don't find a dress, you might just have to go in your overalls and hiking boots."

"Not a bad idea."

"Your mother will *kill me* if I let you show up to her shower in hiking boots."

"It's *my* shower."

"Sibby, Sibby, Sibby. Did you learn nothing from your wedding?"

"What, all of my most important life moments are all about her now?"

"There ya go. So do us all a favor, pick an Easter-egg-colored dress and call it a day. And remember, everyone is going to think you're beautiful no matter what you wear."

"Because I'm the mother-to-be?"

"Well, that. But also because they'll be afraid to anger you for fear that you'll sit on them and destroy them."

"You really suck as a best friend."

"Buy you chicken wings to make up for it?"

"You're great at this best friend thing, you know that?"

"Okay. The next store is the one where you will find a dress—and shoes—I can feel it."

I sighed.

"What?"

"My feet grew two sizes."

"Cheer up. Maybe you can just become a champion swimmer or something, you know, 'cause big feet are basically flippers."

"Chicken wings *and* garlic knots."

"Dude. I'm in awe of your skills," Annie said in amazement.

I finished the last bite of the chocolate cake—which had come on the house, for winning the chicken wing-eating contest.

"If only I could use my powers for good instead of expanding my waistline."

"I shouldn't have let you get the Parmesan garlic dipping sauce. Aidan might never forgive me."

"He takes me any way he can get me. Garlic breath won't stop him." I leaned back against the booth and rested my hands across my belly. "There are things they don't tell you about being pregnant."

"They, who?"

"They, American culture. Everyone wants you to think it's nothing but a miracle and you're this gorgeous vessel of creation and life."

"That sounds—yeah."

"I snore."

"You snore?"

I nodded. "Yeah. And not in a cute, I-have-allergies, don't-you-find-me-hilarious kind of way. I mean, full-on trucker-with-a-gut-and-sleep-apnea snoring. I've woken up so many mornings to find Aidan on the couch. Just to escape me. And normally, I wouldn't be offended by such a thing. Sleep is sleep, right? But I'm already the size of an orca whale, and him sleeping on the couch makes me feel abandoned."

"Are you sure I'm the one who needs therapy?" she teased.

"I've had to start wearing nose strips."

She leaned forward really close to my face. "Is that what that indentation on your nose is from?"

"See? I'm a hideous creature. I won't let Aidan have sex with me if the lights are on. I'm Sibzilla right now and he can't see me that way."

"You are quite dramatic. Anyone ever tell you that?"

"You don't have to sound so amused by it."

"Sibby," she began, like she was about to school me on the ways of life, "you found a man who loves you unconditionally. Right?"

I squirmed in the booth. "Yeah."

"Well, doesn't it stand to reason that he's going to love you no matter what?"

"You're missing the point. This isn't about love. This is about traumatizing my husband so badly that he'll never want to have sex with me again."

Of course the young college-aged guy with effortlessly swept hair and a chiseled jaw arrived at our table at that exact moment.

His grin took up his entire face as he reached down to clear away my empty dessert plate. "I think you're gorgeous and I'd have sex with you."

Annie laughed into her water glass and a bit sloshed out the side.

I looked up at the server. "Are you in college?"

"Yeah."

"What are you studying?"

"Acting." His face fell. "Damn. I walked right into that one, didn't I?"

"Yep," Annie said.

"Well, I wasn't lying," he said, trying to salvage the conversation—and his tip.

I sighed. "I appreciate it. Honestly, I do. Even if it is a lie."

"It's not a lie. I like a woman who can put away an insane amount of chicken wings." He smiled and set the bill down on the table. "Whenever you're ready."

He walked away and Annie stared after him. "Solid ten out of ten on the rear end."

"He's a fetus."

"Hey, he could be prime boy toy material. You know, when you have your mid-life crisis, decide to get your boobs done, and fake tan yourself until you're orange, he might be the perfect play thing."

"You paint a lovely picture of me in my later years," I remarked dryly.

She threw down her credit card and Boy Toy came back and swooped it up. He returned a few minutes later with the check presenter, flashed me a smile, and then left. When Annie went to sign the credit card slip, she laughed.

"What?" I demanded.

She showed me the receipt.

I let out a laugh. "Shane left his number and a little heart. You're obligated to give him a thirty percent tip. You know that right?"

"He played us well." She quickly scribbled her signature and a tip.

I scooted out of the booth and made sure to grab all my shopping bags. Gone were the days where retail therapy made me feel better. Now it just reminded me that I didn't fit into any of my skinny-leg jeans.

I waved to Shane on our way out, causing Annie to laugh. She started to hum.

"Are you humming *Mrs. Robinson?*" I demanded.

"Maybe."

"You're worse than a five-year-old."

Annie grinned. "I'm preparing you for your offspring."

My current furry offspring was spinning in circles by the time I came home. Annie reached down to pet him while I set the shopping bags aside and reached for his leash.

"Someone has cabin fever," Annie commented, finally dropping her bags.

I clipped the leash to Jasper's collar. "Aidan is going to be pretty busy the next few months with the expansion. And then when the babies come... I just hope Jasper gets enough exercise and attention."

"Maybe Jasper needs a friend. You could get your dog a dog."

"Right, that's all we need. Another dog in this tiny apartment."

"It's not that tiny."

"Well, either way, I don't have the energy to handle a puppy. Even if it would benefit Jasper." The mutt pawed the front door. "I was going to walk Jasper to Veritas to see Aidan—"

"So that's your way of telling me not to come so Caleb won't throw things at my face?"

"Wow, you hardly stuttered over his name. Good for you."

She gave me a half smile. "Progress, right? I have to call your mother anyway."

"Um, why?"

"She wants to make sure all the stuff for the baby shower gets delivered and she needs me to oversee it."

I pinched the bridge of my nose. This weekend was going to be exhausting. Not only was my mother coming up for my baby shower, but Aidan's mom and sisters were driving down from Upstate.

"This is going to be rough, isn't it?" I asked her.

"Oh, yeah. For sure. I'll walk out with you," Annie said. "I have to head into the city, so I'll call your mom on the way to the train."

"Aren't you tired after our marathon shopping expedition?" I queried as I locked the front door.

"Meeting," she said cryptically.

"Does it have anything to do with your uncle's restaurant?"

"It might."

"And you really won't tell me?"

"Not yet. I will as soon as I can, okay?"

We hugged when we got down to the sidewalk and then walked in opposite directions. While Jasper took his time sniffing the bushes, I thought about how great it was to have Annie back in the city. I had really missed my best friend.

I envied Aidan. He got to work with Caleb. They were buddies as well as business partners. They trusted each other, and when things got heated they just duked it out until they were doing shots and laughing over how stupid it all was.

Veritas had just opened for the evening, but I didn't see

Aidan. Caleb was unloading a supply of bourbon and setting the bottles onto the bar.

"Hey. Where's Aidan?" I asked.

Caleb set a bottle on the bar and came around to give Jasper some love. "You know dogs aren't allowed in bars anymore, right?"

"He's my service animal. I have anxiety."

He grinned. "Your husband went to the bodega to grab us sandwiches. He should be back any minute. Sit." He gestured to the stool in the corner. Before I'd managed to hoist myself up onto the stool, Caleb had placed a glass of water in front of me. Jasper settled down at my feet.

"So," he began, "you excited for the baby shower?"

"Um. Sure?"

"That was lackluster."

"My mom is coming, which is a blessing and a curse. I'm preparing for the crazy." I cocked my head to the side. "Did I tell you that I think you're looking really good? Healthy."

"Thanks. I've been working out."

"Yeah, now that I look at you, I can tell you're bulkier. You're not becoming a meathead, are you?"

"Nah. Not my style."

I sighed. "This idle chitchat is making me crazy. I need to ask you something."

"Shoot."

I looked him dead in the eye when I asked, "Are you still in love with Annie?"

"Wow. No lube. Thanks for that," he remarked dryly. "I thought by tacit agreement we weren't going to mention her anymore."

"I think that rule is between you and Aidan."

"We talk about shit," Caleb admitted. "But only after

one too many beers. And that hasn't happened in a while. We haven't had a solid hangout in weeks."

I frowned. "Really? Why not?"

"We've been busy with the bar. Now the expansion. Plus—"

"Plus he comes home right away because of me and my uterus."

"I don't think it's about your uterus per se, just what's in it." He paused. "This went in a really weird direction."

"Story of my life. So if I don't want to talk about the baby shower, and you don't want to talk about Annie, what does that leave us to talk about?"

"I dunno. The Knicks?"

"Who?"

"Oh, man. Seriously?"

I grinned.

"You *are* kidding."

The bar's front door opened and Aidan strolled inside. He carried two wrapped sandwiches and tossed one at Caleb. Jasper jumped up off the ground and pawed Aidan's thighs. It seemed I wasn't the only one missing Aidan. And I knew that feeling was just going to get worse. When the sale of the property went through in about a month or so, then Aidan and Caleb would be even busier —like that was even possible.

"This is a nice surprise," Aidan said, scratching Jasper's head as he leaned over to kiss my cheek.

"Just coming to say hi," I said. "And ask if you wanted to go to dinner. But obviously you already planned on eating."

"Ah, yeah. I was going to call," he said. "Caleb asked if I could fill in behind the bar for him tonight."

"Why?" My eyes darted between both of them.

Aidan glanced at his buddy, who had the grace to look uncomfortable. He rubbed the back of his neck.

"I have a date."

"Someone new?" I ventured to ask.

"Yeah."

Awkward silence.

"Well, good for you." I rummaged up a smile.

"You're a shitty liar, Sibby," Caleb said with a chuckle.

"No, I mean it. I want you to be happy. You just caught me by surprise." I looked at Aidan. "I guess I'll see you later tonight. Way later."

"Or you could drop Jasper off at home and come back here. Read on your Kindle," he suggested.

"Read," I repeated. "Pregnant woman reading alone at a bar? Sounds kinda…ya know. Pathetic."

"You wouldn't be alone—I'll entertain you. And then I can stare at your pretty face."

I smiled up at him. "That sounds nice."

"You fucking guys," Caleb muttered. "You're like a Disney-movie couple."

"Hipster and the Beast?" I joked. "One guess who the beast is." I gestured to my body.

"Sibby," Aidan warned.

"Sorry, sorry." I held up my hands. "I'll run Jasper home and be back in an hour." I brushed my lips across his. I turned to Caleb. "Have fun tonight. But not too much fun. And just remember, putting out on the first date is considered forward."

"Wow, you're so antiquated, Sibby. Guess you've forgotten that you went home with Aidan on the first night you guys met?"

I remembered that night fondly. It had been the start of something truly wonderful; I just hadn't known it at the time.

Annie and Caleb had met then too; they'd had a very different outcome to their relationship.

The thought made me sad. Maybe it had been naive of me to think that their relationship could've turned out any other way. Not everyone got the happily ever after. Not everyone found their Aidan, who would love them through all their faults and all the hard times they would have together.

"Not that it's any of your business, Caleb, but I kept my knees together. Aidan wasn't that charming." I winked at my husband.

"You married me in the end. And you're pregnant, so I think it worked out okay."

"You grew on me like a fungus."

"And that's my cue," Caleb said. "Time to put these bourbon bottles away."

I kissed Aidan goodbye and headed out with Jasper. I got home just as the sun was beginning to set. Aidan and I had both been so busy we hadn't spent a lot of time together. Before I headed back to the bar, I got on my computer and searched a bunch of online-deal sites for a weekend vacation package.

"Boom!" I yelled, startling Jasper. "High-five me. I just found us a Poconos deal!" I held my hand up to Jasper, who looked at me in confusion. "Oh sure, you can figure out how to nose off the Xbox, but a high-five for your mother is too much to handle?" I scratched his ears and he laid back down, and a moment later he was snoring.

This was perfect.

I was going to kidnap my own husband for a romantic getaway.

## Chapter 8

Holishkes: [hole-ish-kes]

1. Stuffed cabbage, often filled with meatballs in a tomato based sweet and sour sauce.

2. Great, more peasant food.

"Pierogis!" my mother bellowed as she leaned over and hugged me around the middle.

Sometimes, I felt like I was put on this earth to make my mother a *bubbe*.

I exchanged an amused glance with my father who stood patiently next to her.

"Okay, time to let me go," I said.

"One more minute," she pled.

"If you let me go, I'll show you the nursery."

She dropped me like a sweet *kugel* and backed away. She'd just gotten off a plane and she looked incredible. I did not inherit that gene. The moment I stepped on a plane my hair frizzed and my clothes rumpled. My mother's lipstick was still completely intact and not a single hair was out of place. She had a way with hairspray that I'd never mastered.

"Hi, Dad," I said, embracing him. "You look good."

"Thanks, Sibby. So do you."

"Hmmm." I arched an eyebrow in disbelief.

"He's healthy too. Colon is clean as a whistle," Mom announced.

"Um, yay?"

"Where's Aidan?" she asked.

"Meeting with the bank," I said.

"So it's full steam ahead on buying the building, eh?" Dad asked.

I nodded.

"I'm so proud of him," Mom said, puffing out her chest. "He really went for it and now look at him."

"Yeah. He's a superstar in a beard. So do you want to see the nursery?" I asked, waving them toward the converted office. "We're still waiting on the furniture from Aidan's uncle, but we got the rest of it sorted. So, what do you think?" I opened the nursery door and gestured for them to go in.

"It looks great, Sibby," Dad said.

"Mom?" I looked at her.

Her eyes scanned over the walls. "It's nice."

That was Mama Goldstein's code for *meh*.

"What's wrong with it?" I demanded.

Out of the corner of my eye, I saw my father back out of the nursery and shoot me an apologetic look.

Traitor.

Letting me handle my mother on my own. That must've meant she'd been in fine form this past week and he knew something was coming. Full-on crazy *bubbe* mode.

"I just think it's a little...dull."

"Dull?"

She nodded. "There's no mural."

"I stenciled."

"The colors aren't bright. It's muted. And honey, once you get the baby furniture in here, there won't be any room left. You should really think about moving out of the city. You need more space for the twins, and whoever comes after the twins."

I blinked. "Whoever comes after the twins? What do you mean by that?"

"More babies, of course."

Hello, high blood pressure.

"Mom," I said as calmly as I could. "Our life is in the city. We are not moving to suburbia just to fulfill your dream of having a brood of grandchildren. Two is plenty. And may I remind you that you only had me."

"Not for lack of trying, Sibby."

"Yuck."

"You've already proven to be more fertile than me."

"Double yuck. So you're saying it's my job to have more children because you could only have me? That's a lot of pressure, Mother."

"Don't *mother* me, Sibyl Ruth."

"Don't *middle name* me!"

She arched perfectly waxed eyebrows, which only infuriated me more. That was Mom. No matter how frequently I got my eyebrows waxed I looked like the missing link.

I had a habitual Jewnibrow.

"How long are you going to be a city dweller?" she demanded. "Think of their development. The smog, the hustle and bustle, and—"

"You mean exposing the twins to jazz and Broadway, world-class food, an endless stream of art, culture, and creative options for their minds is an awful way to grow up?"

"Where are they going to learn to ride their bikes?"

"We live near parks."

"They'll have to take the subway to Montessori school and that will expose them to all kinds of cretins. Sibby, the suburbs are a better place to raise a family."

"Nothing is good enough for you," I blurted out.

"What do you mean, nothing is good enough for me?"

"I mean, you come in here, say the nursery is *nice* which we all know is your bullshit code for *this sucks.*"

"Language, Sibby."

"No. You don't get to language me, Mom. I'm an adult. And if I don't want to make the nursery look like Toys "R" Us upchucked in here, then that's my prerogative. And if Aidan and I want to raise our babies in the city, then that's our prerogative, too."

"Why are you so upset?"

"Have you been listening?"

"Yes, Sibby, I've been listening," she said, her tone calm and placating. "I don't think you're really mad at me. I think you're mad at yourself."

"Oh, did you suddenly become a psychologist as well as a matchmaker?"

"You're picking a fight with me, just like when you were a teenager."

"You came into *my* apartment and instead of hugging me, you hugged my belly. Do you know what that feels like?"

She looked taken aback, like it had never occurred to her that maybe I found it offensive.

"You're proud of Aidan. You're excited to be a grand-mother. But what about me, Mom? What about *me*?"

"I told you I was proud of you and your book. I read it. We sent you a gift basket. I'm still waiting on that thank you note, by the way. I taught you better than that."

"You have to send a thank you note to your own parents? That seems a little formal."

"We all like to be appreciated." She sniffed.

"All we talk about is baby stuff. Why don't you ask me how I am doing independently of motherhood? I haven't stopped being my own person, you know."

Her skin paled. "I'm sorry, Sibby. I didn't—I mean, I know I get overexcited…"

Pomeranians got overexcited. My baby-hungry Jewish mother got *verklempt*. At least my mother didn't pee on the carpet when that happened.

"I think I need some air," she said softly. She turned and walked out of the nursery.

I heard the front door of the apartment close and only then did I go into the living room. My father was on the couch, his coat was off, and Jasper was already lying across my father's trousers. The TV was on, but it was low. My dad muted the television and looked at me with a knowing expression.

I took a seat on the couch next to him, moving Jasper so I could sit. "Am I wrong?"

"No."

"Really?"

"You're not. But you and your mother do this. You get

into fights because neither of you can hear one another. You've always been that way, you know. She also doesn't like that she's so far away from you and can't help out."

"I don't want her help," I muttered.

"She knows that too. Which also hurts her feelings."

"I'm trying to figure all this out. I know she's there if I need help, but I want to do this with Aidan. Me and Aidan. Not me, Aidan, and Mom. Does that make sense?"

"Yes."

"My wedding was about her," I pointed out. "I had the wedding *she* wanted me to have. I was fine with it because Aidan was fine with it. But this. This is different. This is me learning how to be a mother. I don't want any judgment over it."

"She's going through a transition."

"What, like menopause? I thought she went through that already."

"Not menopause. But—well—she started this match-making business because she needs to be needed."

"She insulted my nursery and then had the audacity to tell me where I should live, how I should raise my babies. The muffins aren't even baked yet, you know?"

"Cut her some slack. She's just very excited." He hugged me to him. "Can you do that for me, Wapa Bug?"

"If you stop calling me that odious nickname from my childhood, I will."

110

I woke up the next morning to a sight of taffeta and tissue paper. And ribbons. So many ribbons. Aidan wasn't around and neither was Jasper, so I assumed they'd gone for a walk to escape the apartment.

"Morning, sunshine," Annie said with a wry grin.

"What time is it?" I asked.

"Seven," my mother said without looking up from the mason jars in front of her.

"In the morning?" I blurted out. "Such an ungodly hour."

Annie was sitting on the floor. She was still in her pajamas, her hair in a messy top bun. But Mom had a full face of makeup and perfect hair.

How, just how?

I suddenly had a flashback to the days leading up to my wedding. I'd had a panic attack. Not about marriage or Aidan. But because of all the taffeta. I'd dreamt I was drowning in a cream puff of a dress.

And now those feelings of panic were coming back full-throttle.

"What is all this?" I asked, moving aside fabric so I could take a seat on the couch.

"We're making gifts and decorations for your baby shower." Mom poured clear liquid into mason jars which Annie then took and added wicks.

"Homemade oil lanterns?" I remarked. "Those are really freakin' cool!"

"Your mother's idea," Annie said with a smile. "I blew her mind with Pinterest."

"I'm obsessed." Mom looked at me and grinned. It faded quickly.

We couldn't have an honest conversation with Annie in the room, but I didn't want to be at odds with my mother. Not now, and definitely not during the baby shower.

"It looks amazing. Thank you for doing all of this —for me."

Her gaze softened in understanding. "It's my pleasure. Thank you for letting me."

Annie pretended to be busy tying a bow around a mason jar. She wasn't completely oblivious about what went on between me and my mother. I'd told Annie everything when she'd gotten back to the apartment last night.

My relationship with my mother was an ongoing saga, and most of the time I could laugh it off. We didn't live near each other, so it was easy to deal with it from a distance. But with all the hormones running rampant through my ever-expanding body, I just didn't have the bandwidth to handle our usual MO.

I got up off the couch and went to get myself a cup of coffee. "Where's Aidan and Jasper?"

"Jasper is with Mrs. Nowacki, and Aidan is with your father having breakfast."

"How much more do you have to do?" I wondered.

"A few hours' worth."

I tapped the rim of my mug as I inhaled the fragrant aroma. "Caffeinated?" I asked Annie.

"Yup."

"Awesome." My doctor had told me I was allowed one cup of caffeinated coffee a day, and most of the time I didn't need it, but something told me that for the next couple of days, I'd need the fortification.

"Want some help?" I asked.

"You can't help with your own baby shower," Annie said with an eye roll.

"So what, I'm just supposed to sit and talk with you guys but not help?"

"You have an appointment at nine," Annie said.

"I do?" I reached for my phone to pull up my calendar, but there was nothing there.

"Yes. Aidan got you a spa day."

"A spa day? Really?" I felt tears prick my eyes.

"No," Annie whispered. "No, no, no. Please don't cry."

"I can't help it!" I wailed.

Mom handed me a box of tissues from the end table. I plucked a few and blotted my eyes.

"I remember when I was pregnant with you and it was near the end. And I was so miserable and I was ready for you to come out. I couldn't sleep and I'd get up out of bed and head downstairs to the couch to read. I didn't want to wake your father up, you know? He had rounds and he needed his sleep. Anyway, he came down one morning to find me on the couch. I'd fallen asleep sitting up. He didn't like that I wasn't sleeping in our bed; he bought me a book light so I could read next to him in bed. I burst into tears at his thoughtfulness." She shook her head and smiled at the memory. "Funny. What you remember."

"What a good guy," Annie said with a sigh.

"You looking for a good guy?" Mom asked. "I know one. A nice Jewish boy who helped me set up my website. He lives in Atlanta."

"It's a nice idea, but I don't do long distance," Annie said.

"He'd be worth the move," Mom assured her. "He has a nice *tuchus*."

"Should've led with that, Mama Goldstein," Annie said with a grin. "I'm totally sold."

The babies were playing my bladder like a set of bongos. I shifted uncomfortably on the couch and contemplated getting up, but Aidan was rubbing my feet and we were watching a rom-com.

"You okay?" he asked, dragging his eyes away from the screen to look at me.

I nodded. "My bladder is being squashed by your children."

He grinned.

"And I don't want to move because you're rubbing my feet and this is my favorite part of the movie."

"I can pause the movie, and I promise to rub your feet when you get back."

I wiggled my toes and showed off the bright red polish. "Thank you. For the spa day."

He tweaked my big toe. "You're welcome."

"It was really sweet of you."

"I know."

I laughed. "Are you ready for your surprise?"

"Sex?" he asked hopefully. "Wait, is Annie coming back here?"

"No. She's staying with friends in the city tonight."

"We have the apartment to ourselves?"

"Yes, we have the apartment to ourselves, but I wasn't offering sex. I mean, I am. But just—hold on." I reached for my phone on the coffee table and pulled up the reservation at the hotel in the Poconos and showed it to him.

"What's this?" He took the phone and looked at the screen.

"It's going to be our reward for surviving our families. Can you get away next weekend?"

"You set this up? Without checking with me first?"

My face fell. "Aidan, I—"

He lifted my legs off of him and then leaned across the couch to hug me. It was awkward because my belly got in the way, but somehow we made it work.

"Thanks, Sib. This is—well, it's been a while since we've done anything for just the two of us, out of the city. This is perfect."

I sighed in relief. "Our free time is about to become nonexistent. For years. I just figured, get it while we still can."

His hand slithered its way under my shirt. "Oh, I'll get it," he leered. "If you let me."

"Oof! Someone just kicked my bladder."

I struggled to sit up and Aidan had to help. I went to the bathroom and then came out a few minutes later, prepared to put the movie on hold to seduce my husband. Dinner had finally settled and I was getting my second wind.

Unfortunately, Aidan was conked out on the couch, Jasper next to him. I studied him for a moment, noticing the lines of fatigue around his mouth and eyes. He worked all the time now and what spare time he did have, we were always doing baby stuff. Birthing class, baby shopping, baby reading, preparing for the baby shower.

Baby, baby, baby.

Was I giving Aidan enough attention? Did he feel loved? The last thing I wanted to do was ignore him. Sure,

I was growing two humans inside of me and trying to balance my needs with theirs, but what about Aidan?

He was taking care of me—of us. But who was taking care of him?

I burst into tears, startling him awake.

"Wha—what is it?" he asked, looking around to see if I'd set something on fire again.

"I'm sorry!" I blubbered.

Poor guy looked completely at a loss. "For what?"

"For ignoring you!"

"You think you've been ignoring me? Sibby, you've been amazing. I don't know how you do it." He took me into his arms and let me cry it out. This was the second time I'd cried today. A pigeon with a broken wing had set me off earlier, and I *hated* pigeons.

"You just booked us a romantic weekend in the Poconos. Clearly you're thinking about me—about us."

"I don't want to do that thing where I miss you even though we live together."

"Okay," he said in a tone that clearly meant he had no idea what I was talking about.

"When was the last time we talked about something that wasn't bar-related, book-related, or baby-related?"

He rubbed my back. "It's going to be okay, you know. The bar will go through its growing pains with the expansion; we'll go through growing pains when our family dynamic changes. We'll have to find a new normal, but we'll be okay. We're Aidan and Sibby."

I sniffled. "Does Caleb like this new girl?"

"I'm getting conversation whiplash here," Aidan said, pulling away. He went and turned off the Xbox and TV.

I continued, "If he starts dating this girl, then that's it. He and Annie won't have a chance to reconcile."

His face screwed up in confusion. "He was dating another girl before this one…"

"No. He was sleeping with her to help his ego. But she was his rebound. He's done rebounding."

"You seem to have some very clear insight into the male brain."

"Are you saying I'm wrong?"

"I'm saying it doesn't matter if Caleb dates this girl or another because this thing with Annie is done."

"You're such a guy. Have you learned nothing from watching rom-coms these past many years?"

"I know you write them, Sibby, but let's be honest: rom-coms aren't real life."

"Take it back."

"No."

"Take it back or no sex for you," I said jokingly.

"Fine, I take it back," he said with a grin.

I paused. "You don't really take it back, do you?"

"Nope. And you're not really withholding sex, are you?"

"Nope. We'd both lose." I paused for a moment. "They still have feelings for each other."

"Of course. Caleb is still feeling a lot of anger about the whole thing."

"That bodes well for his new relationship…"

"They're not in a relationship. They're dating—there's a difference." He looked at Jasper, who had escaped to his dog bed when I'd burst into tears. Jasper was on his back, spread-eagle, junk on display. Or what was left of his junk since he'd been snipped.

"I should take him out before we…ya know." He waggled his eyebrows. "Do you want to come with us?"

"How cold is it?"

Aidan reached for his phone and pulled up the weather app. "Eighteen degrees."

"How many?"

"Eighteen," he repeated with a grin. "Prime hunting-hat weather."

"No thanks. I'm good."

"I won't be long." He called Jasper and quickly leashed him, not bothering to put Jasper in his dog sweater for a quick walk around the block.

Aidan's hand was on the doorknob when he said, "Promise me something."

"I swear I'll be awake when you get home."

"Not that."

"You don't want me to stay awake?"

"Sibby," he growled. "Promise me you won't meddle."

My mouth gaped. "But I'm Jewish. It's what we do. *And* my mother is a matchmaker. It's in my DNA!"

"Leave him be, Sibby," Aidan said softly. "He couldn't get out of bed for two weeks after they broke up, remember?"

I grimaced. "Yeah, I remember."

"You could make it worse. He's finally starting to act like himself. Please don't put him through that again."

"Okay, I'll stay out of it."

"I want your word. No meddling in other people's business."

"Okay, Ricky Ricardo. I hear you. Loud and clear."

He sighed. "Lucy never listened to Ricky. I have a feeling you won't listen to me either."

## Chapter 9

Challah: [KHala—say it with the back of your throat, and if you spit on the person next to you, you did it right]

1. Egg-bread. Golden brown on the outside, and delicious and doughy in the center.

2. Holla!

My alarm went off the next morning. I was already awake, flipped over onto my back, and staring at the ceiling.

Today was the day.

BS-day.

Baby Shower day.

I smelled freshly brewed coffee and wondered how early Aidan had gotten up.

As I washed my hands in the bathroom sink, I took a moment to look in the mirror. I gripped porcelain as my mouth dropped open.

"No. No, no, no!" I cried in horror.

Directly in the center of my head, in the spot between my newly waxed eyebrows was a massive zit. It was red and angry and I knew, without a shadow of a doubt, concealer wouldn't do anything to actually conceal it.

"Why, God, why?" I bemoaned.

I heard the front door open and close and then the sound of Jasper running across the wood floor to his water bowl.

"Sibby?" Aidan called.

"Yeah," I called back. "I'm up."

"Do you want some coffee?"

"All right."

"Are you okay? You sound weird. Like you swallowed a ferret."

I stared at my forehead. Jeez, was it growing? It looked like it was growing. I closed my eyes. Why? Why did this have to happen today? On a day where I was going to be the center of attention. With photos! And for crying out loud, the monster zit couldn't be in a place easily hidden? Like my hairline or on my *tuchus*?

This was worse than being a teenager. As a teenager, I'd had a few acne flare-ups that resulted in a laugh or two, but all-in-all my teenage years hadn't been too emotionally damaging.

But at age twenty-nine I was fat and oily, and sharing my body with two babies that used my organs as hacky sacks, and my hormones were causing all sorts of things to happen.

I washed my face and then came out of the bathroom just as Aidan sauntered into the living room, holding two cups of coffee.

"Here you go—oh." His eyes immediately went to the zit. "What happened?"

"What happened? What do you mean *what happened?* My hormones have run amok."

"It's not that bad," he lied, his eyes still riveted to my forehead.

"Not that bad?" I glared. "I look like a cyclops."

Aidan closed his eyes and turned away, but not before I saw him stifling his laughter. His shoulders began to shake.

"Shut up!" I cried. "What am I going to do? I can't go out looking like this!"

"Sibby, you can absolutely go outside."

"No. It's not Halloween. I need to sit at home in the dark where I won't scare little children and old people with heart conditions."

If I looked like a troll under a bridge, then damn it, I was going to act like one too.

Aidan had just taken a sip of his coffee, but my comment made him spit it out. "You're killing me here."

"Good. This is your fault."

He sighed, but his blue eyes were still lit with humor. "Because I'm the one that got you pregnant, and therefore indirectly responsible for the monster zit on your face?"

"*Monster?* You said it wasn't that bad! You"—I pointed at him—"lied to me!"

"Oy."

"No. You don't get to *oy* me."

"What do you want me to say? You can't skip your own baby shower." He looked at his watch. "Your mother should be here any minute to get the decorations."

"Oh, great. More people to witness my shame."

"Shame? What's the shame? You're human. This happens to everyone."

"Not you," I snapped. "I've seen photos of you as a teenager. You were hot then. You're hotter now. And other women think you're hot and with me looking like a swamp creature, you're no doubt thinking about other options."

He looked heavenward, but wisely said nothing.

"This is the kind of zit where if we had a teenage daughter I'd let her stay home from school so she wouldn't have to deal with the psychological abuse from bullying."

"Good thing we're having two boys then," he said.

I shook my head. "I hope they're good at sports."

"What does that have to do with anything?"

"They'll be popular. Life is easier for popular kids."

"It wasn't easy," he said. "I still felt alone and misunderstood."

"Oh, man. You had that James Dean thing going for you, didn't you?" I rolled my eyes. "I married the popular jock. How did that happen?"

"Because I'm sweet and kind, and *amazing* in bed." I laughed and he smiled. "And we have a pretty good life, don't we?"

"What does that have to do with anything?" I demanded.

"If you can be nonsensical, so can I."

"Do you know anything about women?"

"I know everything about you, Sib. Who cares about other women?"

I sighed. "Rats."

"What?"

"You make it impossible to get irrationally mad at you."

His grin was broad and sexy. How he managed to look like that so early in the day, I'd never know.

"Remind me to thank your parents," I muttered.

"For what?"

"Never mind." The buzzer sounded. "Bet that's Mom."

Aidan pressed the buzzer. A few moments later, he opened the door. Not just my mother—but my aunt *and* my *bubbe.*

"Surprise!" my mother greeted. "Look who just got in from LaGuardia!"

"Sibby!" Aunt Rebecca boomed, embracing me. She leaned back. "What happened to your face?"

"Ugh!" I moaned, trying to cover my forehead with my hands.

*Bubbe* shoved my aunt aside and grasped my chin in her hands. "I know old country recipe," she said in her thick German accent. "I need potato, oil, egg, flour, and onion."

"To make a potato *latke?*" I asked in bemusement.

"I have potato," Mrs. Nowacki said, appearing in the open doorway.

*Bubbe* and Mrs. Nowacki spent a moment sizing each other up. Was there going to be an Eastern European rumble?

*Bubbe* said something in German. Mrs. Nowacki answered in the same language. Then Mrs. Nowacki said something in Polish. *Bubbe* answered back in Polish. The two of them hugged and began chattering, switching between Polish and German and completely ignoring the rest of us.

"You come with me, I have all the ingredients," Mrs. Nowacki finally said in English, grabbing onto *Bubbe's* hand and pulling her toward her apartment.

"Might be time for me to take Jasper and head to Caleb's," Aidan said.

"If you leave me alone with them, I'll divorce you," I threatened.

"Empty threat," he said and kissed my cheek. He whispered in my ear, "Self-preservation. You get it, right?"

I glared at him in jealousy.

With a quick hello and goodbye to my mother and aunt, Aidan managed to get into his boots and coat, suited up Jasper, and was out the door before Mrs. Nowacki and *Bubbe* came back.

"Now I need potato peeler," *Bubbe* announced.

My eye began to twitch.

"Annie!" I heard my mother greet.

"Hi," Annie said. "What's going on in here?"

I didn't move from my position on the couch because I was currently holding a potato pancake poultice to the center of my forehead.

"The apartment has been invaded," I said.

"Hush, you," my aunt Rebecca said from somewhere behind the couch. "*Bubbe* and I flew in this morning to surprise Sibby."

"I didn't think you were going to be able to attend the baby shower," Annie said.

"Last-minute schedule change," Aunt Rebecca said.

"What's Sibby doing—and what's on her face?"

"A big zit," my mother said without mincing words. "*Bubbe* has a recipe to get rid of it."

"I'm sure it's not that—"

I slowly removed the poultice, made sure it wouldn't fall apart, and showed her.

"Damn," she murmured.

"I guess that means it's not any smaller," I muttered, trying not to cry.

"Put it back on your forehead," Aunt Rebecca commanded.

It was sometimes difficult to tell her and my mother apart. Aunt Becca was only ten months older than my mother. People always thought they were twins. Not to mention, they were both dramatic and loud, and really good at the guilt thing.

I put the poultice back on my forehead and leaned back.

"Where's Aidan?" Annie asked.

"He took the dog and went to Caleb's," Mom said. I heard a phone ring. "Oh, that's mine, let me grab it. It's work!"

"Work?" I asked. "You mean—wait, was that the matchmaker song from *Fiddler on the Roof?*"

"Yes. It was my idea," Aunt Becca said, sounding proud of herself.

"And what's that delicious aroma?" Annie asked. I felt her tap my feet and I moved them aside so she could sit down.

"The cooked version of what's on my face."

"I don't follow."

"*Latkes*," Aunt Becca clarified. "Though it does feel weird to be eating *latkes* in February."

"They're a Hanukkah food, right?" Annie asked.

"Ding, ding, ding! You win the Jewish *Jeopardy!* category!"

"Are you being snarky or hormonal?" Annie demanded.

"Yes."

"Oh, great. Snark on steroids."

"Snark with a side of bitterness, thank you very much."

"So what's exactly in this zit-be-gone recipe?" Annie wondered. "So I know for next time."

"I haven't seen a pimple on your face in years."

"Now the true feelings come out," she said, humor in her tone. "You hate me for my perfect skin."

"Among other reasons—you wet dream."

Awkward pause.

"Too far?" I asked.

"Just far enough."

Mom interjected, "I've been asked to organize the Purim Carnival at the Temple, and they want me to include a matchmaking session for the old people."

"Mom, they're all people in your age bracket. Does that mean you're—"

"Don't finish that sentence, Sibyl Ruth."

"Go you!" Aunt Becca said.

I heard a slapping of hands.

"Did they just high-five?" I asked Annie.

"Yup."

"This is utterly ridiculous." I sat up. "*Bubbe!* When can I take off this compress?"

"In a little while," *Bubbe* called back from the confines of the kitchen.

"*Latkes* are cooked!" Mrs. Nowacki added.

The two of them had become fast friends and spoke to each other in a mixture of Polish and German. It made me realize how lonely Mrs. Nowacki truly was. Her children didn't live in New York any more, and her husband had passed at least a decade prior. *Bubbe* still had *Zayde*, and they lived close to my parents and other extended family so she didn't feel that loneliness.

I was glad that Mrs. Nowacki had become a part of our family. She looked out for me and Aidan, and for Jasper, and one day soon, she'd get to meet the twins and be a part of their lives too.

There wasn't enough space around the kitchen table for all of us, so we ate in the living room. As I finished the last bite of my *latke*, *Bubbe* got up from the living room chair and went to the coffee table where the serving dish of *latkes* rested.

She looked at my empty plate and without bothering to ask if I was still hungry, she slid a *latke* onto it. Then she took it upon herself to slather the *latke* with sour cream and applesauce.

"Oh, I'm full—"

"Eat, you too thin," *Bubbe* commanded, leaving no room for argument.

"Much too thin," Mrs. Nowacki agreed.

"I've already had five," I protested.

"Four for twins, one for you. Eat another and make it even." *Bubbe* winked.

I looked down at my plate, wondering if I had just enough room to shovel it in. Oh, who was I kidding? These were potato *latkes*!

*Bubbe* retook her seat and began *kibbitzing* with Mrs. Nowacki about *kreplach* recipes. Mom and Aunt Becca were on the opposite side of the living room, sitting in twin kitchen chairs, brainstorming about the Purim Carnival. That left me and Annie on the couch. We looked at each other and tried not to laugh.

"You know, if I didn't have a front-row seat to your life, I wouldn't believe it," she said, wheezing on a chuckle.

"Right?" I'd been holding the poultice with one hand and eating with the other. I removed the potato mash from my face and pointed to my forehead. "Is it smaller?"

She peered closer. "You know what? It really is."

"Awesome." I shoved the poultice back onto my forehead. "I have four more hours to get rid of this thing."

Annie leaned over toward my plate. She cut off a piece of *latke* and ate it. "Or, you could charge it rent since it looks like it moved in."

"Bite me."

## Chapter 10

Chopped liver: [cH-ahp'd liv-er]

1. A savory spread made from sautéed liver and onions.

2. Ick. And really, who doesn't know how to pronounce chopped.²

"Well, what do you think?" Annie asked as I gaped at the decorations. We were standing in the dining room of a quaint West Village restaurant that Zeb managed.

"I think it's the most beautiful thing I've ever seen," I stated. "Thank you."

"Thank your mom. She organized the hell out of this party. I just did as I was told."

"And collaborated with Zeb on the menu. Are those baby quiches over there?"

"Yep. All the food is in mini form. Except for the cake." She gestured to a wedding-sized, four-tiered, blue-frosting cake in the corner of the room.

Would it be bad form to stick my face in the top layer and eat until I hit the table? Maybe that would cover my zit which I hadn't been able to fully get rid of, but luckily it had shrunk in size enough to be covered by makeup.

"Are you sure you like it, Sibby?" Annie asked, biting her lip in apprehension.

"I love it," I assured her.

I had worried that I was going to walk into an overly girly, tulle-infested nightmare. But it wasn't anything like that. A mason jar candle and a bouquet of flowers graced the center of each table. The accent colors were three different shades of blue and the tablecloths were cream.

"She listened," I murmured. "Didn't she? She thought about what I'd like versus what she'd like, and she made this about me."

"She's trying, Sib," Annie admitted. "It's hard for her."

My mother was currently flitting around the room, ensuring that everything was in its place before guests arrived. My family was already here, having all trekked together from my apartment into the city.

Mrs. Nowacki and *Bubbe* were glued to one another, *schmoozing* in the corner, holding flutes of something bubbly.

"Uh oh. *Bubbe* has a glass of champagne," I muttered.

"Uh oh," Annie repeated.

"How can that woman hold her vodka, but not her champagne? Do you remember what happened at my wedding?"

"Oh yes, I was there."

We thought we'd managed to cut *Bubbe* off from the champagne, but only later did we find out she'd been sneaking it. Many glasses of bubbly liquid later she'd decided to get up on stage and publicly bless Aidan's sperm in a mixture of broken English, Yiddish, and Hebrew. The next day she didn't even remember she'd done it.

"But what can she do now?" Annie asked. "You're already knocked up with twins. So it would seem that her blessing on Aidan's virility did the trick. She's like a Jewish shaman."

"If that's the case, then let's prevent her from making another public blessing. Who knows the strength of her powers."

My phone vibrated with a text from Aidan's mother. She, along with Aidan's two older sisters, were trying to find a place to park.

"Sibby!" Mom greeted, striding closer. "You look beautiful."

"Thank you." I hugged her. "And thank you for this. It's more than I—just wow. You're going to knock it out of the park with the Purim Carnival."

She beamed.

"Where's Aunt Becca?" I looked around. I'd seen her a few minutes ago, arranging the platters of food, but she'd disappeared.

"On the phone with your uncle Michael. She wants to make sure he's eating those low-carb meals she made for him before she left."

I knew my uncle. No way was that man eating low-carb anything. If Aunt Becca wasn't there to slap a baked good out of his hand, he would succumb to the temptation.

"Grab yourself a mocktail from the hunky bartender. People will start showing up any moment. Annie? Will you help me move the gift table?"

"Sure thing," Annie said.

When my mom and Annie left to tend to hostess duties, I was left alone. I stood for a moment before wandering over to the bar. The bartender was cute, but I didn't recognize him—and I had eaten at the bar plenty of times in the last many months. It was the only time I could see Zeb. Between his busy schedule, his blissful state of domestic cohabitation, and my pregnancy, we never found time to go out anymore.

Not that I enjoyed the gay-club scene before I was pregnant, but I definitely wouldn't enjoy it now. Gay men had amazing bodies. I didn't need to be reminded that what minor abs I'd once possessed were now gone.

"Hi," the bartender greeted with a smile. "Guest of honor?"

"Something like that. I'm Sibby."

He reached over the bar to shake my hand. "Mills. What can I get you?"

"Oh, um. Cranberry seltzer. With a lime and a cherry, please."

Mills winked. He was really cute. Tall, broad. Dark hair that fell across his forehead. Once upon a time, I would've tried to awkwardly flirt with him. But I had my own husband to awkwardly flirt with—and he found me adorable and irresistible for some unknown reason.

The bartender was completely charming and his eyes kept straying to Annie, who was in the corner of the room, helping my mother move the gift table.

Mills handed me my drink. "So your friend—"

"Taken," I lied with a commiserating smile.

He nodded good-naturedly. I took my drink and left. Did I feel remorse lying to the bartender about Annie's relationship status? A little. But she was on a testosterone sabbatical, so what did it matter?

Aidan told me not to get involved, but our two best friends were heartbroken and still in love with each other. I didn't care what any of them said. I knew better. And damn if I wasn't going to use every trick in the book to get them back together. Or at least in the same room so they could work out their feelings. If only I could find a way to lock them in an elevator together…

Friends started to arrive. Jess, my old manager from Antonio's showed up on the heels of Katrina, a Russian waitress who'd scared the living daylights out of me when I'd first started working with her. But once I'd made her laugh and shared my chocolate, she'd become, well, not warm, exactly. But she tolerated me and for her that was a meaningful thing.

After we caught up for a few minutes, Katrina wandered over to *Bubbe* and Mrs. Nowacki and started talking with them.

"It's like an Eastern European party over there," I said to Jess.

"Only Kat could get away with wearing black to a baby shower." Jess shook her head. She, however, was wearing a plum sweater dress and rocking knee-high black boots.

"Right? I'll never forget. I gave her a book recommendation and you know what she said to me? The book was almost perfect. The only way it would have been better is if they had all died."

"Well, her favorite book is *Anna Karenina*," Jess pointed out.

"She makes it so easy, doesn't she?" I said with a laugh.

"That she does. Maybe we're all just walking clichés, you know?"

Speaking of clichés.

My Jewish mother had somehow cornered Annie and

was talking to her about something uncomfortable. I knew that because I could literally see Annie looking around for someone to rescue her.

Her gaze landed on mine and she widened her eyes in desperation.

"I have to go save my best friend," I said to Jess.

"Do it. I'm going to get a mimosa."

Jess headed to the bar and I went to liberate Annie from my mother's meddling presence. As I approached, I heard my mom, once again, telling Annie about the nice Jewish web designer in Atlanta.

Was I no different from my own mother? I wanted Annie and Caleb back together, but did I really know what was best for them?

Me, a clone of my mother.

Now *that* was a truly terrifying thought.

Aidan's mother and sisters arrived, immediately taking the party to the next level. My family and his family absolutely adored each other, despite the fact that they had nothing in common. Aidan's mom and sisters were totally down to earth. They were into camping and gardening, and rocked the ponytail and makeup-free face routine.

My mother and aunt on the other hand…

My feet hurt just thinking about the amount of heels the both of them possessed. They were Southern women, through and through. They went to the hair salon every five weeks to touch up their gray roots, lipstick was mandatory, and they could get away with almost anything due to the light Southern drawls and the *bless her hearts*.

They were so different, and yet our families mingled easily and had truly become *mishpacha*.

Our Jewish wedding had been an epic celebration of the blending of families. Not to mention all the drinking. So much drinking. My father and Aidan's father doing tequila shots, my mother and Aidan's mother drinking Caleb's signature cocktail and planning a pregnancy we hadn't even given them yet. If it had been left up to them, I would've gotten knocked up on my wedding night.

"Your mother did a wonderful job," Nancy said with a smile as she took a sip of her drink.

"I agree. You're not offended, are you?" I asked suddenly. "That she kinda took over and—"

Nancy patted my arm. "No. I understand. I have three girls." She gestured with her chin to two of Aidan's sisters, Janet and Melanie, who were talking to Jess. "Though I doubt I'll get to throw Kara a baby shower any time soon."

"Where is she now?" I asked, thinking about the youngest Kincaid.

"Vietnam. We think?" She sighed. "I wish she'd stop traveling and settle down. But"—she shrugged—"not my life."

Aidan's youngest sister popped up randomly, whenever she had a few free days. She had come to our wedding, but she was a photojournalist and traveled to crazy remote places all over the world. Some of them were very dangerous. That wasn't something she was ever going to just get over or stop doing. She liked the excitement.

I liked excitement every now and again too. Sometimes, I even wore mismatching socks.

On purpose.

"Sibby!" Stacy greeted.

I whirled and was quickly embraced. I introduced her to Nancy, but then Aidan's mom excused herself so she could mingle.

My eyes raked over her. "You look great."

"I started eating red meat again," she confided.

"Ah, that must be it," I said with a smile.

"Beautiful party."

"Isn't it? My mom did a great job with Annie's help."

"They totally nailed it," she mused.

We caught up for a few minutes—I hadn't seen Stacy in a few weeks, since she'd decided to follow her boyfriend to a few of his cross-country gigs. I had thoughts on that matter, but I wisely kept them to myself.

"Cute bartender," Stacy commented.

"Good mixologist too," I stated, lifting my glass to show her. "Perfect amount of cranberry juice."

She laughed. "It doesn't bug you that everyone is drinking but you?"

"I've gotten used to it. I don't even miss the booze anymore."

"Huh. Really?"

I grinned. "No. I'm totally lying. I can't wait to have a glass of wine."

"Ooooh wine! You mind?"

"Be my guest," I said, waving her toward the dreamy bartender.

I was sipping on my drink when someone behind me said, "This party is way tamer than your bachelorette party!"

Nat's voice startled me and liquid went up my nose and splashed out of the glass onto my cleavage.

"Sorry," she said with a chuckle. She quickly hopped

over to the bar, grabbed some napkins, and brought them back to me.

I mopped at my face and then my chest. "You know how to pull off one hell of a surprise." For weeks Nat had told me she wouldn't be able to make it to New York for my baby shower. "How did you keep it a secret?"

"Sheer willpower. Totally worth it since I got you to spill your drink." She looked around. "I'm impressed, Sibby."

"It's all too Sibbilized if you ask me," I said with a laugh. "Is it horrible?"

"Nah," she said. "But you won't be getting drunk at your own baby shower and then texting Aidan really awful poetry."

"Ah, my bachelorette party. Such a good night…from what I can remember. Though, to be honest, I haven't been that drunk since. That hangover was one for the books."

"Dude," she said with a nod.

"Drink?" I suggested. We went to the bar and I set aside the soiled napkins while Nat ordered a cocktail. "So how did you escape Houston?"

"Tad is handling the beast. For three whole days!"

"Wahoo! Any grand plans?"

"Meeting up with you so we can catch up, obviously."

I grinned. "Obviously."

"And then I plan on eating my way through the city. God, I miss the food here so much." She took a sip of her drink, her eyes wandering around the room. And then her lips widened into a huge smile because she saw Zeb and his boyfriend walk in. Terry carried a beautiful cream paper-wrapped present with a big, silver bow.

Zeb pressed a kiss to my cheek in greeting and hugged Nat tightly. "I can't believe I'm at one of these things," he teased, plucking the gift from Terry's hands. He took it over to the present table and then got waylaid by my mother.

"He does know that this will be you guys in a few years when you adopt a cute Asian baby, right?" I said to Terry.

Terry smiled. "Yeah, but he likes to live in denial."

"You mean he still likes to pretend he's twenty-two and a rager?"

"Pretty much."

"Wow. None of us are that anymore. Bonkers."

Nat nodded. "No kidding. Sometimes, I'm like, whoa, I have a kid and a husband, and a mortgage, and going to Costco when they hand out samples is like adult Disneyland."

"That's because their samples are amazing," Zeb stated, returning to our group and hearing the tail end of Nat's comment. "Ah-ma-zing!"

"Totally," Terry agreed.

"I heart Costco," I said with a dreamy sigh. "We went a few months ago for all of our paper needs and walked out with a three-hundred-dollar blender."

"Three hundred dollars?" Zeb exclaimed. "For a blender? What's this appliance do?"

"Everything. Dice, purée, whisk, make nut butter, rice flour, ice cream—"

"Okay, but three hundred dollars? That's a bit excessive."

"Uh, you spent twice that on your entire drag-queen ensemble for last year's Halloween party," I reminded him.

He grinned. "But I won the costume contest. I drank for free all night long. Top shelf."

The Antonio's crew naturally gravitated to each other. It was just like old times, except we were all paired up now.

Even Kat, who had recently started dating a retired fencer, who'd once been a Russian Olympian.

My stomach growled and from across the room, my mother called out, "I think it's time we cut the cake!"

"Did she *hear* your stomach?" Zeb asked in amazement.

"Probably. Jewish mothers have a sixth sense when any of their children are hungry," I quipped. "She even calls me from Atlanta when she senses I'm thinking about food."

Zeb raised an eyebrow. "Really?"

"Hey, Zeb, the sky is falling," Nat teased.

"Oh hush, you," he said and wrapped her in a side hug.

"What's up with your blond buddies?" Nat asked me with a chin gesture at Annie and Stacy.

"They look ready to go all *West Side Story*," Terry remarked.

"As long as there's snapping, I'm into the live show," I said. "Though, I think they're making peace with one another."

"Everyone wants to be Sibby's best friend!" Zeb joked. "Sibby is sooooo fun."

"I am fun," I said. "Well, I used to be. Now I fall asleep at seven-thirty to the Hallmark Channel."

"That's my worst nightmare," Zeb said. "Asleep before midnight?"

"Nights you don't work at the restaurant, you're in bed at ten-thirty. In red silk pajamas. Nursing warm milk."

"Wow. Way to expose me for the boring adult that I am. And for the record, I was referring to the Hallmark Channel situation. That's the true nightmare."

I stared at him. "Oh my God."

"What?" Zeb demanded.

"You're a closet Hallmark junkie."

"I am not."

"You so are! I bet your favorite movies are the ones that take place in Alaska with the big city girls finding romance in a small town."

"Shut up," Zeb groaned.

"Actually, he's a sucker for *When Calls the Heart*," Terry said with a wide smile. "Sorry, honey, but I've outed you."

"Let your Hallmark-love flag fly!"

Kat rolled her eyes. I wondered how she tolerated us.

"I'll give someone a hundred dollars to change the subject," Zeb muttered, looking highly embarrassed now that we all knew about his love for Hallmark.

"That cake is insane," Terry stated, obviously taking pity on his significant other.

My mother sliced into the four-tiered confection. It was far more decadent than my Bat Mitzvah cake, which had been a layered lemon poppy-seed with a raspberry jam filling.

But this cake was chocolate, and I salivated at the thought of it. I was granted the first piece and then I moaned aloud after I took a bite.

"She doesn't even make that noise when Aidan's on top of her," Zeb blurted out.

"Okay, no more bellinis for you," Terry said, plucking Zeb's flute from his fingers. "You're done."

"Yeah, maybe keep the sex jokes about my husband on the DL. His mother is right over there." I pointed.

"So no virility jokes," he asked.

I shoved a bite of cake into his mouth to silence him. He chewed and swallowed.

"Damn, that's amazing. What is it?"

"Chocolate coconut cake with a—"

"Coconut?" Zeb demanded. "Did you say coconut?"

"Yes, why?"

"I'm allergic to coconut. Really, dangerously allergic…"

His eyes widened in fear, showing the whites of them. After a few moments he started to wheeze, his skin turning red and blotchy.

"Shit!" I yelled, tossing my paper plate onto the table behind me.

"I'm calling an ambulance!" Jess cried, sounding just as hysterical as me.

As Zeb continued to pant, Terry shoved him into a chair. "EpiPen!" Terry called.

Zeb tried to reach into his pocket, but he was wearing skinny jeans and it was impossible to get into them when he was sitting.

"Move," Kat bellowed. She stepped forward and pushed Zeb's hand away from his pants. She ripped the pocket open with her bare hands like she had the strength of a Russian logger.

"Who knows how to do this?" she asked, holding up the EpiPen.

Nat swiped the pen from her. "My nephew has a severe peanut allergy. I do this all the time. Parenting one-oh-one —maybe you don't leave jars of peanut butter open for Ralph to get into?"

"His name is Ralph?" I asked. "So when he vomits people can say, 'Hey, Ralph just Ralph'd!'"

Zeb made a noise that sounded like a feral cat in heat and glared at us, gesturing to his throat.

"Oh, right," Nat said, shaking her head and turning back to the matter at hand. She jabbed the EpiPen into Zeb's thigh. He squealed like a stuck pig.

"Sibby!" Jess called.

"What?" I asked, not looking away from Zeb, watching as his breathing slowly became easier.

"Sibby! Sibby! The tablecloth!"

I turned to see that the tablecloth behind me was on fire, thanks in part to the paper plate I'd chucked onto the table when I tried to help Zeb—only my plate, and the chunk of chocolate cake that was on it, had somehow landed on top of one of the mason jar candles my mom had made, and knocked it over, spilling liquid wax everywhere. There was the whoosh of a small inferno as the flames licked a dry wicker basket of flowers and everything around the mason jar went up in flames.

"Someone call the fire department!" I screamed as smoke billowed up to the ceiling.

"On it!" Annie called out.

Mills jumped over the bar with a bucket of dirty dishwater. He ran to the fire and dumped the entirety of the bucket onto the flames. The fire sputtered and then went out.

Smoke and steam curled into the air, and chocolate icing and cake chunks, mixed into the dishwater, spilled off the table onto the floor in globs.

Then the fire alarm went off.

*Bubbe* and Mrs. Nowacki had their arms wrapped around one another, staring as one.

Nancy and her daughters stood by with wide eyes.

Mom's jaw was nearly on the floor.

I looked around the room as I heard sirens blaring in the distance over the sound of the fire alarm.

It was up to me to rally the troops.

So I lifted my head and forced a grin. "Can I get another piece of that cake?"

## Chapter 11

Kishke: [kish-kah]

1. Beef intestine stuffed with a seasoned filling of carrots, celery and onions.

2. Beef intestine, huh? That's one big bag of nope.

"Sibby, I'm fine," Zeb assured me. "You didn't have to leave your party to come with us to the hospital."

"Um, yes I did. Not only did I injure you, but I set your restaurant on fire."

"It's not *my* restaurant. I just manage it. And for the record, you didn't set the entire thing on fire, just a tablecloth."

I'd ridden in the ambulance with Zeb and Terry, leaving everyone else to decorate baby onesies and drink without me there. No reason they shouldn't get to enjoy themselves because I was an accidental arsonist.

"It was a lovely party," Terry said from the hospital chair in the exam room. "Up until the fire, that is."

"Agreed." Zeb looked to the door. "Can't I go home yet? They checked me out—I'm fine."

"Patience," I said.

"Stupid paperwork," Zeb muttered.

"Speaking of paperwork, how are you going to explain to the owner what happened?"

"I'll tell him we had a minor snafu."

"Under the claims section, just write *Sibby's Law*," I said.

"Contrary to popular belief,"—Zeb smiled—"that's not a universal term."

"It should be," Terry said. "In fact, I'd love to get bumper stickers made."

"We don't have a car," Zeb reminded him.

"I have a car. Maybe instead of baby-on-board stickers, we can put up a Sibby's Law sticker."

"I'm sure your Instagram followers would love the hell out of that," Zeb remarked.

My phone vibrated with a text from Annie.

Annie: Why did you tell Mills I was in a relationship?

"Crap."

"What?" Zeb asked.

"Nothing."

"Is it the restaurant?" Terry inquired. "Is everything okay?"

"Not the restaurant—everything is good." I slipped my phone back into my purse, even though it was buzzing every few seconds.

"Aidan? Or your other life partner?" Zeb asked.

"Who? Annie?"

"That would be the one." Zeb grinned.

I bit my lip. "It's Annie." I clamped my mouth shut and pretended to read the poster on the wall showing how to do the Heimlich maneuver.

"Sibby, what shenanigans have you gotten yourself into?" Zeb demanded.

"No shenanigans."

"Uh huh. I don't believe you."

"If it helps, I don't believe you either," Terry added.

"Talk. I know you're dying to," Zeb said.

"Well—" I paused. "I'm trying to get Annie and Caleb back together."

They exchanged a look.

"Is that a good idea?" Terry hedged.

"Probably not. Aidan says to stay out of it. But Caleb just started dating a woman, and Mills asked about Annie and I told him she was already involved with someone." I pointed to my purse. "She just found out that I cock-blocked her—"

"I never understood that term," Terry interjected. "Not when it comes to women wanting to get some. Shouldn't it be vagina-blocking?"

"That sounds so clinical," Zeb stated. "I think cunt-blocking is better."

"I'll alert the masses to the change," I remarked dryly. "And we'll add it as an entry to Wikipedia and Urban Dictionary."

"Could you?" Zeb got up from the bed. "Fuck this, I'm going to see what's taking so long. I need to get out of here. My windpipe is no longer in danger of closing."

I winced and he patted me on his way out.

"I think I agree," Terry said.

"About cunt-blocking?"

"About not interfering. No good can come of this."

"But it's like, in the rom-com bylaws," I protested. "I have to do something!"

"Why?" He tilted his head to one side. "That was a messy breakup. Would it make your life easier if they got back together? Yes, but she really hurt him."

My Antonio's friends had become Annie's friends. Aidan and Caleb had a long history of working together and they were tight, so it was inevitable that people had heard through the grapevine what had gone down.

"She's my best friend," I said. "And Caleb is Aidan's best friend. I want them both to be godparents, but what happens when Aidan and I die in a flaming car accident on New Year's Eve and the two of them have to raise Murgatroyd and Agamemnon together? What then, Terry? Because right now they're mortal enemies and can't even be in the same room as one another." I let out a long exhale, my heart beating rapidly at my winded explanation.

Terry's mouth hung open, but he quickly closed it. "Okay, there are so many things I need to address. Let's start at the beginning. Why do you think you and Aidan are going to die in a car accident—on New Year's Eve, no less—which is very specific. I'll give you that."

"Because life can't be this good!" I stated dramatically. "It's all too perfect. If I don't fuck this up, then the universe surely will! Don't you see? My life is basically a romantic comedy and what happens in those movies?"

"They live happily ever after?"

"Yes, until some drunk idiot plows into our car."

"Riiiiiight. Sure. So after losing their parents in a flaming car crash, they're going to have to live with the names Murgatroyd and Agamemnon? Forever? That's how

146

you want to be remembered? As the parents who died and then gave them those awful names?"

"Those names are amazing!"

"Agamemnon died because his wife and her lover killed him. That's quite a legacy to put onto a child. And Murgatroyd? You're not giving birth to a cartoon character. Did Aidan sign off on these names?"

"Not yet. But he will."

He grinned. "I still think they should be working titles. You know, works in progress. Come up with some alternatives. Like Ham Hock and Hashtag."

"This isn't funny. My feelings—and fears—are warranted."

He sobered. "Emotions are emotions. Fear is fear. But maybe, you should talk to your husband about all of this?"

"I've tried."

"Really?"

"Well…I have been waking him up in the middle of the night because my nightmares make me cry hysterically."

"Yeah, that's not the same as having a dialogue. I know Aidan. If you talk to him, really talk to him, he'll help you through all of this. He's your husband, right? That's what they're supposed to do."

"Yeah."

"Find a quiet time to talk to him. And please, for all of our sakes, think about what you're doing before you mess with Caleb and Annie."

I got out of the cab just as Aidan was walking toward our apartment building with Jasper in tow. Both my boys stopped and waited for me.

"You're back," I said in surprise.

"You're back. I wasn't expecting you for a few more hours." He looked to the cab as it drove away. "No presents?"

"Still at the restaurant."

He raised his eyebrows. "What happened?"

"Um…"

"Okay which one: flood, fire—"

"Fire," I interrupted.

"Again? What is it with you and fire?" he demanded.

"The turkey wasn't my fault. Jasper had gotten loose and we'd gone to look for him. Mrs. Nowacki was the one who fell asleep."

"Way to throw our elderly neighbor under the bus. So there was a fire…"

"Not just a fire," I said with a sigh. "There was an EpiPen incident. I just left the hospital."

He rushed toward me. "What's wrong? What happened? Why didn't you call me?"

I placed my hand on his cheek. "It wasn't *me* who had to go to the hospital. It was Zeb. Let's go inside and I'll tell you everything."

When we got upstairs, we quickly shucked our coats.

Tights in the winter were a terrible idea even when you weren't pregnant. I sighed in relief as I undressed in the living room.

"Sibby?" Aidan asked in humor.

"What?"

"Are you trying to distract me?"

"No." I looked at him. His blue eyes blazed with heat, and I wondered how he could ever find me attractive in this form. But I wasn't going to ask.

I quickly explained the breakdown of the party, which had him in stitches, even though he tried—and then failed miserably—to hold in his laughter.

"Our moms are going to bring the gifts over once the party ends."

"Why didn't you go back?"

"I set a tablecloth on fire," I reminded him. "Who knows what else I might've destroyed had I gone back. Why aren't you at Caleb's anyway? And where's my dad? And your dad?"

"Our dads went to a sports bar. Caleb had plans to meet up with the girl he's dating, so we all cleared out. He needed some time to get ready."

"How much time does he need?" I asked in amusement.

"He likes to primp. He's kinda girly that way." His hand came up to rest on my shoulder. "You look really tired, love."

"That's not very nice."

He chuckled. "You didn't let me finish. Why don't you change into your sweats and I'll give you a back massage?"

"How were you single when we met?" I demanded. "You're like the holy grail of husbands. You don't get mad when I spill things or set things on fire, and you do back rubs—that's special."

"As long as you don't set yourself on fire, we're good. Go change. I'll make some tea."

I sighed. "You really do win all the points. Sometimes I don't think I'm a good enough wife."

"We've been over this, Sib."

"I'm not a good cook."

"You've gotten better."

"Really?"

"Sure."

I glared at him. He grinned.

"I shrank all your polos by drying them on high heat."

"Yeah, that wasn't ideal. They were expensive."

"I ignore you."

"You don't."

"I *do*," I insisted. "I use the excuse that I'm tired or pregnant."

"Those aren't excuses, they're facts. While we're playing this game, don't you think I feel the same way? Do you know how guilty I feel about this expansion?"

"I've known that was coming since you opened the bar."

"Still—"

"And the space next door became available and that just doesn't happen every day."

He hugged me to him. "I think we're both very hard on ourselves. Too hard."

"Sometimes I feel like a useless lump."

"Sometimes I feel like all I do is work."

We fell silent for a moment and then I said, "I'm really looking forward to getting away next weekend."

"That reminds me. Caleb said he can watch Jasper."

"You sure? Mrs. Nowacki wouldn't mind."

"I worry about her walking on ice with our squirrel-chasing dog. One wrong step, she could go down, break a hip. I'd never forgive myself."

I nodded. "I know."

"I don't like that we live on a second-floor apartment without an elevator. For so many reasons. The major one being—"

"The major one being that I already can't see my feet and you worry about me slipping down the stairs."

"Yep."

"And then there's the added issue of the double stroller we have to get through the narrow hallway and down the stairs."

He rubbed a hand over his face. "We have to figure out a better solution."

"We could turn the stairs into a slide. I can slide down with the babies in tow."

"Done and done," he said with a smile.

"I'm not moving again. Not until we buy the house Upstate. I've just gotten the kitchen arranged the way I like it."

"That's because *I* organized the kitchen," he said with a laugh.

The buzzer went off.

"Bet that's Mom, Annie, and the gang," I said, heading to the door.

Sure enough it was the baby-shower entourage including Aidan's mother and sisters, my aunt, mother, grandmother, Mrs. Nowacki, and Annie. Each and every one of them had their arms full with presents.

"Look at that haul!" Aidan said with a grin, and then waved them toward the nursery.

They marched in line like lemmings. Jasper woofed and happily wagged his tail. We hadn't had this many people in our apartment ever. It wasn't like we had a ton of space to host.

"Where's your father?" Nancy asked Aidan.

"With my father," I answered. "At a sports bar, apparently."

"They do know they have cell phones and can call their husbands, right?" Annie whispered to me.

"A sporting event is on TV. All bets are off on actually answering the cell phone," I whispered back.

"We need to get going if we want to make it home before the snow," Nancy said.

"The city isn't supposed to get snow," Annie said.

"Upstate," Nancy clarified. "Bud listened to the weather on the HAM radio as we drove into the city. Storm's a comin'. Gotta get home and see to the chickens."

"Oh, um, sure." Annie shot me a look.

I hugged Nancy goodbye. "I'm really sorry I didn't get to spend more time at the shower."

"Well, you didn't plan on setting a table on fire and sending your friend to the hospital," she said with a teasing grin.

"Tablecloth. I set a *tablecloth* on fire."

"Actually, it was the table," Annie interjected. "I saw the damage when I helped Mills move it downstairs."

"You helped Mills?"

Her cheeks pinkened. "Maybe. Oh, look, someone else to talk to." She immediately darted away and went to speak to my aunt who was on the other side of the room.

"What was that about?" Nancy wondered.

"No idea," I lied.

I refused to meet Aidan's eyes because I so didn't want to have to explain what I'd been up to.

"That wench," I muttered.

"What?" Aidan asked.

"Annie." I held up my phone. "She snuck out of here right as your mother and sisters left."

"Why did she sneak out?"

"Because she doesn't want to answer questions about Mills."

"Mills would be who, exactly?"

"The hot bartender who worked my baby shower…"

"You had a bartender at your baby shower? Doesn't that seem—I don't know—bad form?"

"Just because I couldn't drink didn't mean others had to forgo the pleasure."

"So how hot was he?" he demanded.

"On a scale of one to hotness, I'd say he was firmly in the Chris Pine zone."

"That's pretty hot," he said in amusement. "And Annie flirted with him? You sound upset about it…"

"I *am* upset about it."

"Why?"

"Because."

Aidan sighed. "Sibby, don't. Don't go there."

"Where? I'm not going anywhere."

"Annie and Caleb are not getting back together. It's not going to happen."

"Fine." I leaned over, attempting to reach the TV

remote; only it was impossible because my belly was in the way.

"Sibby."

"Don't take that tone with me, Aidan."

His mouth slackened. "What tone?"

"You know. That Aidan tone."

"I'm gonna need you to clarify."

"That Aidan tone that says you know better than me."

He looked at me for a moment and then he got up and left the room.

"Where are you going?" I demanded. "We were having a discussion."

"I'm getting Aspirin," he called back.

"I don't need Aspirin."

"It's not for you!"

I fell silent and stared at my clasped hands. My husband needed medication. Because of me. Sure, it was only Aspirin, but what if he eventually needed something stronger? Like Ibuprofen?

I knew I sounded crazy, and yet I had the hardest time corralling my emotions and thoughts. They all just spewed out every which direction. There was no scooping them up and shoving them back inside.

Aidan returned to the living room. He stood over the couch, looking down at me.

"Tell me why you want Caleb and Annie together so badly."

"I've already told you. They're our best friends. They're good together. Mostly."

"Yeah, when Annie has her head screwed on straight," he pointed out. "And you know I love your best friend. She's become a good friend to me too, but she fucked up, Sibby. Caleb isn't the same after that."

"He's dating.

"She's dating."

"She's thinking about dating," I corrected. "She didn't drink at my shower. Can you believe that? She's really on this healthier, exercise and figure-her-shit-out kick."

"Doesn't mean the newer, better version of her is good enough for him. Why do you want them back together so badly? You still haven't told me." His eyes bore into mine.

I waited and then, "Oh my God."

"What?"

"Terry called you."

"What? No—"

"YES. He totally called you."

Aidan's shoulders slumped ever so slightly. "He might've called me. He might've told me about your—eh —monologue."

"Monologue? Is that a fancier word for rant?" I asked.

He threaded his fingers through his hair. "I can't. I just can't do this right now."

"Can't *do what* exactly?"

Before I knew it, Aidan was striding toward the door. He grabbed his coat off the rack. "I need to take a walk."

The door shut behind him.

I looked at Jasper as he lifted his head from his doggie bed to stare at the door, whining at Aidan's departure.

"Do you think it was something I said?" I queried the dog.

He woofed and wagged his tail.

"Yeah." I sighed and patted the couch. Jasper bounded over and hopped up. "I'll apologize for my insanity when he comes home."

After a few minutes I got up from the couch, which was a monumental struggle, and grabbed my laptop. I wrote a post on my pregnancy blog, telling everyone about the disaster of my baby shower. But in a moment of total vulnerability and neediness, I talked about the stupid arguments Aidan and I were getting into because I couldn't control my hormones and irrational fears.

Only they didn't feel so irrational. I worried about pretty much everything now, and then I picked dumb fights over the love lives of our two best friends.

Aidan was right. It wasn't my place to get involved in Annie and Caleb's relationship, or lack thereof. But knowing that and really *knowing* that, was something else entirely.

When I had visions of being Annie's matron of honor, she would be standing next to Caleb, not Mills. Then again, Annie had never been the girl who dreamed of her wedding. Never picked out her colors or thought of being a princess for a day. Hell, she didn't really even believe in marriage. Caleb had been her first serious relationship, and that only happened because Caleb had led the way and she'd loved him enough to follow. But in the end, she blew the whole thing up.

Speaking of things blowing up…

Aidan had left the apartment without his cell phone and it was currently vibrating across the coffee table in my direction.

With the name Aria flashing on the screen.

I didn't consider myself a jealous woman. Not under normal circumstances.

These weren't normal circumstances.

My ankles were the size of small tree trunks. I'd gained thirty-five pounds and counting. My jeans were actually jeggings and I wore spandex every day. And we all knew spandex was a privilege, not a right.

To say I was as angry as a sow, resemblance intended, was an understatement.

Aidan and I liked to joke about women hitting on him, with or without me present.

But this…

This felt different.

This felt like an attack on my already unstable hoofing. Not only did I feel like I was pushing away my husband, but also that I was driving him into the arms of some buxom blonde.

I didn't know what this Aria woman looked like, but I had a vivid imagination and it was in overdrive.

I knew Aidan had gone to Veritas. It was his home away from home, even when Caleb wasn't working.

It was on.

I worked myself into a fit of rage as I marched to Veritas. When I opened the door to the bar, I expected to find him sitting in the corner of the bar, nursing a beer. I was not prepared for the woman sitting next to him.

Only she wasn't a buxom blonde, she was a buxom redhead.

A total Jessica Rabbit, curves and all.

Without a thought, I marched over to them. Everything happened in slow motion as I watched her throw her head back and laugh and then place a hand on my husband's arm.

"Unhand him, you hussy!" I yelled.

The redhead looked at me, her mouth gaping. Her blue eyes caught the light of a candle on the bar. It only made her prettier and it pissed me off even more.

"Sibby," Aidan began.

"Quiet, you! I'll deal with you and your straying ways later! First you get a call from Aria"—I slammed his cell phone down onto the bar between them—"and then I find you here with this—this—"

"Sibby," Aidan growled. "This is Aria. Our wine rep."

The air escaped my lungs and I let out a squeak. "Wine rep?"

Aria turned to look at me, her jaw closing. And then her lips pulled into a knowing grin. "Nice to meet you. Sibby, is it?"

I nodded, sure that something had rattled loose inside my mind.

Oh, right. My marbles. I'd lost my freakin' marbles.

"Sibby, I was just commiserating with your husband."

"Oh?" My voice sounded very far away.

She nodded. "My wife is pregnant. We've been trading war stories."

I wanted the earth to open up and swallow me whole. It would be a true feat, considering I was a behemoth, but I was sure nature would find a way.

I was a complete idiot. An insecure idiot.

"Your hair is really shiny," I blurted out.

"Thank you," she said with a wry grin. She hopped up off the stool. "Aidan, I'll have those new wine samples in next week."

"Great. Can't wait to taste them. Give my regards to Tess," he said.

"I will."

With a final wave, she left Veritas. All the patrons sitting at the bar had already gone back to their drinks, but I could tell a few of them were eyeing me curiously.

"Okay, before you say anything—"

Aidan's shoulders shook with laughter.

"Wait, what?" I asked. "You're not mad at me? I drove you to Aspirin and you left our apartment like a husband in the 1950s."

"I don't understand that last part," Aidan said, trying to get his mirth under control.

"Husbands in the 1950s. You know, when they'd go

bowling to escape the wife and children. Or they'd head down to the local watering hole while the wife cleaned up the dinner table."

"That's quite a picture."

"You good, Aidan?" the bartender asked.

He was new and I didn't recognize him.

"I'm good. Dan, I'd like you to meet my wife, Sibby."

Dan reached over the bar to shake my hand. "Pleasure."

"Yeah. You too." I leaned close to Aidan. "Can we please leave now? Everyone is looking at me."

"No one is looking at you."

"Rotten liar."

He chuckled. Reaching for his coat, he gave Dan a final wave. We were outside on the sidewalk when he slipped a hand into his coat and pulled out his beanie.

We walked in silence toward home. I kept my eyes down. Partly so that I could watch out for icy patches, but also so I didn't have to look at Aidan. Every now and again he grasped my elbow and held on to me so that I wouldn't slip over a tricky part of the slick sidewalk.

"So are you going to yell at me?" I blurted out. "I can't take being frozen out!"

"Who's freezing you out?"

"You are!"

"I'm not. I swear."

"Why aren't you?"

He looked heavenward. He'd been doing that a lot lately. Ever since I'd gotten pregnant, he seemed to always be looking at the sky. Maybe he prayed for strength. Maybe he prayed that I'd spontaneously fall silent for the next four months. If he wasn't careful he'd wind up with a crick.

"I'm not mad at you, Sibby."

"Why not? I accused you of cheating. No, scratch that.

I came to your place of business, called a business associate a hussy, and *publicly* accused you of cheating."

"It's nice that you still find me attractive."

"Will you stop joking?"

"No. Let me ask you a question. Are you embarrassed about your behavior?"

"Eighty percent embarrassed, twenty percent I stand by the crazy."

He laughed. "Can you promise it won't happen again?"

"Definitely…not. If wreaking havoc was an Olympic sport, I'd take the gold."

"I think you're perfect."

I started to cry.

"Ah, don't do that, love."

"I'm an insane person."

"You're also the mother of my children. You get a free pass."

"For how long?"

"Have you figured out a way to get my children out of your body without going through labor?"

I smiled slightly. "Free pass, huh?"

"Free pass."

I rested my head against his shoulder as we turned down our street. "Do we have ice cream at home?"

"We do. I also picked up hot fudge the other day."

"It's official. I don't deserve you."

## Chapter 12

Macaroons: [mac-ah-roons]

1. A small cookie, typically made from ground almonds and coconut.

2. These are eaten at Passover, and they always seem to come out of their tin container in one giant, sticky lump. They are gooey and gross.

I opened the bathroom door in the deli to find my husband leaning against the opposite wall. He was trying not to look amused, but he wasn't doing a very good job of it.

"You think my vomiting is funny?" I demanded,

crossing my arms over my chest and simultaneously wincing at the soreness of my ginormous breasts. Yeah, pregnancy was a hoot. I was already wearing a nursing bra because my boobs had a propensity to leak.

Way to go, biology.

I was never doing this again. These kids were gonna come out of me. They'd be cute and I'd love them, but that was it. If Aidan wanted another, he could have it himself.

Where was I?

Oh, yes. Berating my husband in the 2nd Avenue Deli. The scent of fresh rye bread and *gribenes* teased my nostrils, and immediately my mouth filled with saliva. The urge to puke again came over me.

I forced it down.

The twins were not taking my love of rye bread from me. They could have my big feet and the hair in odd places if they wanted, but if they took my love of deli food, I'd never forgive them—and I'd make sure to tell them that when they were old enough.

"Are you okay?" he asked.

"I think so." I pressed a fist to my closed mouth.

Mind over matter. My ancestors were Maccabees. I would not succumb!

"What set you off?" he asked as we headed back into the main dining room toward our large table in the back.

"Watching my father eat his pastrami sandwich. It was that last bite, where the chicken liver oozed out from between the bread, glopping onto the plate."

"Stop, you're going to make me lose *my* appetite."

"I don't know if I can keep anything down except for matzo ball soup. If your children revolt at the thought, then there's no safe place for them."

"You do realize that you're talking about fetuses who can't yet know the meaning of Jewish guilt, right?"

"It's never too early to learn."

We arrived back at the table. Mrs. Nowacki had joined the family and was currently eating her blueberry blintzes and talking to *Bubbe*. Those two had become fast friends and I hated the idea that they would be separated when *Bubbe* went home with my aunt later that evening.

Mom looked up from her sandwich—how that woman managed to keep it from falling apart I'd never know. I always mangled my food. It was an art form, really. Aidan didn't share food with me because of it.

"You okay?" she asked.

I nodded. "Yeah, but I don't think I can sit across from Dad. The smell of the Russian dressing and chicken liver—"

"Switch places with me," Aunt Becca said.

We did a round of musical chairs. I sat across from *Bubbe* and breathed in the scent of her brisket. It smelled good, but I didn't want any—even after she put some on a side plate for me.

I picked at it while I sipped on my Dr. Brown's Black Cherry Soda, letting the carbonation settle my stomach.

Aidan pulled up a chair at the end of the table and sat down next to me. "I found the waitress and put in an order for matzo ball soup for you."

"Thank you," I said.

"Will it bother you if I finish my Reuben?"

I shook my head. "I don't think so."

"I thought you were past the morning sickness phase," he said, taking a big, juicy bite of his sandwich.

"This isn't morning sickness, this is Jewish Deli sickness, which is terrifying."

"They'll take away your Jew card if you don't get over that," he said blithely.

"Seriously." I sighed and tapped my fingers across the table.

My food arrived and I ate it slowly, making sure it stayed down. It did. Thankfully.

Mom and Aunt Becca *kibbitzed* about the upcoming Purim Carnival while my dad pulled out his phone to check their flight status.

"No delays," he said, setting it down. "So we should get going soon."

My dad paid the check and then a bunch of to-go boxes showed up at our table.

"Are you guys really going to take chicken liver on an airplane? Isn't that mean?" I asked.

"You don't leave chicken liver behind," *Bubbe* said in thickly accented English.

We got out onto the sidewalk. Mrs. Nowacki and *Bubbe* jabbered like two birds and then embraced. I hugged my mother, thanking her again for the party, and apologizing one last time for setting the table on fire.

She was fairly subdued, simply waving away the apology. "Thanks for letting me throw you the shower. I know there are other people who could've done it, but it meant a lot to me."

I hugged Aunt Becca and my father, and then we loaded them into a cab to take them back to their hotel.

Mrs. Nowacki, Aidan, and I grabbed our own cab back to Brooklyn. Mrs. Nowacki sat in the middle seat because she was the smallest of us. She grabbed my hand, her fingers gnarled with cold.

"Change," she said. "Change is coming."

I glanced at Aidan and he grinned nervously.

How much more change could we possibly deal with?

I logged on to my anonymous pregnancy blog and my eyes nearly bugged out of my head when I saw all the comments on the last post—where I'd shared the epic failure of my baby shower, and then all of my fears.

The responses were overwhelmingly positive and thoughtful. Why was it that these strangers through a screen managed to offer me such a beautiful community?

My phone buzzed. A text from Nat.

She was still in town and she wanted to hang out. Part of me wanted to unload on her because if anyone would understand, it would've been her. She'd already gone through pregnancy. She understood the highs and lows.

My life, before getting pregnant, had felt like I was riding a bike that was on fire. Now, I was still riding that flaming bike, but I was also juggling knives.

I called Nat.

"Do you want to come over here for tea?" I asked her.

"I could do that," she said. "I'm already in your hood."

"Why?"

"Beacon's Closet."

"How you manage to find true vintage treasures there is beyond me. Every time I go into Beacon's it's a zoo."

"You've gotta fight for what you want."

"And you fight for Pucci, Dior, and Alexander McQueen."

"To name a few. See you in twenty."

We hung up and then I managed to hoist myself off the couch. I put on the kettle for tea and unwrapped the cookies Mrs. Nowacki had made us a few days ago. There were only four left, but Nat very rarely ate carbs anyway. She had willpower, I'd give her that.

I buzzed her up and she came into the apartment loaded down with bags from Beacon's Closet.

"God, I love New York," she said with a grin. She tossed the bags down and hugged me. Jasper leaped off the couch to greet her and Nat gave him a good snuggle before even removing her coat.

"You could always move back," I suggested.

"Nah. It's a great place to visit, but my time living here is done."

"You don't miss it?"

"Of course I miss it." She smiled. "But then I think about all the things I've gained since leaving."

"A mortgage and a two-car garage?"

"Oh, someone's snide." She looked at my belly. "Just you wait."

"Wait? Wait for what?"

"The moving bug to hit you. You'll crave the space and fresh air. The quiet. You'll want the twins to learn to ride their bikes on your street and not in a park packed with five hundred people."

"Bite your tongue," I muttered.

She grinned. "Do you know I'm more creative in Houston?"

"What? Really?"

Nat nodded and then took off her ankle boots and set them aside. Despite the frigid temperatures, she was dressed to kill. Black skinny-leg jeans, flowing, black sheer top. Her angular bob hit just below the chin.

There wasn't enough hair product on the planet to get my hair to do that.

"This city is great," she said, picking up the conversation where we left off. "Don't get me wrong. It's one of the most dynamic, expressive cities in the world. At one point, I really thought I wanted to move back, but after being in Houston for a while, I was able to unwind. Manhattan made me feel like I was constantly swimming upstream. Do you know what happens to your creativity when you're no longer fighting where you live?"

I shook my head.

"It *explodes*. All over the place. I can barely keep up with it."

"That sounds messy."

She grinned.

"How did you deal with your artist stuff while you were pregnant?" I asked.

"I was creative when I wanted to be creative. Otherwise I slept."

"So you didn't beat yourself up for not wanting to be you?"

"What's going on, Sibby?"

The kettle began to whistle and I went into the kitchen to fix us two mugs. I brought them back and set them down on the coffee table. Nat had taken a seat in the chair, Jasper across her lap.

I grinned. That dog had no shame. Which I loved. We should all act more like dogs. Well, not the sniffing other people's butts part. Or eating the random stuff at the dog park. Okay, maybe acting like a dog wasn't a great idea.

"Sibby?"

"Huh?"

"Are you going to explain what you meant? About not wanting to be you?"

I nodded and handed her a mug so she didn't have to disturb Jasper.

Getting comfortable on the couch, I thought about my words. If anyone would understand, it would be Nat. She was a mother. She was an artist and made her living that way.

"I'd just gotten into the groove of writing, ya know?" When she nodded, I went on. "I was feeling it. I was having fun. I was totally blown away by the fact that I got paid to make up stories. And here's the kicker—I have fans who actually read and liked my books. I mean, I feel like I made some mortal enemies with this last book, but overall I'm chalking it up to a good learning experience. My fans —the ones I haven't alienated—send me emails and tweet at me."

"I don't think you tweet *at* someone. Not unless it's hostile."

"Fair. So anyway, I'm living this life. This really good life. Aidan and I are in a great routine. We have the dog. We're focused on our careers—"

"And then you get pregnant…"

"And then I get pregnant," I repeated. "All of a sudden everything I thought I knew is suddenly in the reevaluation stage. I still want to write, I do. I still want to do all that, but I'm afraid that I want the other stuff more."

"It comes back," she said. "You get lost in this time and the pregnancy because you're supposed to. Can you imagine dedicating all the time to your career that you dedicate to growing a human? Or in your case two? Your body will go back to the way it was. Not completely, but it does go back. You'll fit into the skinny jeans again. You just have to work really hard for it. It's the same with your art. You'll get back to it. You won't ever be the same—you can't be. But you will feel like a different version of you. A stronger version of you."

I let out a deep exhale that felt like it had come from my lower belly.

"How long have you been feeling this way?" she asked.

"Ever since this book flop. It would be easy, you know? To quit…"

She grinned.

"What?"

"You *really* think I haven't tried to quit?"

I frowned. "I don't understand."

"I've *tried* to quit. Many times. When I've gone through creative blocks and I can't draw or paint, or if I can do those things, it's all crap anyway. But I come back to it. Every time. That's what happens when you're meant to do something. And you are meant to be a writer. So if you want to quit for a little while, okay, quit. But it won't quit you."

"You sure you went to art school? Or are you hiding a PhD in Psychology in your back pocket?"

She took a sip of her tea. "A diploma would never fit in these jeans."

"I'm so glad I have you to talk to."

She grinned. "I know."

# Chapter 13

Kugel: [koogel]

1. A kind of sweet or savory pudding of noodles or potatoes.

2. Did you say kegel?

"You do realize we're only going out of town for the weekend," Aidan said, looking at the luggage by the front door. "And most of the time we'll be inside—naked, by a fire."

I shuddered. "You're going to see me naked in fire-light? Don't scream when you see the shadow of a monster on the wall."

He chuckled. "Seriously, are you sure you need all this?"

"Don't we have room in the Subaru?"

"Of course we have room."

"Then why are you bugging me about my packing choices?"

Aidan sighed. "You're right. When will I learn?"

"No idea."

He grabbed two of the four suitcases and left the apartment to load up. Luckily we found a parking spot right in front of the apartment. It was like the parking gods had smiled down on us because that almost never happened. There'd been days when neither one of us had the energy to get up and deal with Alternate Side Parking and had decided to sleep in and eat the forty-five dollar ticket.

One of the many joys of city living.

I looked at Jasper. "You ready to see Uncle Caleb?"

He woofed and wagged his tail. I leashed him up and put the last two suitcases out into the hall so I could lock up.

I knocked on Mrs. Nowacki's door to tell her we were leaving. She said a quick goodbye, considering she was Skyping with my *Bubbe*. I said hello to *Bubbe*, shook my head, and then waited for Aidan to come back up and get the last two suitcases.

An hour later, Jasper was asleep on Caleb's couch and we were on our way to the Poconos for our romantic weekend.

"We're supposed to get snow while we're there," I said, looking at my phone's weather app.

"Put that thing away," he said.

"What? Why?"

"Because you're missing the drive."

"We're still in the city. Which isn't super pretty."

He smiled. "Want to make a bet?"

"What kind of bet?"

"I bet you can't turn your phone off for three hours."

"Not fair," I whined. "We're using your phone for GPS."

"Okay, I'll tell you what. You can have use of your phone until we get to the hotel. And then both our phones go off. *All weekend.*"

I gasped. "What are you saying?"

"I'm saying, we wanted time away from the city to really connect. So let's connect."

"Leave it to you to make it dirty."

He laughed. "I wasn't even thinking about making it dirty. But now that we're on the topic of dirty stuff, I wouldn't say no to doing that thing—"

"That involves bright light and coconut oil. No. That will be our celebration after I give birth and the doctor clears me for sexual exercise."

"You're such an odd duck."

"Yup."

"So, what do you say? No phones for the weekend?"

"But if a millennial doesn't take photos of their food and share them on Instagram, then did it really happen?"

"I fear for our children."

"As do I. But you were the one that wanted them."

"Deny it all you want. Your uterus was hungry for my baby batter."

"Um, ew. And how do you even know that terrible, vile, disgusting phrase?"

"I don't know. Must've read it somewhere."

I looked at him. "Oh my God."

"What?"

"You've read a romance novel aside from mine, haven't you?"

"What? No, I haven't!"

"Oh, you lie!" I started to laugh. "Which one? Please, oh please, oh please tell me which one?"

"You won't judge me?"

"Oh, no, I will."

"It was on *your* Kindle. So if anything, I should judge you for your smutty, smutty taste in books."

"My smutty taste in books is how we wound up in this situation." I pointed to my belly in a circling motion for dramatic affect.

"Actually, we wound up in this situation because of a failed contraceptive."

"You're trying to turn the conversation. Title of the book, please."

"*Claimed by My Alien Mates*."

"You're into sci-fi reverse harem? Aidan, I never would've guessed that."

"Not going to lie, there were some sex scenes where I wondered what went where and how."

I began to giggle and then Aidan started to laugh. He didn't even look embarrassed, which was one of the many reasons I loved him. He didn't take himself too seriously and I needed that. Especially as of late.

"When did you read it?" I asked.

"I've been reading it this past week. When you fall asleep with your head in my lap, I turn off the TV, reach for the Kindle, since I can't get up and you've always got it nearby, and then an hour or so later I'm wishing I had a cigarette."

"Romance novels save marriages."

"Put that on a T-shirt."

Somewhere in New Jersey I fell asleep, and I didn't wake up until Aidan was pulling into the resort parking lot.

"You are the worst entertainer ever," Aidan said with a wry grin.

"Aw, man! I wanted to play road trip games with you." My mouth was dry because I'd slept with it open. I'd probably snored the entire way, too.

I was a real prize.

I grabbed a bottle of water from the center console and guzzled it, and then immediately had to pee. We got out of the car and headed for the main lodge to check in. It was an expansive wooden cabin with bright lighting, a lit fireplace with a huge fire, and comfortable couches.

Aidan waited for me while I hit the bathroom and then we wandered up to the check-in desk, the smiling attendant waiting to greet us. Her fair cheeks were rosy, like she enjoyed time outdoors. Skiing, snowshoeing, that sort of thing. I didn't get it, but whatever.

"Welcome to Haven Resorts," she chirped. "Checking in?"

"Yes, please," I said, stepping up to the counter. "The reservation is under the name Sibby Goldstein-Kincaid."

She typed on the keyboard. "Oh, yes, there you are. We have you in one of our deluxe romantic suites. I'll need to see your credit card and ID."

"Ah, Sibby?" Aidan asked.

"Hold on a second," I called back as I searched my purse for my wallet, which was at the bottom of my bag.

"Sib, did you happen to read the fine print?"

I stopped hunting for my wallet and looked up at him. "Fine print? Fine print about what?"

His eyes sparkled with amusement. "You booked us a romantic weekend at a nudist resort."

"Clothing is optional," the check-in attendant voiced just as I saw a man in a backpack walking through the lobby with his dangly bits on display.

Why would anyone choose to go nude in winter?

And why was it the nudists were people you never wanted to actually see naked?

"Will you excuse us just for a second," I said with a smile, dragging Aidan to the corner of the lobby. His back was to the wall and I faced him. I didn't want any more surprises.

"What's up?" he asked with a knowing grin.

"You're enjoying the hell out of this, aren't you?"

"Not yet. But I do like the idea of wandering around in the buff."

I rolled my eyes. "We're *not* staying."

"Like hell we're not," he said, tone calm. "We haven't had a weekend together just the two of us in a long time. We drove three hours. Actually, *I* drove three hours, over an hour of which was dead-stop traffic trying to get out of the city. You slept most of the way. You didn't entertain me and that was your only job as the passenger."

"I'll be damned if I watch you walk around naked in public. Just waiting for some hot cougar to attempt to steal you away."

"Cougar? I don't even get the luxury of a young co-ed hitting on me?"

"Young co-eds don't come to places like this." I shook my head. "So weird. All the young people with bangin' bodies wouldn't be caught dead here."

"That's because young people have body issues. I imagine after a couple of kids and twenty years of marriage, you don't really care how your body looks anymore, so you're not embarrassed to show it off."

"Well, I guess we have something to look forward to."

"When did you become such a termagant?"

"Termagant? What are you doing? Studying for the GRE?"

"We put word-of-the-day toilet paper in the bathroom at the bar…"

"So you can educate the inebriated?" I asked. "Am I really a termagant?"

"No. Well, not usually."

"Just lately?"

He shrugged. "Don't look now, but your second husband is walking through the lobby as we speak."

I attempted to be discreet when I turned to look over my shoulder. A man, north of seventy, with white ear hair protruding like it was trying to escape his head, sauntered through the lobby toward the coffee bar, stark naked. He caught my eye and winked.

I quickly glanced away. "You really want to stay here?"

"We can hang out in our own private cabin. We don't even have to leave. In fact, I'm banking on it."

"But there's all this couple's stuff to do. Couples massages and—"

"So we'll stay?"

"Two conditions."

He grinned. "What are they?"

"One, we keep our clothes on in public."

"Fine. And the other condition?"

"We don't tell anyone about my snafu."

His shoulders shook with laughter.

"I'm serious," I said.

"Fine."

"I mean it. No reveling in my mess-up over beers with Caleb. It's too much. The fire, the zit, I just can't—"

He put his hand to the back of my neck and gently dragged me to him. His kiss was brief, but no less enjoyable. It gave me shivers down to my toes.

"Tell you what. Let's check in, get to our cabin, and have a naked party of our own."

"By naked party do you mean sit and talk and enjoy a nice artisanal soda?"

"Cut that hipster shit out right now, Mrs. Kincaid."

"Oooh, I like it when you call me Mrs."

He shook his head and then linked his fingers through mine. We went back to the desk, I slapped a smile on my face, and we finished checking in.

Our cabin was at the end of the property and it was secluded, nestled among the trees. "This is very Hansel and Gretel," he remarked.

"Gah, what I wouldn't give for a gingerbread loaf right now."

"I can make that happen."

"Really?"

"Sibby gets what Sibby wants."

I grinned. "This weekend is going to be fun."

"Damn right. I plan on doting on you every moment."

"You just want to get into my pants."

"Well, that's a given."

"It's nice to be desired. Oh, wow," I said the moment we stepped inside our cabin. It was gorgeous. It was an open-floor plan with huge windows, a gas fireplace, and two leather couches in the front room. There was another door that led to the bedroom and bathroom.

"Hey, this is great," Aidan said, wheeling the suitcases inside. "Let me grab the rest of the luggage from the car."

"I'll get the fireplace going."

Before he left he said, "They have a fur-skinned rug…"

"Someone is feeling frisky."

"What can I say? The woods make me horny."

While Aidan grabbed the rest of our luggage, I used the bathroom.

Again.

I looked forlornly at the Jacuzzi in the corner. Once

upon a time, in the early part of our relationship and marriage, we'd taken sensual baths together. But now that I was pregnant, I couldn't take baths anymore. Along with soft cheeses, bivalves, alcohol, and certain types of meat, baths and sauna steams were off the table.

I turned on the fireplace in the living room, unzipped one of the suitcases, and pulled out my comfortable sweats. Screw it. It would make getting into my knickers a hell of a lot easier for Aidan, so it was a win-win.

There was a welcome basket on one of the end tables near the couch and I grabbed an apple. Taking a bite, I dug through the basket and found a half bottle of wine. Just because I couldn't imbibe didn't mean Aidan shouldn't. I found a wineglass, poured the bottle, and let the wine breathe.

Aidan finally returned, letting in a bluster of cold air. He set the suitcases by the door and bent over to remove his boots.

"That took a while," I said.

"Ah, yeah, I ran into another guest. She wanted to stop and chat."

"She? What was she wearing?"

"A trench coat. And if I had to guess, there was nothing on beneath it."

"Do I have anything to worry about?"

"Ah—no. She was definitely a septuagenarian."

"Look at you and your second big word of the day."

"That toilet paper is useful in so many ways."

Once he'd taken off his outerwear and was sitting on the couch facing the fireplace, I handed him the glass of wine.

"You sure?"

I nodded and then sat down next to him. I curled into his side and his arm came around me. We snuggled like that for a long while as the fake logs burned in the gas fireplace.

Finally, he asked, "Sibby, are you happy?"

"Of course I'm happy. Why would you ask that?"

"We've just gone through a lot of changes recently. And I noticed…"

"Yes?"

"You haven't started writing another book. I know this last release had you reeling. Is that why you haven't written anything new?"

"I'm just taking some time off."

"Is that all it is? I worry about you, Sibby. Working from home with only Mrs. Nowacki and Jasper for company."

"I'm okay," I assured him. "Really."

"You're not just placating me?"

"No."

He let out a sigh of relief.

"Though, maybe now is a good time to discuss paternity leave."

He nodded. "Yeah. Caleb and I have already been interviewing candidates to take over temporarily. I was thinking I'd take the first two months off."

I let out a breath. Suddenly it didn't seem so overwhelming. "That would be great, actually."

"The expansion will be underway, so there will be meetings I'll have to attend. No way around it. But I don't need to work sixty hours a week right as the twins arrive. Caleb can run the bar side of things and the expansion won't be done until my leave is over."

"Agamemnon and Murgatroyd," I said. "We should really start calling them by their names. I don't want to just call them *the twins* or the pierogis."

"Uh, yeah, about those names? I'm vetoing them."

"I thought you were considering them," I said, looking at him with my brows raised.

"Yeah, that was just to mollify you. We're not doing the Brooklyn parent thing where we name our kids something ridiculous just so they'll stand out. This special-snowflake thing has got to go."

I leaned over and pressed my lips to his. "You're the best. You know that, right?"

"You really think so? After I just nixed your name choices?"

"You keep me in check. In a way that no one else does."

"Not even Annie?"

"Are you jealous of Annie?"

"Jealous? No. But I know you talk to her in ways that you don't talk to me."

"Some stuff is just for the girls. Now, can we stop talking? I'd like to distract you with sex."

"I'm in."

I plucked the glass of wine from his hand and set it down on the coffee table. Then I straddled him. Or tried to straddle him.

I sighed.

"Need some help seducing me?" he asked with a grin.

"Please."

I sat up in bed and reached for my sweater.

"What are you doing?" Aidan asked.

I looked at him over my shoulder. His arm was under his head and his blue eyes were dreamy with satisfaction. The sheet was pulled up to his waist, but his well-defined chest was still on display.

"You don't have a dad bod at all."

"Uh, thanks?"

He reached for me, but I evaded his grasp. "I'm hungry. I need food."

"Guess that means I have to get up."

"Did I render you immobile?" I asked with a cheeky grin.

"You're a regular succubus."

I beamed with pride.

"I'm just surprised you let me keep the lights on," he said with a wink as he finally climbed out of bed.

"I was overcome with lust. I wasn't thinking clearly."

"What about later tonight? Maybe you won't be thinking clearly then too?"

"Hmmm. I imagine if I find some good hearty food— some meat-and-potato sort of thing—I'll be down for the count."

"And here I'd hoped that we'd get another round in before we both succumbed to exhaustion."

"You read too many romance novels," I quipped.

"I've read one, Sibby. Besides your trilogy. That hardly equates to *many*. But I'm curious about the direction of this conversation."

"Romance-novel characters all wake up multiple times a night to get down and dirty. I call bullshit."

He snorted. "Judging by your own experience?"

I crossed my arms over my chest. "Are you saying you'd

enjoy waking up in the middle of the night for some hanky-panky?"

"Who wouldn't want hanky-panky in the middle of the night? And now I have to give back my dude card because I just said hanky-panky."

"I'll make you a deal. The next time you wake up in the middle of the night and you want to get randy, let me know."

"Great, I'll set an alarm," he stated.

"Nope, that's cheating. You have to naturally wake up to have sex with me."

He laughed. "Fine, we'll play it your way. By the way, who would've thought these would've been the kinds of conversations we'd have in our marriage. Not very romantic, huh?"

"I think, after living in a five-hundred square-foot apartment, it's nearly impossible to have romance in your marriage," I quipped. "You hear everything. And I mean *everything.*"

"And on that lovely note, I think we should get dinner while we still have the energy."

We headed to the front room and grabbed our coats. "Before we leave, give me your cell phone," he commanded.

"You sure about this?"

"Yes. We're going to turn them off and lock them in the safe."

"What if Caleb needs to reach us because of Jasper or the bar?"

"He has the lodge's main phone number. And there's a vet hospital around the corner from his apartment. As far as the bar goes, there's nothing to deal with right now. The construction crew starts work on the place next week.

We've got a lull. Any other excuses for why you can't give me your phone?"

"Not any good ones," I grumbled and then handed him my cell.

After he locked up both our phones in the safe with a passcode he wouldn't tell me, he asked, "Are we planning on eating at the lodge's restaurant?"

"Are clothes optional there?"

He smiled. "No. Clothes are mandatory in all dining areas."

"Probably something to do with health-code violations," I mused.

Aidan laughed and then grabbed the door for me. We stepped out onto the porch and I looked up at the sky. "We'll get snow tonight."

"Then your wish was granted, huh? You wanted snow while we were here."

"Snow makes it cozy, you know?"

We walked hand in hand to the main lodge. There were two restaurants: one was a breakfast and dinner spot with a fancy dining experience and the other was a pub. We opted for the pub's casual vibe.

A hostess sat us at a table in the corner and left menus for us to peruse. While I was deciding between fish and chips or the chili mac and cheese, a band set up in the corner. "Hey, we get some live music while we eat," I said with a nod in their direction.

"That will be fun. Did you decide what you wanted?"

"Er—no."

His mouth quirked up with humor. "What two entrées do you want?"

I told him. "But I also want the jalapeño popper appetizer."

"We'll get all three." He closed his menu and set it aside.

"Oh, you know how to treat a lady."

He leaned across the table and whispered, "What you did back there was hardly ladylike behavior."

I sat up straighter. "Thank you."

Aidan took my hand that rested on the table. We gazed at each other like two lovestruck idiots. The waitress took our order and then scooped up the menus, sighing just a little too loud. But not in a lamenting sort of way. Yeah, we either made people sigh in dreamy longing, or in that vocal curse-in-rage-at-the-bitterness-of-their-own-love-lives kind of way.

"I think the band is starting," I said.

Sure enough, a mandolin player walked up to the mic and said, "Hey y'all. We're Smokey Mokey and the Turkey Burpers. Thanks for joining us tonight. We've got a fun set for you, so sit back and enjoy it!"

"Smokey Mokey and the Turkey Burpers?" I asked. "That's not a real band name."

"It is," Aidan said with a huge grin. "These guys are *awesome*."

"You've got to be kidding me. You've heard of them?"

"Caleb and I saw them a few years ago when we were crashing with my parents. They're a riot. They opened for Lesbian Alpaca Orgy. It was a good night."

"Sounds like a hoot."

One guy had a washboard, another pulled out a jug, and one even held a saw and a cello bow to play it with.

"A saw? What's he going to—"

The man with the saw bent it, dragged the bow across the back side opposite the teeth, and then the band joined in.

"Wow." I blinked and looked at Aidan. "And here I

thought living in New York meant I'd already seen everything."

"Careful. You're in danger of becoming a true New Yorker, where you don't think there's anything outside of the city."

"Yeah, you're right. I need to expand my horizons. Travel to other cities."

"I heard there are vampire bars in New Orleans."

"When are we going?"

## Chapter 14

Brisket: [briskit]

1. Slow cooked, cheap cuts of beef from the front of a cow.

2. If we can make cheap cuts of beef taste so good, why are we still suffering through gefilte fish?

"They have naked yoga here," I said the next morning, reading the list of activities offered by the resort. I shuddered. "Can you imagine being behind someone and seeing, well, *everything*? Yuck."

Aidan scratched his bearded jaw and grinned. "What other activities are there?"

"Naked charades."

Pause.

"You're kidding?"

I grinned and he laughed.

"What should we do with our entire day to ourselves?" he asked.

"We could go on a hike," I suggested.

"Are you feeling okay?"

I rolled my eyes. "Yes. I'm feeling fine. You know this happens to me. I complain about nature and then once you get me out into it, I enjoy it."

"Yeah. It would be nice if you remembered that you enjoyed it. It would make my job a lot easier."

"I'm ignoring that comment," I said. "It snowed. Good thing I brought three suitcases. Where would I be without my ski pants?"

He shook his head. "I managed to pack all my outdoor weather gear into one suitcase."

"You're not a woman."

"Good point."

We dressed in our warmest clothes and snow boots, and then tromped to the main lodge to grab breakfast. I was glad to see that because the temperature had dropped and snow had fallen, that people were choosing clothing over skin.

I sounded like such a prude. They went topless in France. And I loved the French. So why did I have such a hang-up about it?

A part of me was truly glad to be having two boys. Body image was such a huge issue for young women, and I wasn't sure how I would've even handled the situations that came about in junior high due to changing bodies and periods and all of that.

"Sibby?" Aidan asked from across the table as he laid

down bills to pay our check. "You okay?"

"Huh? Oh, yeah."

"You sure? You zoned out. What were you thinking about?"

"Body image," I said.

He stood and helped me into my coat. I bundled up and then, with my red-mittened hand, grasped his and we headed out into the cold weather. The sun was shining, but the snow wouldn't melt anytime soon. Already I felt my cheeks bristle with the chill. I found it oddly invigorating.

"Explain that," he said.

As we headed toward the frozen lake, I told him where my mind had gone.

"So you're not disappointed about two boys?" he asked.

"Nope. Promise."

He breathed a sigh. "Good. I thought maybe you'd want a girl."

"Yikes, no."

"I grew up with three sisters. They were holy terrors. More so than even I was. Janet was the type of teenager that snuck out, stayed out past curfew, and dated guys who drove motorcycles. Melanie would wear cardigans and pearls to school and then change into revealing clothing in the bathroom before first period—and then change back before going home. She was also fond of bright blue eye shadow."

"Gotta love the eighties."

"Kara is still a hell-raiser," he pointed out. "She hasn't outgrown that phase. Never will."

"She's the black sheep. Marches to the beat of her own drummer. Not everyone wants marriage, a home in the suburbs, and babies."

"I know."

We got to the lake. No one was out walking the path around the body of water, so we had a nice moment of seclusion and intimacy. It was probably better that way, since I wanted to bring up a sensitive topic.

"I want Annie to be the twins' godmother. And for Caleb to be their godfather. But that might not be the best idea."

Aidan opened his mouth, but I immediately cut him off. "Do not do your Marlon Brando impression."

"But I'm good at it."

"Uh huh. Sure."

He rolled his eyes. "What's the problem with both of them being godmother and godfather?"

"What if we die?" I blurted out. "And they have to raise the kids together? But they're not a couple. That will cause so many problems."

"By the way, I really love how you're thinking our deaths are a foregone conclusion. You're morbid. Anyone ever tell you that?"

"I'm serious."

"So am I. You're morbid as hell."

"Aidan—"

"Then we'll ask other people to be our children's godparents if you're so worried about it. And frankly, I don't get the feeling that Annie's into the kid idea. Are we really going to leave our children with her?"

"Her and Caleb," I reminded him.

"Which is why I stand behind asking other people," Aidan said.

"We can't ask anyone else. We can't ask my parents because that will offend your parents. We can't ask your parents because that will offend my parents. We can't ask either of your sisters because they have broods of their own, and adding twins to the mix—twins that spawn from *my* loins, will be a full-time job all on its own."

"Don't you think you're being just a tad dramatic?"

I came to a stop and placed my hands on my hips. He walked a few feet, before realizing I wasn't following, and stopped.

He turned.

I waited a moment before speaking.

"You're not taking me seriously," I said.

"Sibby," he said gently. "I don't know how to combat this irrational fear that we're going to die and leave our children alone. That's not something I can talk you down from."

"You're not afraid of dying?"

There was a cacophony of honking and I looked around, trying to discern the cause of the noise. A gaggle of geese was coming up behind us. The birds flapped their wings and made a great show of the fact that we were in their territory.

"This seems like odd timing, don't you think?" Aidan asked.

We looked at each other and immediately started power walking away from the geese. But they were fast and furious, and they did not want us there.

"Faster!" Aidan called, grasping my hand.

"I don't go any faster!" I yelled back.

Abruptly, I stopped.

"What are you doing?"

"Facing them!" I turned toward the flock of geese and waved my arms. "Go away, demons!"

"They're not evil spirits."

"Yes, they are!"

I continued flailing my arms like a maniac. Aidan managed to dart in front of me in a gentlemanly show of protection. The geese slowed their roll and one by one they took off into the sky, honking and beating their wings.

I grinned at Aidan. "See? You just gotta tell them who's boss."

Just when I thought the coast was clear, one goose flew back down, dive bombing us like an aircraft.

"Gahhhhh!" I yelled, covering my head in a motion to protect it.

But the goose didn't want me—and a moment later I saw the bird flapping in midair, pecking at Aidan's shoulder.

With one final jab at Aidan, it beat its wings in his face and then took off.

"Oh my God, I didn't know they could do that!" I stated, rushing to Aidan so I could examine him for damage.

He grimaced as we looked at his coat, which had been shredded by the goose's beak.

"Are you okay?" I asked.

"I think so." He winced when I ran a hand down his neck. There was an angry red blotch on his skin.

"I think that goose gave you a hickey." I took his hand and brought it to my lips.

"You jealous?" he teased.

"That you were goose-pecked?"

"Better than being hen-pecked."

"Why didn't the goose attack me?" I asked.

"I don't know. Maybe you had a spell of safety on you. Who knows what *Bubbe* mutters at you in Yiddish."

"Those are overall blessings, Aidan. You know, happy, healthy life, etcetera. I don't think they include, 'Please God, protect my granddaughter from irrational geese.'"

"Maybe it was a blanket blessing."

When we stopped off in the main lodge, after our trip to the hospital so Aidan could get checked out, the resort owner himself had come out of the concierge's office. He'd gotten one look at Aidan in his ruined coat, and in a gesture of true hospitality he comped our entire stay, and even called REI and told them to send over a brand new Mountain Hardware winter coat for Aidan.

Nice people, the nudists.

"How are you feeling?" I asked, glancing at the bandage on his neck. It hadn't been a deep wound, but it had broken the skin and since it was a wild animal, the doctor had prescribed him antibiotics.

"Okay, I think." He took another sip of his microbrew and stared up at me. His eyes reflected the firelight in our cabin. He grinned and then stood up. "This has been quite the romantic weekend, hasn't it?"

"Well, it wasn't dull, that's for sure."

"If a romantic weekend is dull then we're doing it wrong."

I laughed. "Are you hungry?"

"Not yet."

"Hmmm."

"Sibby, if you're hungry, go ahead and order something."

"No, it's fine, I'll nosh on this fruit basket they left us." I picked up an orange, but really I wanted a brownie sundae.

I sat down on the couch in front of the fire and peeled the fruit. I sectioned it out and gave Aidan a sliver.

He popped the piece into his mouth and chewed. "It's good. Sweet."

I ate my own piece and agreed. "I've had a really good time just being with you, muffin top. I feel like I got to really talk to you."

"Why do you have to call me muffin top?" he asked, filching another slice of orange.

"Because it's the best part of the muffin. No one eats the bottom. It's messy and dry and you have to deal with the sticky wrapper."

He shook his head. "It's the least masculine nickname *ever*."

"I think by definition, terms of endearment are meant to be sappy, gross, and decidedly non-masculine."

"You could call me tiger," he said and then growled.

"Or instead of muffin top, I could call you schnookums, honey bunny, or schmoopy—"

"Muffin top it is then."

I grinned. "Just admit it, you'll never win. Besides, I don't call you muffin top in public."

"You called me muffin top in front of your entire family at your cousin Aaron's wedding…"

I shrugged. "Shit happens."

"You mean wine happens."

The cabin phone rang and Aidan made a move to get up, but I put a hand on his thigh to stop him.

"Can you give me a little push?" I asked.

He helped me get up and then I went to answer the phone. "Hello?"

"Sibby?"

"Mrs. Nowacki?" I frowned.

"Yes. I try your cell phone. Then I try your *mąż*. No answer."

"We turned our phones off to unplug. What's wrong? Are you okay?"

"Oh, yes. I am fine. I am staying with Dorota across the street."

"Why?" She started jabbering in Polish and I interrupted, "English, Mrs. Nowacki. I need you to speak English."

"Bed bugs! Our building has bed bugs!"

"No," I whispered.

"Sibby? What's wrong?" Aidan called from the couch.

I looked over at him as I clutched the receiver in my hand. I put my finger up to my lips to buy myself a moment and then went back to listening to Mrs. Nowacki as she phased in and out of English.

"They spray this morning, but we stay out of apartment for twenty-four hour. Kill all the bugs. But it is worse…"

"How can it be worse?" I asked, already thinking about the nightmare we were going to come home to. The hours of steaming furniture and washing clothes and—

"The buildings on both sides of us have them too. Building super say we pass bed bugs back and forth like communal disease and it never go away."

"Communicable," I corrected. "Communicable disease." I pinched the bridge of my nose. "Thank you for calling."

"You are coming home tomorrow, yes?"

"We were, yeah. I don't know what we'll do now. I have to go. I'll call you back in a little while."

I hung up and took a deep breath.

"Sibby, you're scaring the shit out of me," Aidan said from behind me.

I jumped. "Gah! Don't creep!"

"Sorry. What's going on?"

"Our building has bed bugs."

Aidan let out a long stream of curses that would make a pirate proud.

"I know."

I quickly told him all that Mrs. Nowacki had relayed.

"This is bad. So bad. Bed bugs are the *worst* thing that can happen to a New Yorker."

"So in a way, it's a right of passage?" I asked, still bemused.

His frown deepened. "You're not going to like what I'm gonna suggest."

I sighed. "We're going to move apartments, aren't we?"

## Chapter 15

Rugelach: [roo-ge-lach]

    1. Croissant-like pastry, made with cream cheese or yogurt in the dough mixture.

    2. Cover that bitch in chocolate and eat your heart out.

    I stared out the window. Everything was white. The snow hadn't melted because it hadn't gotten above twenty degrees. But out here, at least, the snow stayed pristine and beautiful instead of turning to black slush in the matter of minutes like it did in the city.

    Why did I love living in Brooklyn again?

    Even if bed bugs made me want to say *screw this shit*

and buy a house and move to the burbs—we couldn't do that now. Not after we'd thrown all of Aidan's inheritance into the bar's expansion. I had some book money saved, and it was a good amount, but it wouldn't even make a dent in a down payment. Not for a house on the east coast.

"You've been quiet for an hour," Aidan said.

I sighed. "Been thinking."

"About?"

"How we can't afford our lifestyle."

"Can anyone really afford their lifestyle?"

I rubbed my eyes and tried to calm my breathing. "This was the last thing we needed."

"Well, to be fair, people need bed bugs like they need syphilis."

"Where are we going to move? *When* are we going to move?" I demanded. "How is anyone going to let us move into an apartment? We've got the worst thing to contend with and it's easy to bring it to our new place if we're not careful."

"Sibby, breathe."

"I am breathing!"

"No, you're hyperventilating. There's a distinct difference."

I closed my eyes and pretended I was on a tropical-island beach where there were no such things as bed bugs and mirrors. Where I looked amazing in a polka-dot bikini. A place without stretch marks or mortgages.

"Okay, I'm calm."

"Lie. Maybe if you didn't squeak when you talked, I'd believe you."

"What are we going to do? We can't go home to our apartment right away. And even if we could—"

"I have a plan."

"You do?" I flipped my eyelids open and peered at him.

"I have a friend who's the concierge at the Manhattan Hotel. He can hook us up with a room for the night. I need to talk to the super of our building and find out how bad it all is. I need to know what they sprayed our apartment with. I can't imagine it's anything good for a pregnant woman and a dog."

I moaned. "This is a total nightmare. How are we ever going to truly get rid of them? They can live for years in a mattress, even if you put a mattress cover on it."

"How do you know that?" he asked.

"Annie got them the first year she moved up here when she was living in Manhattan."

"That sucks."

"Did you text Caleb and ask him if he can keep Jasper for another night?"

I missed my fur baby and I'd been excited to pick him up and sniff his belly. Nibble his ears. Generally be gross with him.

"Yeah, he's fine with it."

"Did you tell him why?"

He sighed. "No."

"You know how hard it is to find a dog-friendly apartment in Greenpoint?"

"So we're staying in Greenpoint, then?"

"Where else would we move? Williamsburg is still Hipsterburg. Bushwick is expensive but dicey, and it's not our style anyway. Long Island City is—"

"Too far from Veritas unless I want to start driving all the time. And anything in South Brooklyn is too far away from both the city *and* Greenpoint. We didn't even discuss living in Sunnyside or Astoria…"

"That's because they're too deep in Queens." I ventured a smile, feeling some of my humor come back.

He chuckled. "You're such a Greenpoint snob. There are those apartments available on Eagle Street."

"Those apartments *start* at five thousand dollars a month."

He cursed. "Never mind then."

"No."

"Yes."

"Bed bugs?" Annie gasped over the phone. "Seriously?"

"Yep. In all their disgusting glory." I brought the mug of tea to my mouth and awkwardly shuffled my position on the couch.

"When did this all happen?"

"Three days ago."

"And you're just now telling me this?"

"You've been MIA," I reminded her.

"Have not."

"Have too."

"Let's not do this," she stated.

"Because you'll lose."

"Probably. You've been MIA too, you know. On your romantic weekend getaway. Where are you guys staying? How bad is it? Do you have to throw out your furniture? What are you going to do?"

"Slow down, Speed Racer. We're staying at Caleb's."

She paused and then, "That's good."

"Aidan talked to the exterminator and the super. Both said it wasn't a bad infestation, but both buildings on either side of us have it too. They've already been fumigated multiple times. The bugs just flee the poison and take up shop in another building."

"So you'll get them again?"

"Pretty much. Aidan won't let me into the apartment because—"

"Because you're pregnant. Yeah, that makes sense."

"He's over there now, examining our furniture. I'm at Caleb's looking at apartment listings."

"Oh man."

"Tell me about it. Every apartment in Greenpoint is overpriced—even the ones that are prewar and haven't been modernized since—well, ever."

"You're gung-ho about staying in Greenpoint?"

"Yes. I'm thinking of Aidan and his commute."

"Eh, okay."

"Our whole life is in Greenpoint. His bar. My prenatal yoga class. My birthing class. Mrs. Nowacki."

"It's sweet that she's really become a part of your tribe. I kind of love that. How's she doing with all this bed-bug stuff?"

"She staying with a friend across the street who will help her with all the laundering." I bit my lip. "I don't want her moving back into that apartment."

"She's been in that place, what? Thirty years?"

"Yeah."

"Yeah, I don't think you'll get her out of there anytime soon."

"Probably not," I said. "Okay, I'm shot. I can't talk about this anymore, I'm way too stressed."

"What else do you want to talk about?"

"Uh, how about the fact that you skipped out of town without even a goodbye?"

"Or we could talk about the fact that you cock-blocked me," Annie responded.

"Cunt-blocked," I corrected.

"What?"

"Never mind. It's a Zeb thing."

"Why did you tell Mills I wasn't single?"

"Because if you start dating then it means this thing with you and Caleb is really over."

"Sibby," she said gently. "It was over the minute I flirted with another guy. He was done. Last straw. There's no coming back from that. Even if I wanted to—which I don't—I need to move on. He needs to move on."

Oh, he was moving on all right. Aidan and I were having dinner with Caleb and his new girlfriend that night.

"Are you dating Mills?" I asked her.

"Kind of hard to date someone you just met when he lives in the City and you live in Montauk."

"So you're not dating him?" I pressed.

"We're texting. Happy, Ms. Nosey?"

"Mrs. Nosey Hyphen Snarky," I told her. "That's my married name."

"You're weird."

"Yep." I paused. "Are we good?"

"Of course we're good. Why wouldn't we be?"

"Because I've tried to control your love life."

"You're stopping now, though, right?"

"Right. Because as much as I love my mother, I don't want to be her." I groaned. "Crap. I have to call my parents and tell them everything."

"May I suggest waiting until you're settled into your new place? The last thing you need is your mother's stress and anxiety coming through all the way from Atlanta."

"Yeah, her emotions transcend time and space," I said.

"Besides, she's still really busy with her new business. I'm not sure she's ready to hear it all."

"Yeah, she is. Wait, how do you know that?"

"Because she keeps emailing me pictures of candidates for my next relationship," Annie said.

"You're kidding? She's sending you photos of her sixty-year-old clients?"

"No, their grandsons."

"Oh. I don't know if that's better or worse," I replied.

"I'm pretty sure she wants me to have her grandchildren by proxy."

"That's weird."

"Your mother is the craziest, baby-hungry woman I've ever encountered." She paused. "It's kind of nice, though. Having a mother figure wanting me to be happy."

"Oy. Let's not go there."

"You're right. Talking about my mother is a surefire way of making me crack my no-drinking promise to myself."

"I'm proud of you, you know? For getting your head on straight."

"Eh, I'm a work in progress."

"Aren't we all? Call you later, mother shucker."

"Ha! I knew you'd cave. Later, mother shucker."

As I hung up, I heard something rustling in the kitchen. Frowning, I looked around for Jasper. He wasn't on his dog bed in the living room. I somehow managed to get myself up from the couch and went into the kitchen to investigate.

The refrigerator door was open, along with the middle drawer. Jasper was currently licking plastic wrap.

"What did you do?" I asked him, hands on my hips.

He looked up at me and wagged his tail. One of his ears flopped down over his forehead.

"How the hell did you even get into the fridge?" I demanded.

When he failed to suddenly learn how to speak, I leaned over to pick up the wrapper. I sniffed it.

"Cheddar? You deleted the cheese? Ate. I meant, you ate an entire block of cheese?"

He whined.

"Oh, this isn't good. This isn't good at all."

He dashed toward the front door and began to paw at it. I hustled as fast as I could and grabbed his leash and my coat. I quickly slipped into my clogs and then we were out of the apartment.

It wasn't until we were halfway down the block and Jasper was chewing on a patch of city grass that I remembered that Caleb's front door auto-locked and I'd left my key on the coffee table. Key and phone.

I looked up at the sky. "Are you smiting me?"

"Um, Sib? You doing okay?"

I jumped when I heard Aidan's voice behind me. "What are you doing here?"

"I needed a break from the apartment crap and I missed you." He leaned over and kissed me. "You forgot your hat."

"Yeah. Your furry son decided to eat an entire block of cheese."

"Seriously?" He grinned and took the leash from me. We started walking together and he grasped my hand. "You're cold, love. Zip up your coat."

I did as he commanded. He was so cute when he was bossy, trying to take care of me.

"Is he going to be okay?" I asked with a nervous glance at our dog.

"Yeah, he'll be fine. He's going to have really bad gas, though."

"Worse than normal?"

"Oh, yeah."

"He's lucky he's so cute," I stated. "How did Jasper even get into the fridge? That's what I want to know."

"Caleb was trying to teach Jasper how to bring him a beer from the fridge."

"He's a terrible influence on our child," I quipped. "All he managed to do was teach Jasper to get into the cheese drawer."

"Well, he's committed. Have to give him props for that."

"Yeah, he destroyed the hell out of that cheese. Like mother, like son."

Aidan laughed. "How's the apartment hunting going?"

"Terrible." I hunched lower in my coat when an errant gust of wind blew across the street. "Did you know that Greenpoint got really expensive?"

He snorted. "Yeah, I'm aware. You do know that Brooklyn is officially more expensive than Manhattan now? We could find something reasonable in the East Village. The commute wouldn't be awful."

"They're working on the L line," I reminded him. "What happens when they shut that down? It would take you *forever* to get over the bridge. We'd be much better off moving to Long Island City or Sunnyside and we already vetoed those neighborhoods. And I'm no Manhattan girl. I'm a Brooklyn girl."

I moaned dramatically as we walked up the front steps of Caleb's building. He lived on the third floor. Jasper raced up the stairwell and was patiently waiting at the door by the time we made it.

Aidan unlocked the apartment and we went inside. I cleaned up the mess in the kitchen, closed the drawer and refrigerator, and put on the kettle for tea.

"My uncle called to tell me the baby furniture is ready," Aidan said, taking off his coat and hanging it on the hook by the door. "He doesn't have a problem holding it for us."

"Good because I only want to move that heavy stuff once and it can't come into the apartment now." I rubbed the back of my neck.

"Come here," Aidan said, patting the couch. "Crick from the crummy mattress?"

"Yeah."

I sat down and his hands moved to my neck. He gently massaged my skin and I felt like Silly Putty.

My phone rang and I immediately reached for it.

"Let it go to voicemail."

"I'm waiting on some realtors to call me back."

He sighed. "Fine."

I grabbed my phone, but it wasn't a realtor. It was Stacy.

"You can definitely ignore that," Aidan teased.

I rolled my eyes and answered my cell. All I heard was sobbing.

"Oh my God, what's wrong?" I demanded.

"Joe. His band—they're moving to Las Vegas!" she wailed.

"Did you guys break up?" I asked gently.

I heard her blow her nose. "No."

"So…long distance then?"

"Yeah, until he decides he likes groupies better than me."

I didn't have the heart to tell her that he'd already been playing out-of-town gigs, and I wouldn't have been surprised if he'd already sampled some groupies. But I wasn't going to be an asshole just for the sake of being an asshole. But he was a guy in his mid-twenties whose band was taking off. Even mediocre musicians couldn't be counted on for their fidelity.

It was a thing.

"When does he leave?"

"A week from tomorrow."

An idea suddenly came to me and I looked at Aidan. His brows were furrowed in curiosity.

I tried to sound calm as I asked, "What's he doing with his apartment?"

"Bow to me, for I am the master," I said with a grin.

Aidan raised his beer and clinked it against my soda glass. "You are the queen of all that is awesome."

It had taken us five minutes to decide we wanted Joe's apartment. It had stairwell access to a rooftop view of the Manhattan skyline, it was on the first floor, it was dog friendly, it had enough street parking that we'd be able to find a place for our car, and the price and timing had been right. Best of all? The landlord was completely absent—he lived in Europe. So there was no chance of him breathing down our necks. He had a building superintendent tend to any issues.

We'd gone to Veritas to celebrate. We were sitting in the corner booth, rejoicing over the fact that we were about to have three separate rooms in our apartment.

We were basically going to live like New York royalty.

"You get to have an office again," he said with a smile.

"And a nursery. That middle bedroom is *huge*."

"Not as big as our bedroom." He shook his head. "Just…wow."

"What?"

"Who would've thought that bed bugs would lead us to an even more amazing apartment?"

"I hate leaving Mrs. Nowacki," I said with a sigh.

"We'll still see her. She's one of us now." He winked.

"We need to get back to Caleb's," I said, taking a sip of my club soda. "I want to change before dinner."

"Promise me one thing—scratch that, promise me two things."

I raised an eyebrow and waited.

"You will be nice to Caleb's new girlfriend."

I rolled my eyes. "Yes, I'll be nice."

"And you won't bring up Annie."

"Do you really think I don't know how to behave in polite society?" I demanded.

"This pregnancy has dismantled your filter," he reminded me. "Just be aware of that."

"What if she sucks?" I asked. "And I hate her?"

"You can't hate Emmeline. It's impossible."

"Emmeline? Ugh. That name."

"What's wrong with that name?"

"Nothing—I fucking love that name."

"Ah, now I get it. You're not upset that you think you'll hate her. You're worried you're going to like her."

"You think you know me so well." I attempted to scoot out of the booth so I could make a dramatic exit, but it was impossible since I couldn't get up on my own.

Aidan chuckled, slid out of the booth all suave-like, and then came to my aid. Beggars couldn't be choosers, so

I let him help me. We held hands the entire way back to Caleb's apartment, but didn't talk much.

My mind was occupied with the dinner we were supposed to go to. Meeting Emmeline was the nail in the coffin. Sure, for the past few months, Annie, Caleb, and Aidan had all said the relationship was over. Repeatedly. But call me a hopeful romantic; I'd expected Annie to pull a Hail Mary. I anticipated the boom-box-over-the-head-outside-the-bedroom-window moment.

Never came.

She was texting Mills. She was into him.

And Caleb was dating Emmeline.

"If she goes by some cutesy nickname, I'm gonna vomit," I blurted out when we got up the stairs to Caleb's apartment.

Aidan didn't reply.

"Oh, man—she does, doesn't she? Have a cute nickname?"

"Everyone calls her Em. Caleb—ah—calls her Emmie."

"Moses save me."

"What?"

"Emmie? Annie? Don't you think that's an odd coincidence?"

"No, I don't." He squeezed my hand.

I was already planning on how to use my pregnancy to leave dinner early. I felt like a traitor to Annie, having dinner with Caleb and his new girlfriend.

"It's going to be okay," Aidan said.

"If I want to leave, I need to be able to leave, okay?"

He sighed. "Okay."

"Let's have a secret code word."

"Let's not. You do remember that we're staying at Caleb's apartment for another week until we get to move into Joe's place? If you make this dinner awkward, then our living situation is going to get super uncomfortable."

"Damn it," I muttered. "You're so right."

"Also remember that you love Caleb."

I felt my heart soften. "Yeah, I do."

"And you want him to be happy."

"I guess," I muttered.

"Will you try? For me?"

I moaned. "Oh, man! You know I can't refuse you anything. Fine, I'll be on my best behavior."

He grinned. "And sell it, Sibby."

"I'll sell it," I agreed. "Rats."

We went to one of our favorite restaurants in Greenpoint. It was a prewar warehouse with a massive open floor plan and glass windows surrounding the upper portion of the walls that let in a ton of natural light, and it had been converted into a chic, trendy spot with amazing food.

Aidan and I arrived before Caleb and Em. The hostess sat us in the garden out back. It would've been chilly, but there were heating lamps in every corner. It was actually so warm that I felt comfortable enough to remove my coat.

"Did I tell you that you look really pretty?" Aidan asked, his eyes dipping down my body.

I was wearing a long black sweater that was formfitting. It strained over my belly, but it was comfortable and it covered me. My jeans had an elastic band and I'd had to settle for my new, roomy UGGs. There was no way I could've fit my feet into my favorite pair of Converse sneakers anymore. Not with the sudden foot growth.

"You look pretty good too." I ran my hand down the side of his face, over his beard. He turned his head and kissed my palm. His dark hair had grown out substantially and he hadn't bothered to get it cut.

"You look very Kurt Russell. The hair," I remarked.

He grinned. "You're a sucker for Kurt."

"Dude, he's so hot."

"You know he played Santa in a movie recently, right?"

"Then I guess Santa has got it going on."

Just as we were about to get into a debate over the hotness of Santa, Em and Caleb arrived. Caleb and Aidan shook hands, and then Aidan slapped Caleb on the back.

Total bro moment.

"Hi Em," Aidan greeted and then embraced her, much to my surprise. Clearly, he felt comfortable. He gestured toward me. "My wife, Sibby."

The petite, glossy-haired brunette smiled widely when she looked at me. "It's nice to meet you, Sibby."

"You too," I said, somehow not choking on the words.

"I heard you're having twins?"

I nodded.

"You look amazing."

*Do not fall for flattery because your self-esteem is low,* I thought. Her smile was genuine.

"Thank you," I said, reluctantly smiling back. "It's been kind of crazy, but it's amazing too."

Her gaze went back to my belly. The twins were currently playing air hockey with my organs.

"Would you like to feel?" I asked.

"Oh, no, you just met me—that would be weird, right?"

I grabbed her hand and placed it on my stomach. "Strangers come up and touch me like I'm a fertility statue."

"Boundaries, people," she muttered. "Wow. I've never felt anything like that. Thank you."

Dammit.

She was nice and genuine, and she also wanted people to have boundaries. And without even thinking I had already brought her into my comfort zone.

Failing.

"Why don't you two sit next to each other," Aidan suggested, gesturing to the chair next to me.

"You sure?" Em asked.

"Yeah, go for it. I'll sit across from Sibby and play footsie with her."

"Oh, you're the cutest, my little muffin top," I said, laying it on thick.

Caleb groaned. "Didn't I tell you they were gross?"

"I think it's sweet," Em said.

I watched her exchange a knowing look with Caleb. Then I glanced at Aidan who'd seen it too. He shrugged.

We all took our seats and the waiter came by for our drink orders. The three of them went for a bottle of wine. I asked for a good old ginger ale.

Em and I naturally broke off into our own conversation. She was the oldest of three, she was from Colorado, she liked camping, nature, and sports. Yet she was dainty and feminine, and when she looked at Caleb I could tell how much she liked him.

"How did you guys meet?" I asked.

"I'm a wine rep. I work with Aria."

I couldn't stop the grimace that worked its way across my face. "Aria. Yeah. Um—"

"It's okay," she laughed. "I heard about the, ah, misunderstanding? Can't say I blame you. Aria is hot."

I let out a chuckle.

"Are you guys ready to order?" the server asked.

"Oh, we haven't had a chance to look yet," I said.

"Sibby, why don't you order some stuff for the table and get us going?" Aidan suggested.

"Anyone have any food allergies?" I asked, opening the menu.

"I eat everything," Em said. "Bacon is in my blood."

I glared at Aidan, clearly sending the message that Em was awesome.

He grinned and mouthed *told ya.*

## Chapter 16

Falafel: [felafel]

1. Fried, seasoned chickpea cakes, often formed into balls before cooking and then pressed flat to open them up immediately before serving. Typically served over rice, and sometimes with lamb or chicken as well as other middle eastern garnishes.

2. I'm dancing to this food right now, you just can't see it.

Caleb went home with Em, so Aidan and I had the apartment to ourselves. Not that we were going to try anything—there was no way I was going to have uncomfortable pregnancy sex on a pullout couch that wasn't even ours.

Unfortunately, the couch wasn't enough of a deterrent for Aidan, who after a couple of glasses of wine had started getting handsy.

"Aidan," I said, attempting to move away from him

"Are you too full to get frisky?" His lips brushed my neck and I couldn't say it was the worst thing in the world.

"Among other things. I'm afraid we'll break the couch."

"So, let's get creative." He stayed close to me for a moment, but when he saw that I wasn't in the mood he backed off. Aidan wrapped himself around me and we cuddled. That was nice. Sometimes you just wanted to be held. And because he was much bigger than me, he could still get his arms around my massive middle.

He splayed his hands across my belly and I covered his hands with mine.

"I like her," I said softly.

"I knew you would."

Em had been the perfect blend between genuine and sassy. She was smart and kept Caleb on his toes, but there was sincere affection between them. It was easy, like they didn't have to try too hard.

It had been a constant push and pull between Annie and Caleb. So much strife. So much drama. It hadn't been healthy.

For any of us.

"Think it'll get serious?" I asked him.

"If he knows what's good for him."

I snorted. "Do you think he's ready for that? Or even thinking of that?"

"He's over his breakup with Annie. He sowed his oats. That's not what he's doing with Em."

"You mean he sowed his oats with Gemma?"

"Yes. Gemma was the last of it. He got out his hurt and anger and he got his mojo back." Aidan paused. "Just don't be surprised if he and Em get serious really fast."

"That's not good, is it? Getting serious too fast?"

"Sibby, *we* got serious almost immediately."

"Naw uh."

"Yeah huh. You don't want to admit it, but it's true. We were exclusive long before the actual talk of being exclusive. We had all the feelings."

"Any feelings I had for you were in my pants."

He snorted out a laugh. "Okay, whatever you say."

I thought for a moment. "Men and women are different."

"So I've heard."

"You're telling me he's ready for something serious so soon after his breakup?"

"I'm saying when a man is ready, he's ready. And Caleb is ready. Ready to settle down. Get a dog. Ready for kids."

At the mention of the word dog, ours lifted his furry head to stare at us and then we heard the unmistakable sound of breaking wind.

"Oh, God, dog!" I waved a hand in front of my nose. "That was noxious. No more cheese for you. Ever."

Jasper whined.

"He's gotta go outside. I'll take him. You stay here. Try not to stew."

"I'm not stewing. I'm contemplating. There's a difference."

"Sure." Aidan called Jasper to him.

"Aren't you going to put on your coat?" I asked.

"It's only forty-five out. Besides, my virility will keep me warm."

I rolled my eyes. They left the apartment and I got up

to get some water. My phone vibrated as I came back into the living room.

It was a text from Annie.

Annie: What are you doing the first week in April?

Me: Nothing that I know of. Why?

Three little dots appeared and then disappeared, followed by the phone ringing.

"This is too much to text," she said. "Hi."

"Hello."

"You sound weird."

"No, I don't."

"Did I interrupt married dirty-time?"

"Do you really think I'd make Aidan pause so I could answer your call?"

"Uh, yeah. We're Mer and Christina. They paused all the time."

"I don't want to be Mer and Christina. Mer has had, like, everyone she loves, die. Or leave her. You're totally Christina, by the way. She leaves Mer. You left me."

"Way to spoil the show."

"There are fifteen seasons. If people don't know that by now, then they should catch up on Netflix. No excuses." I paused. "Why did you call again?"

"I don't remember," she said in bemusement. "Oh wait, yes I do. The first week in April. Can you and Aidan get away?"

"What's going on?"

"Remember how I had a plan to save my uncle's restaurant?"

"Yes."

"Well, it came to fruition. When I was in the city for your baby shower, I contacted my friend Dylan who works at Oyster Life Magazine."

"That's really a magazine? Wow, you can do anything in this city."

"It's truly the city of dreams," she commented. "Where was I? Oh yeah. Every year in Montauk my uncle's restaurant participates in an oyster-shucking competition and festival. All the money made from the festival gets donated to the Billion Dollar Oyster project—you know, that project that restores natural oyster reefs in New York Harbor?"

"Uh, sure."

"Dylan says she'll come to the competition and do a write-up about the restaurant, and all the stuff my uncle does for the community, as well as his charity to the city."

"That's great, but it's a magazine write-up in a magazine no one has ever heard of."

"Hold on there, Snarky Pants. Dylan said that if I could get a celebrity to participate in the competition then she'd get someone from *The New York Times* to show up."

"Wow, *The New York Times.* That's actually a big deal. Do you know any celebrities? What about Gordon Ramsey? I bet he could shuck an oyster fast—"

"Sibby—"

"Or Mario Batali? Danny Meyer? Oh wait, maybe you don't want a celebrity chef. How about—"

"SIBBY!"

"What?"

"You."

"What about me?"

"*You're* the celebrity I want."

"I'm not a celebrity."

"You have an insane amount of Instagram followers, and people know your face."

"That's because I hit people in the eyes with corks and

tell people to stick it where the sun don't shine. All by accident, mind you."

"It was just one eye, and it was just one cork."

"I'm not a celebrity. You want someone famous. I'm not famous."

"Right, you're infamous."

"Not funny."

"Kinda funny."

"Are you sure you want me there? Are you sure I'm a big enough draw?" I asked.

"I know you are. I told Dylan I was going to ask you and she was super excited. She's a legit fan of yours."

"Are you lying?" I asked in suspicion.

"I'm not, I swear. She's a fan—she loves your videos. She didn't even know we were best friends until I told her."

I sighed. "I don't know how to shuck oysters."

"Don't worry. I'll show you. I'll turn you into one badass—"

"—don't say it—"

"Mother shucker!"

Aidan came back just as I hung up with Annie. He unleashed the mutt, who bounded toward me and gave me a wet kiss on my nose.

What a cutie patootie!

"What have I told you?" I asked, wiping the slobber

from my face. "It's important to ask. Not everyone likes sloppy kisses."

"You do realize you're trying to rationalize with a dog."

"Just the other day I heard you trying to explain the rules of football to him. So don't play that game with me."

He grinned. "Who was on the phone? Your mom?"

I shuddered. "Please. If I talk to my mom, then I'm going to have to tell her about the bed bugs. That means she'll know about the move. She'll want to fly up here and help me decorate the new nursery."

"Wouldn't be such a bad idea. Considering it's going to be a lot of work setting the place up."

"She's too busy. What with her Rent-a-Yenta matchmaking service and the Purim Carnival…"

"You don't think that your mother would drop everything to fly up here to help with the nursery?"

"Of course she would. Which is why she's on a need-to-know basis. Better to ask for forgiveness, not permission."

"Right." He snapped his fingers. "So if that wasn't your mother calling this late, then it must've been Annie."

"Yup."

"How is she?"

"Good."

"Did you tell her about Em?"

"No."

"Sibby?"

"Yeah?"

"Stop giving me one word answers."

It was my turn to grin. "You're not going to believe this, but…" I told him what Annie needed and how I was supposed to help.

"She asked both of us to come, but I know you'll never

be able to get away. Not with the move and the bar expansion."

"And miss you shuck oysters in a competition? Yeah, I don't think so. I'm not missing that for anything."

"Why do you sound so amused by the prospect?"

"Because it's you."

"Oh. Right."

"I'll be there—at least for the competition."

I grinned. "Promise?"

"Definitely."

I ran my hand across Jasper's head. "I think I'll take him with me."

"That's a great idea."

"What do you think? Are you a beach dog? Or a mountain dog?"

He looked at me with sweet brown eyes and then hopped up on the pullout bed. He turned in a circle a few times and then laid down, resting his face on my leg.

"It's going to come out, you know," I said to Aidan as he walked to the kitchen.

I heard a cabinet open. "What will come out?"

"Em and Caleb. It will inevitably come up."

The faucet turned on for a moment, and then off again before he came back into the living room. "I'd assume that would be the case, yes. But if she's texting this Mills guy—and what kind of name is Mills anyway—why would she care?"

"If you have to ask that question then you don't really know Annie."

"I think you're projecting. I think *you* would freak out if we broke up and you found out I was dating someone else. Even if you were, too."

"Why would you even say that?"

"Sibby—"

"No one's breaking up! We are not breaking up. We don't do that!"

"Whoa. I didn't mean—what's happening right now?"

"Right now, I'm utterly fragile so you can't make sweeping statements like the one you just made."

His blue eyes stared into mine. "Are you really worried about this? Or is this the result of an influx of hormones. Tell me, honestly. Do you worry about us?"

I shook my head and looked down.

"Sibby…"

"I don't. Not really. I just sometimes have these dreams."

"Dreams?"

"Nightmares," I corrected. "Where we have the twins and they're like, six weeks old. I'm tired and haggard and my boobs are hanging down to my knees. My hair hasn't been brushed in days and my legs aren't shaved and you come into the apartment—the babies are wailing—and you announce you're leaving me."

"Oh, Sib, no…"

I nodded. "And you tell me you're in love with someone else and then you take the dog."

"Holy shit, Dream Aidan is an *asshole*," he said, taking a seat on the pullout couch and setting his glass on the end table. He wrapped his arms around me and I pressed my face into the crook of his neck. Things always seemed better after I nuzzled into his beard. Didn't really know why, but I went with it anyway.

"Dream Aidan *is* a total asshole," I agreed.

"How often have you been having this dream?"

"I've been having some rendition of it for"—I paused —"at least two months."

"Why didn't you tell me sooner?"

"Remember a few weeks ago when I woke you up by hitting you with a pillow?"

He blinked. "That's what that was about? I thought you said I was snoring…"

"You weren't snoring. I woke myself up because *I* was snoring. And when I came to, I remembered the dream. Thus, pillow in your face."

"You made Eggs Benedict that morning for breakfast," he realized.

I pointed to myself. "Yeah, I felt guilty and had to make something for you that actually took effort."

"You don't have to worry about me being with anyone else."

"I know, but—"

"But?"

"Is Annie right? Are marriages destined to fail?"

"Do you want the romantic answer or the realistic answer?"

"How about realistic with the side of romance?"

"I can do that." He took a moment, clearly gathering his thoughts, knowing his audience had a habit of flying off the handle.

I hated saying this about myself, but I was kinda irrational. Even before the flood of pregnancy hormones.

What, are you actually surprised? I do have *some* awareness about myself. Not a lot, but some.

"Cavemen used to die really early," Aidan announced. "They lived long enough to spread their seed around and then they got eaten by wild animals or—"

"Or, cavewives killed them out of sheer frustration."

He smiled. "All I'm saying is, we're not biologically created to be with one person for sixty years. Marriage is a relatively modern social construct. People aren't designed for fidelity, for one partner forever. We're literally fighting our DNA by choosing monogamy."

"You're not winning any points—in fact, you're making me even more worried that, once I give birth to your little seedlings that I won't be desirable anymore, and you'll want to go start another family with someone else. Someone younger. Someone *blonder*."

"What is it with you and thinking I'd choose a blonde?" he asked, attempting to hide his amusement.

"Because I could never pull off being a blonde. Ergo, you'd choose my antithesis. But for the love of all that is holy, don't leave me for a woman with a name that ends in an *I*."

"I'm not following."

"Tiffani, Candi, Bambi—"

"If I ever left you for a woman named Bambi, then I deserve to get eaten by bears."

I grinned.

"Marriage in general is designed to fail unless people work really, really hard at keeping it all together," he said again as his hand reached up to cup my cheek. "But marriage to you? It's the best thing I've ever done. I'm in, Sib; all the way. Through bed bugs and book flops, through soccer games and braces, through houses and mortgages and all the things in between."

I sighed. "That's nice."

## Chapter 17

Halva: [hall-va]

1. A sweet, dense confection made of sesame flour and honey, originating in the Middle East.

2. I'll halva some more, please.

We moved into our new apartment a week later. The movers had just brought in the last of the furniture. Aidan gave them a cash tip before closing the front door. He leaned against it, looked around at all the boxes, and sighed. We'd packed in a frenzied state. When Aidan had gone back to our old apartment, he'd done at least twenty-five loads of laundry. Clean stuff had gone into plastic garbage bags to quarantine them from anything that might have been contaminated.

Furniture had been examined with flashlights, vacuumed thoroughly, and sprayed with stuff that claimed to kill the bugs. The vacuum bags were thrown out and double-bagged, and the vacuum itself tossed in the trash with a sign that read, DO NOT TAKE and a little drawing of a bug with vampire teeth.

There was no way we were bringing the pests to our new place. Bed bugs had invaded our haven, and it would take a while not to freak out every time I saw a black speck anywhere on linen or the floors.

"I'm exhausted just looking at all this stuff," he said.

"Did we really pack in three days? It's all a blur."

I opened a box labeled *dishes* and examined them. They'd survived the short move of a few blocks.

"We should just push through," I said. "If we don't unpack, we'll still be living here in three years with unopened boxes."

"You're so right. Which room should we start with?"

"Kitchen," I said automatically, standing over the box of dishes.

"Okay, but we have to do this my way—as opposed to your way."

I crossed my arms over my chest. "My way would be what?"

"To shove stuff into cabinets so we can't find anything later."

"I'd be offended if that weren't completely true," I said with a laugh. "You start on unpacking—I'm ordering a pizza."

"We just had breakfast—"

I shot him a look.

"Never mind. Get an extra large."

"What do you think I am? An amateur? Can we get black olives on half of it?"

"If you so desire," Aidan quipped.

"Maybe we should just order two pizzas," I muttered, opening the app on my phone.

Bless technology, I didn't even have to talk to anyone to order food anymore.

We unpacked as we ate steaming, fresh pizzas from Grandpa Pete's. While we devoured two of their pies, we adorably bickered about where to put things. In the end, I didn't really care. Aidan was the organized one.

"Why do we have so many useless kitchen gadgets?" I asked, holding up something I didn't recognize.

"Isn't that the strawberry stem remover you just had to have from Ladle?"

"Oh…yes, it is."

Ladle was a trendy, overpriced kitchen appliance store on Bedford Avenue in Williamsburg. Any and all hipsters were welcome, and unless you were a trust-fund baby, it was easy to spend an entire paycheck on devices you'd use once and then throw into a drawer to collect dust over time—which was exactly what I'd done with the corn-on-the-cob holders, the mini wooden honey rod, and now the strawberry stem remover.

"So forget these things," I said, gesturing to the drawer. "We have every appliance we've ever bought on display. Toaster, toaster oven—which seems ridiculous to have both—the blender, coffee maker, coffee grinder, mixer, and food processor. It's like our wedding registry is having an orgy up in here."

"Aren't you a juicy piece of sass today."

I looked at him. "You did not. Did you just come up with that?"

"I might have."

"Well done. I'm impressed." I grinned and then looked at the counter space again. Or lack thereof. "We just had to have all the things. We don't even use most of these."

"Yeah, that mortar and pestle has been severely neglected."

"Why didn't we purge before we moved?" I asked.

"Because we realized we were getting an upgrade in space."

I reached into a box marked *baking* and pulled out three muffin tins with different shapes. "I've never even used these. I'm starting a donation pile."

"Whoa, hold on. Have you reached the end of your nesting rope? Are you about to go completely Spartan?"

"I don't know," I whined. "Why did you let me go into Ladle at all?"

"Do you not remember what happened?" he demanded.

"No," I lied.

"Yes, you do. You *so* do."

I rolled my eyes. Aidan had tried to physically block me from the entrance. I'd darted around him like a football player holding the ball at the five-yard line, sprinting to score a touchdown.

Where did that sports analogy come from? Weird.

"Fine, I got through your defense," I admitted. "But then you got in there and started grabbing stuff off the shelves, too. Who needs three French presses in different sizes?"

He groaned. "We enable each other. This is a real problem."

Aidan went to the kitchen table and reached for a slice of pizza from his half-eaten pie. He lifted the lid. "You've got to be kidding me."

"What?"

"It's empty."

"Jasper!" I yelled.

The dog wormed his nose through the cracked bathroom door and sauntered out.

Aidan and I looked at each other.

"What was he doing in there?" Aidan asked.

"Your guess is as good as mine, but full disclosure—after he ate that entire block of cheese, he basically destroyed city property. Jasper is lactose intolerant. In like, a big way."

"Is it weird that we talk about our dog's—"

"Not that weird. And it's about to get so much worse." I pointed to my belly.

Aidan's brow furrowed as he marched over to the bathroom to peek his head inside. He groaned.

"Rock, paper, scissors on who gets to clean the bathroom," he suggested, already lifting his hand.

"Does it need bleach?"

"Yeah. Lots of it." He lowered his hand. "Damn. That means I'm up."

"Fetus growing for the win!"

Aidan was nearly done cleaning the bathroom when Jasper and I came back inside from a quick walk. I'd needed a break from all the unpacking and the day was surprisingly sunny. Not at all gloomy. Maybe spring would come early this year.

Aidan came out of the bathroom and removed a pair of yellow gloves. He smelled like cleaning products.

I waved a hand in front of my nose. "Did you use an entire bottle of bleach bubbling-spray stuff?"

"Almost. It was vile in there. How was the walk?"

"Fine, but he was already empty…"

We both looked down at Jasper who was sitting calmly by our feet, shooting us cute brown eyes that pleaded for a belly rub.

"Why's he being so weird lately?" I asked.

"Because he knows something is different. We'd just gotten settled in that apartment only to move again. Not to mention, you're pregnant. You smell different to him. Maybe he's jealous."

"I smell different?"

He nodded. "Yep. I notice it, so of course Jasper smells it a thousand times more."

"And this is a cry for attention?" I looked at our dog. "Eating things you shouldn't and pooping in places that are definitely not yours."

He whined.

"Fine. Go sleep on the couch." I waved him in the direction of the living room. He ran over to the couch and hopped up. And of course made himself comfortable directly in the middle of it.

"You know, he really doesn't help. Like at all," Aidan commented.

"Worst roommate ever. Are we done unpacking yet?"

"Not even close."

"Let's move to the bedroom and set that up."

"Oh, no, you don't. We finish a room and *then* we move on."

"What are you saying? That I start projects and then stop them?"

"That's exactly what I'm saying." He grinned. "There's also a bed in the bedroom which means we'll get distracted."

"Yeah, I could definitely go for a nap—oh, you meant the other thing."

Aidan laughed. "I could go for a nap, too. Wow. Did I just become old?"

"No."

"Really?"

"You've been old for a long time. Come on, let's finish this kitchen and then take an adult nap."

I stared at my cell phone as it vibrated across the kitchen counter with the name *Mom* flashing across the screen.

"It won't answer itself," Aidan said. He put away the last of the glassware and then dismantled the box the glasses had been in.

My mother and I hadn't spoken on the phone since she'd come to New York for the baby shower. We'd exchanged a few text messages, but they'd been short and more of a check-in than anything.

I knew she was trying to give me space and that she had been extremely busy with her new business endeavor, but it seemed so out of character for her. I was truly happy for her. She'd needed something more to do than to fixate completely on the entities growing in my uterus.

While I was contemplating if I had enough energy to talk to her, Aidan swiped my phone and answered it.

"Hey, Mom. It's me." He paused, his eyes meeting mine. "Ah, no we didn't get the package you sent us. Hold on, here's Sibby."

He handed me the phone and I put it to my ear. "Hi, Mom."

"I really hope the post office didn't lose the package I sent to you. I shipped it a few days ago."

"Though I'd love to blame the post office on this one, it's probably more than likely that they haven't dealt with our mail-forwarding request yet."

"Mail-forwarding?"

I held in a sigh. "We—kinda had to move."

"What? Why?"

Our buzzer buzzed. Aidan and I looked at each other. I shook my head, having no idea who that could've been. It was Mrs. Nowacki. I waved to her and she waved back. I headed to the bedroom to finish my conversation in private.

"Sibyl Ruth, are you listening to me?" my mother demanded.

"Yes," I said distractedly. "I'm listening. We moved because we got bed bugs."

"And you didn't think to call me?"

"What could you have done?"

"Flown up there and helped you."

"Helped with what?"

"Bed bugs are a nightmare! And they had to spray, didn't they? That's toxic—you can't be around that! Oh my God, the babies!"

"Mom, calm down—we stayed with Caleb while we looked for a new place." I was surprised by how Zen I felt even though I was trying to calm my mother down.

"So Aidan had to handle all the cleaning of the apartment on his own?"

"It was fine. We didn't have that bad of a problem. We caught it early and got to keep most of our stuff."

"It's all bad, anyway you slice it. They invade. They can live for years because cold doesn't kill them, they—"

"You have to stop reading internet articles about the horrors of living in New York."

"At least I no longer forward them to you," she pointed out.

Before I'd moved to New York in my early twenties, my mother's power of choice had been the email forward button. She'd thought I should be informed. There was information and then there was fearmongering. Mom fearmongered.

"Sibby?"

"Yeah, Mom."

"Are you okay?" Her voice sounded paper thin.

"Yeah. I'm doing okay."

She paused. "When you're all moved in, I'd love to see a video of the new place."

I smiled even though she couldn't see me. "I will. Tell me how everything is with you."

"Everything is good here. The Purim Carnival is going to be a smash. I have a meeting with three clients tomorrow and I'm thinking about not wearing bras anymore."

What did she just say?

"Uh, I'm glad for your success, Mom. Care to explain that last statement?"

"I've been wearing bras since I was eleven years old. I developed early. Now, I want to be free."

Oh, dear.

"How does Dad feel about it?"

"I haven't talked to him about it."

My dad was a well-renowned heart surgeon in Atlanta. My parents entertained his colleagues and members of the hospital board frequently. Mom and Dad had a certain social appearance they had to maintain, and if Mom stopped wearing bras—well, she wasn't the kind of woman that *could* stop wearing bras. She was nearly a D cup.

The world would know.

"Maybe you should talk to him about that."

"Free the nipple!"

"That's not what this is. That was about—"

"It's my own revolution, Sibby. I want to bust out of that box. If I don't want to wear a bra, I shouldn't have to wear a bra."

"How are you going to speed walk in the mornings?" I demanded.

"That doesn't require a bra, just legs."

There was no use trying to rationalize with my mother. Once she got it into her head that she was going to do something—*par exemple*, the matchmaking business—there was no stopping her. You had to admire the *chutzpah*, though.

"That reminds me. You can find me on Snapchat under the name Rent-a-Yenta."

"I thought you didn't want to be on Snapchat, only Facebook."

"I do both now. You have to stay relevant."

"I'm not on Snapchat."

"You're not?"

"Nope."

"You really should be, honey. It's where all the young kids are these days."

"That's why I'm not on there," I pointed out.

Snapchat made me feel like a technological dinosaur. Plus, it was all about selfies. Whenever I had attempted to take selfies, I somehow always wound up with a false double chin or something weird in the background. Now that I actually had a double chin, I stayed away from cameras. And mirrors. It was better for my self-esteem.

"Well, the filters are all super fun," she said. "I make myself look like a fox all the time."

"How did you go from hardly knowing how to use Instagram to knowing about filters on Snapchat?"

"That nice young man at the Temple showed me. The one who built my website. He's such a *mensch.*"

"Right. Okay, Mom. I gotta go. Mrs. Nowacki is here," I said.

"Tell her hello for me."

"I will."

I hung up with my mother and stood up from the bed —during our phone call, I'd wandered into the bedroom, wanting a moment of privacy. The soft hum of conversation reached my ears and I went out to greet Mrs. Nowacki.

She was sitting on the couch, Jasper's head in her lap. When she made a move to get up, I waved her down and came over to give her a hug.

I was glad to note that she still felt comfortable enough to show up, even though we no longer lived across the hall.

"I bring you cookies and a package that was delivered," she said.

"Ah, that must be the Purim Package," I said as I went to the counter. Aidan had already opened it and I pulled out three bags of *Hamantaschen*, masks, and groggers.

"What's with the masks?" Aidan asked. "Is Purim like the Jewish Halloween?"

I grinned. "No. It's not a day of the dead. Purim is a celebration of Queen Esther's bravery. Every year on Purim, we're supposed to go to Temple and reread the story. Whenever the name Haman, the villain, is mentioned, we use the noisemaker—" I demonstrated. "It's like a Jewish boo session."

"Cool! But riddle me this. If Haman is wicked, why do we eat a dessert named after him?" Aidan asked.

"Notice the shape? It's supposed to resemble Haman's three-pointed hat. A reminder of sorts." I pulled out a poppy-seed *Hamantaschen* and took a bite. "Mmmm. My favorite."

"You look cute. Noshin' on *Hamantaschen*."

I grinned. "That was a good one."

"Thank you. Are you going to share the wealth?"

I held out the *Hamantaschen* to his mouth and he took a bite. "Wow. Way better than *gefilte* fish."

"*Gefilte* fish sets the bar really low," I said. I set the *Hamantaschen* onto a plate and took it over to the coffee table. "Dessert is served. Mrs. Nowacki, which one do you want?"

Chapter 18

Cholent: [chol-ent]

    1. Slow cooked stew of beef, beans, barley and sometimes potatoes.

    2. Jew stew.

    My face fell when I opened the door and saw that Stacy was in jeans and a sweater. "I said pajama party!"

    She patted her bag. "Did you really think I was going to wear pajamas on the subway?" She looked me up and down. "Yours are nice, by the way."

    "They're Aidan's. I can't zip up my adult onesie."

    "You have an adult onesie?"

I nodded. "It has a hood. And footies."

"I'm really depressed that you can't fit into it because now I want to see it." She came inside the apartment and Jasper ran over to greet her. Aidan was at the bar so I had the place to myself for a supremely low-key girls' night.

"Wow," she said as she looked around. "It didn't look like this when three dudes lived here."

I'd tried to unpack and put everything away during the day. In the few spare moments that Aidan was home, we hung a picture here and there, because nothing said newly-moved-in like the absence of photos or art on the walls.

Bare walls were for college kids who kept their toiletries in plastic drawers. I was growing two humans inside my body, like some sci-fi gestation pod—it was time to act like an adult.

"I'm going to change and get ready for a night of lounging. I need it," she said as she ducked into the bathroom. "Who else is coming?"

"Caleb's new girlfriend, Emmeline. Everyone calls her Em."

Her eyes widened. "No shit? Are you guys like, friends or something?"

"We just met. We had dinner with them not too long ago and she's actually really nice."

"And you invited her tonight, *why?*"

"Honestly? Because Caleb and Aidan are besties and business partners, so that means Em and I will be around each other a lot."

"Yeah, but haven't they only been dating for a hot second? You could've waited a few months before inviting her to a hang out."

"In a few months I'll have humans sucking on my breasts twenty-four seven. I doubt I'll see another human who isn't the father of my children for a long time."

"Ah, so you're stocking up on your social interaction now, huh?"

"Something like that."

She came out of the bathroom wearing a cute pair of men's plaid pajama bottoms and a black hoodie.

"Joe's?"

She nodded and then looked like she was about to start crying.

I held up a finger. "Wait. Just wait."

"I don't want to talk about Joe in front of a girl I don't even know."

"I wasn't going to tell you not to talk about Joe. I was just going to get you a glass of wine first."

"Oh. That's thoughtful."

I poured her a glass of red and handed it to her. She took a hefty swallow. "I just miss him. Like, a lot. These last two weeks have been really hard without him."

"Which is one of the reasons I wanted to have a girl hang before I go out of town to visit Annie in Montauk for that weird oyster-shucking thing."

"Riiiiight. That's so wild."

She set her glass of wine down so she could put her purple-tipped blond hair into a high ponytail. The oven timer blared and I turned on the oven light to look at the chocolate chip cookies.

"I think these are done," I said. "Do you mind taking them out of the oven for me?"

"Sure." She grabbed the oven mitts and opened the oven, reaching in to pull out the cookie sheets. "Oh, hell yes."

"I've also got Oreos, a jar of peanut butter, and a king-sized bag of Runts."

"I think I love you."

"I know."

The door buzzer sounded and Stacy went to answer it. "I thought it was girls' night," Stacy stated, but I heard the amusement in her tone.

"It's not a girls' night without me," Zeb quipped. "Terry is out of town, I'm flying solo, and there's nothing worse than hanging out in a Chelsea apartment by yourself."

"Thanks for trekking all the way to Brooklyn just so you wouldn't be alone," I teased.

Zeb kissed my cheek as he set the grocery bags he was carrying onto the counter. "I want the tour of the new place. Now."

"I want to do it once. So we wait for Em and then I'll show you."

"Fine." He riffled through one of the grocery totes and pulled out a bag of Bugles.

"You didn't," I stated.

"I did. I knew you'd have the sweets covered. So I brought all things salty." He looked at Stacy. "What did you bring?"

"Myself. And all these new makeup samples I'm supposed to wear and then talk about on my YouTube channel."

"MAKEOVERS!" Zeb yelled.

I put a finger to my ear. "Inside voices, please."

The door buzzer buzzed again.

"Your turn to get it," Stacy said to Zeb. "I answered you, Sibby answered me."

"It's the transitive property of answering doors," I said.

"Transitive what now?" Stacy asked.

"It's a geometry thing." I paused. "Did I just remember something useless from high school?"

"Maybe this is your brain's way of getting ready to help your children with their math homework."

"Perish the thought," I said with a sigh. I reached over and pulled off a half-cooled chocolate chip cookie, broke it in half and gave one part to Stacy.

Zeb came back with Em, who was carrying a pie tin covered in foil. "She's so cute, she's like a Polly Pocket," Zeb gushed.

A blush covered Em's cheeks. "Hope you don't mind. I made a pie."

"And she brought vanilla ice cream," Zeb announced, holding up another grocery bag.

"That was really nice of you." I introduced Em and Stacy, stuck the ice cream in the freezer, and then demanded that those who hadn't changed into pajamas do so immediately.

After we were all appropriately attired, I gave them a tour of the apartment.

"The roof view is awesome," Stacy said.

"How do you know?" Zeb asked.

"This used to be her boyfriend's apartment," I answered. As soon as I said the word *boyfriend*, Stacy's eyes filled with tears.

"We need wine," Zeb said as he patted Stacy on the back in an effort to console her. He just looked awkward though, and shot me a look of pure panic.

I grabbed the glass of wine and shoved it at Stacy, and then I poured two more glasses.

"Better?" Zeb asked her as Stacy got control of herself and wiped the corners of her eyes.

She nodded.

"Your mascara didn't run," Em marveled.

"She's a beauty influencer," I explained. "She gets a bunch of makeup samples from different companies to test out and then she talks about them on her YouTube channel."

Em blinked. "Uh. Wow."

I suppressed a grin. Stacy was eyeing Em like a project. Em instantly backed away, but Stacy needed something to distract her and I was all for throwing Em to the wolves. It would be a good diversion for all of us. I didn't want to say anything more to make Stacy cry.

So while Stacy painted the canvas of Em's perfect face, Zeb and I shoved cookie after cookie into our mouths.

"Don't think you're getting out of a makeover, Sibby," Stacy said, brushing Em's eyebrows with a mini eyebrow brush. "I've been dying to do something awesome with your hair."

"It's so shiny." Zeb stroked my head and I batted his hand away.

"It's not a pelt."

"Damn, your hair is *so* soft!" Zeb commented. "I wish I had pregnancy hair."

"That would mean you'd have to be pregnant."

"And share this body with another entity? No thanks."

"Yeah, didn't think so. Speaking of pregnancy"—I took a drink of my Pellegrino—"when are you and Terry going to adopt an adorable, fat, Asian baby?"

"Ooooh." Stacy painted Em's lips as she said, "You guys would look so cute with an Asian baby."

"I need a wine refill if we're going to talk about babies," Zeb said, jumping up.

"Ah, let me grab another bottle—that one is empty," I said.

I raised my hand to Zeb and he helped me up and then we headed to the kitchen. I picked a bottle of Shiraz from the six-bottle wine rack and removed the foil.

"I won't let Terry talk about babies," Zeb said, picking up the thread of our earlier conversation. "Not until he makes an honest man out of me."

"Why, Zeb, you're strangely old-fashioned," I teased. "Not that I'm trying to pressure you into adopting a baby, but it would be nice, ya know? Some friends of mine actually doing the baby thing too."

"All in due time," he assured me with a pat on my shoulder.

"So have you guys talked about a wedding date?" I refilled his glass of wine and then set the bottle down on the counter.

"We have an idea. We're thinking a fall wedding. December at the latest."

"Next year?" I prodded.

"This year."

"Wait, you're engaged?"

He nodded and grinned. "I mean, not officially or anything. The brute didn't buy me an engagement ring, but since we're talking wedding plans, that means we're pretty much there."

I hugged him. "*Mazel tov!* I'm so happy for you guys."

"That leads me to my next point of conversation… Will you be my best man?"

"Me? You sure?"

He nodded. "I don't know what I'd do without you, Sib."

"Probably go to the hospital a lot less," I choked out. "Of course I'll be your best man." We hugged and I pulled back. "Not that I have any say in your wedding date, but I'd love a December wedding."

"Because New England is enchanting in winter?"

"No, because I'm going to need those six months to lose some of the pregnancy weight."

I took Em and Zeb up to the roof while Stacy stayed behind to call Joe. While we'd been hanging out, she'd only been half paying attention to our conversations. Instead, she'd watch her phone for any and all incoming messages from Joe.

"So, can I be a total dick for like thirty seconds?" Zeb asked.

"Sure," I said, hunching lower into my coat. It was still chilly, especially on the roof, but there was nothing like having an up close and personal view of the Manhattan skyline.

Zeb looked at Em. "You okay with that, too?"

"Yes." She smiled. "I can be a dick if I want to be."

"You, Ms. Polly Pocket? I don't think so." Zeb affectionately rumpled her hair—hair that Stacy had yet to get her hands on.

"Go on, I'm waiting for your prickish comment," I said.

"I was just going to ask if we should take bets on when Joe and Stacy are going to break up."

"You're awful," I said, but couldn't help a laugh that escaped. "They might go the distance…"

"Yeah, and you're good at team sports," he quipped.

"Hey!" I elbowed his ribs. "Be nice. Wait no, don't be nice."

"I won't place a bet," Em said. "But my assessment is

that they won't last much longer. Aside from the fact that they're in their mid-twenties, the whole moving to Vegas with the band thing doesn't bode well for them."

"Yep, so now their relationship is long distance with no end in sight," Zeb stated.

"Ugh, you guys are such realists, it's awful."

"We don't all tell love stories for a living," Zeb pointed out.

"Can we go back down? I'm kinda cold." Em was hopping around like an elf.

Zeb shook his head and then wrapped an arm around her neck and pulled her into his lanky body. "Come on, Polly, I'll keep you warm."

I laughed, enjoying their banter. I had so many friends from different groups, but every time I brought people together, other connections formed. Even though my friends were scattered across the United States, my relationships were solid.

"What's that noise?" Zeb asked with a frown as we stood outside my apartment door.

"She either saw a bug or she's excited," I stated. "I'll go in first. Scope out the scene."

"You're pregnant. I'll go first." He stood up straight.

"Wow, you guys are dramatic," Em noted.

Zeb grinned. "Thank you." He pushed open the door and came to a stop. Em and I peered around him like the Von Trapp children peeking out from behind Maria and Captain Von Trapp when they performed on stage.

"She's happy," Zeb noted.

"She had a lot of wine," I commented. "I wasn't sure it was a good idea for her to talk to Joe in this state, but I guess everything is okay?"

Stacy was currently bouncing around the living room, dancing with Jasper.

"What's going on?" I asked, taking off my jacket and hanging it up.

"Joe just asked me to move to Vegas!" she shrieked.

I winced and put a hand to my eardrum. "Good thing we didn't bet," I whispered to Zeb. "You would've lost."

"This is just the first act, baby," he said back. "Jury's still out. I give it three months. Tops."

A wave of sadness rushed over me, catching me by surprise. How many more friends was I going to have to say goodbye to? I was happy for Stacy—if she wanted to be with Joe, then awesome. Moving was the right choice, but dang? Really?

How was I supposed to have an all-girl band if people kept leaving me?

But this wasn't about me, this was about Stacy.

She was excited to get to packing and could hardly focus. I called her an Uber. She didn't even change back into her street clothes.

"I better go too," Zeb said. "It's a schlep to get to Chelsea."

"It's only 9 p.m.," I protested.

"And past your bedtime, Mama," he teased. He hugged me. "Brunch when you get back?"

"Yeah, sounds good. Aren't you going to change?"

He gestured to his black silk pajamas. "No way. I'm rocking this on the subway." Zeb reached for Em. "Come here, Polly Pocket. I want to pick you up."

Em grinned in amusement and looked at me.

I shrugged. "He used to pick me up all the time too, but then I gained thirty-five pounds."

Zeb's mouth dropped open. "You've gained thirty-five pounds?"

"Shut. Up."

"Just, wow. My mangina hurts for you."

"Thanks for the sympathy."

"I'm waiting," Em said.

Zeb scooped her up into his arms and twirled her around. "I like you, Em." He set her back down. "I don't treat everyone I meet this way."

"I feel special," Em said.

Zeb said goodbye to Jasper and then he was gone.

"Are you leaving too?" I asked Em.

"Er—I thought I'd hang out for a bit. If that's okay, I mean I know—"

"I'd love that," I said in relief. "It gets kinda lonely here at night when Aidan works. More wine?"

"Sure."

I refilled her glass and we went into the living room. I settled myself onto the couch, wedging myself into the cushions.

"Where are you going?" Em asked after she settled in the chair.

"Hmmm?" I murmured distractedly. Jasper slithered his way over to me and rested his head in my lap.

"Zeb said he wanted to have brunch when you got back. Where are you going?"

"I'm going to Montauk to visit my best friend." I peered at Em, wondering how I was supposed to mention Annie. Wondering how I was supposed to be friends with both of them.

"That will be fun," she said.

I nodded. "Yeah."

We fell into an awkward silence.

"Oh, hell," Em muttered. "We might as well get it all on the table, right?"

I let out a small laugh. "Yeah. It's probably better for all parties involved."

"You're best friends with Caleb's ex. I'm the new girlfriend. You're obligated to hate me."

"I was planning on hating you actually," I admitted with a rueful smile. "It would be easy to hate you if you sucked. You don't suck."

She let out a breath. "I just really like him, you know? And I don't want it to be weird between us, but I feel like I have to be honest with you. I'm terrified he still loves her. I'm terrified she still loves him. But not enough to break up with him. Is that stupid?"

I shook my head. "Not stupid at all. I don't know what he told you—that's between you guys. But I think it's done, Em. I think they've both closed the door on that relationship." I paused. "You're really good for him. And *to* him. I was watching you guys at dinner and you mesh. You treat each other well. He's really lucky to have you."

She smiled. "Thanks for saying that, Sibby."

"It's not easy. To find another couple that you get along with, you know? You always like one person or the other. But I do like you, Em. I invited you tonight because I'd like us to be friends."

"You sure? I mean, no hard feelings if you're choosing her—"

"Finding your tribe is hard," I interrupted. "Nearly impossible, really. My tribe is scattered across the States. And now Stacy is moving too. You find your tribe and you hold on to them. I'm not saying we're going to be best friends overnight. But I'm open to getting to know you. Independently of Caleb."

She let out a breath of air. "You're really intimidating. You know that?"

I blinked. "Me? But I spill things. And my socks never match. And I get pregnant by accident. I'm not intimidating. I'm a walking disaster. You should just get out of the way so I don't take you down with me!"

## Chapter 19

Blintz: [blints]

1. A thin, rolled crepe stuffed with cheese and then baked or fried.

2. This is how people get fat. Good thing I'm already pregnant.

"Cheers," Annie said, clinking her glass against mine.

I took a sip of the freshly squeezed OJ and moaned in enjoyment. "That's like, the best thing ever."

She grinned. "I'm so glad you're here."

"Me too," I admitted.

"Does your husband miss you yet?" she asked.

"Doubtful. He gets the bed to himself and Mrs. Nowacki promised to cook him a few meals. He's mostly working and sleeping anyway. Besides, he'll come up for the oyster-shucking contest in a few days."

Jasper and I had arrived in Montauk late the previous afternoon. Annie hadn't been there to greet us because she'd been running all over town, ensuring that everything was in order for the oyster-shucking contest.

It was still early morning and we were having breakfast in the restaurant. It didn't open until later in the day, so we had the place to ourselves. She'd cooked a huge breakfast in the restaurant's kitchen. I viewed it as a personal challenge to eat as much of it as I could.

We were out on the patio. Ocean air teased the hair at my temples and the sound of seagulls cawing in the distance reached my ears.

"Dig into the quiche before it gets cold."

I sliced the quiche and put a sliver onto my plate. I cut off a bite and had it partway into my mouth when I asked, "Are those mushrooms?"

"Yep. And tomatoes."

"That's not a quiche, that's a *yeesh*." I pushed the quiche to the edge of my plate and grabbed the bowl of potatoes.

"I thought you liked mushrooms and tomatoes?"

"I did. Guess I don't anymore." I gave her a lopsided smile. "Sorry. I didn't think to mention it. It was so nice of you to cook breakfast, really."

"It's okay," she said. "Can I make you something else?"

"No, there's more than enough here for me to eat, I promise. Truth? All I really want are Fritos and cream cheese."

"Together?"

I nodded. "You'd think it would be weird, but it's so good. Salty and creamy and delicious."

"If I didn't see the belly, I'd assume you were high."

I laughed. "Right?"

We finished breakfast and then I helped clear the plates. We took them into the kitchen and stuck them in the dishwasher. We wrapped the leftovers and put them in the walk-in.

"See what I mean, though? About the restaurant?" she said as we walked through the main dining room.

It was a great space. Tons of windows that let in light and an incredible ocean view. But it was definitely in need of a spruce.

"Yeah, it's a little dated."

So was the menu, according to Annie. She spent the entire ride back to her aunt and uncle's house gabbing about all the changes she would make if she were in charge.

"How did you get your uncle on board with Oyster Life Magazine coming to do a spread on the restaurants competing in this shucking contest?"

She parked her car in the driveway. "Um…"

"Annie, no," I whispered. "You can't blindside him! You have to give him a chance to prepare!"

"I will," she said. "But I won't give him a lot of time because then he'll worry and find a way to back out of it. I'll tell him the morning of…"

We walked to the stairs over the garage and trekked up to the mother-in-law suite where Annie was staying. Jasper greeted us and I discreetly looked around, hoping he hadn't decided to eat Annie's couch or defile her bathroom. He was weird about new spaces. But everything looked good.

"Walk time?" Annie asked.

"Yeah, I want to take him to the beach. Let him run a bit."

"Sounds like a plan."

"Can I borrow a windbreaker? I forgot mine." Though I'd brought my light jacket, I'd completely forgotten that it was cooler and windier by the water.

"Sure." Annie went over to the coatrack. As she riffled through the jackets, I noticed a man's winter coat. Bright blue. Not at all Caleb's style, so I knew it wasn't one of his that he hadn't gotten back after the breakup.

We strolled out and while she locked the apartment, I pondered whether or not I should even bring it up. Annie hadn't been happy when I interfered with her flirtation with Mills. But now that Caleb was dating Em, I just wasn't going to be the jerk that broke up people to try and get my best friend back together with the love of her life. Even if she wouldn't admit he was the love of her life, I knew he was.

To hell with it.

"So I noticed a masculine-looking jacket hanging on the hook by the door." I looked at her and widened my eyes, feigning innocence.

"Yeah, it's Mills's. He left it here a few weeks ago when he came to visit."

Her aunt and uncle were steps from the beach and it took us only a few minutes to get to the shoreline. I let Jasper off his leash and he immediately took off in an attempt to catch a seagull.

"You had a boy visit you and you didn't tell me?"

She glanced at me as she lifted the collar of her jacket. "Because I wasn't sure I wanted to defend my decision."

Her tone said she was baiting me, but I wasn't going to take it. "Tell me what happened. I really want to know. Please?"

Annie paused and shoved her hands in her coat pockets. She stared out at the ocean. Waves lapped along the sand and despite the fact that it was already late morning, the beach was still quiet.

"Nothing physical happened," she said softly. "Well, we kissed, but that's all."

I leaned closer, trying to hear her over the waves. "That's all? Why?"

"When Caleb and I got together, it was physical from the beginning, you know? And that really confuses how you feel about someone."

"So you didn't really love Caleb because you slept with him immediately?"

"I *did* really love him. It's just—well—how can you truly build a foundation with someone if you sleep with them too fast?"

"The hymen grows back without regular sex."

She rolled her eyes. "It does not."

"But you're holding off on sex with Mills?"

"For the time being…"

"And he's cool with that? I mean, you guys talked about it, right?"

"Yeah, actually we did. I told him before he came up that I wasn't ready to take our relationship further and if he wasn't okay with that, he didn't have to come."

"Wow. Okay."

"I just—you can't do the same thing day in and day out and expect different results. I'm trying to be more thoughtful about my life and my choices."

"You mean you're trying to be an adult?"

"Yeah, that."

"When you get the hang of it, can you tell me how to do it?"

I held up the green T-shirt to my body and grimaced. "You got me an extra large, right?"

"Er—is there a good way to answer this question?"

I sighed. "It's okay. I know I've gained some weight since I got pregnant."

Annie wisely didn't comment on that fact. "Look at the back."

I held the shirt away from me and flipped it around. "Mother Shuckers? Really?" I said with a laugh.

"Badass Mother Shuckers. You ready for your first oyster-shucking lesson?"

"This seems like a terrible idea. I'm a clumsy person. But okay. If you think I can do this."

We headed over to the main house. There was a large kitchen and a table that sat twelve. After laying down newspaper, Annie grabbed a bag of oysters from the refrigerator and dumped them onto the table.

"It's a shame you can't help me eat these," she said.

"Parasites."

"Ugh. Why are you trying to ruin oysters for me?"

"Sorry."

"That's okay, I basically ignore most pregnancy stuff you mention. Otherwise I'm sure I'd never eat my favorite foods again."

"My weirdest craving as of late—you ready for it?"

"Hit me."

"Pickled okra and Mint Oreos."

"That sounds awful."

"I enjoyed it going down, but it gave me heartburn later on."

"So let's see. You've been afflicted with sudden hair growth, morning sickness and all day nausea, the crushing of your internal organs, heartburn, and weight gain. What else?"

"I've become very aware of my lady bits."

She paused her oyster shucking to look at me. "I'm going to need more than that."

"I tried to go for a Brazilian a few weeks ago. You know, to have someone clean me up, since I can't even see down there."

Her shoulders shook with laughter. "Go on."

"Well, they ripped off one patch and I screamed bloody murder. It was, like, the worst pain I've ever felt. It's like all the blood in my body is concentrated down there, and even wearing jeans is tricky. I refused to let her finish. Cut to later that night when Aidan and I are in bed... His hands are wandering and he feels one smooth patch and the rest of it isn't. Then comments on it."

Annie let out a huge laugh. "Oh my God! So you're just like, a wild woman down there?"

"Except for that one patch. I thought about asking Aidan to help me out by using his beard trimmer, but I don't want him near it. I'm afraid he'll get lost in the jungle and never come out."

"We have the weirdest conversations. You know that, right?"

"It's odd, you know? Like, technically I could talk about all this stuff with the other women in my birthing class, but I'd much rather talk to you. Is that okay?"

"Of course it's okay. Look, I know I make jokes—"

"I make jokes too. It's our thing," I said.

"Right. It is our thing."

"Even though I'm having kids and you're still undecided about all that stuff, you're still my best friend and I want you involved. Is that okay?"

"Sibby, you're my best friend in the entire world." She looked down at the oyster she was holding. "I know it's been hard for you—that I left the city. I miss you. I do. I miss being able to walk over to your apartment, split a bottle of wine, talk about life. You stood by me when I was my worst self, and it sorta kills me that I had to move away to get my head on straight. I want to be there when you have the babies. I don't want to miss stuff."

"I don't want you to miss stuff either. You're still good with being their godmother, right?"

"Hell yes. You think I'm going to let someone else take Agamemnon and Troy to get their first tattoos?"

"Troy? You shortened only one of my unborn children's names."

"You try coming up with a nickname for Agamemnon."

"Doesn't matter." I sighed. "Aidan gave a hard veto on those names. Too Brooklyn, he says."

"Damn. They were growing on me. Any other names in the pool?"

"Not yet. I'm thinking we wait until they pop out and then see what they look like."

"Mr. Overprepared won't let you do that," she said with a laugh.

"Probably not."

"Come on, let's pick up the oyster-shucking speed. At this rate, we'll come in last place and that would not go well."

"What do we get if we win?"

"Bragging rights."

"That's it?"

"And a big trophy. Not to mention Dylan will do an extra feature on the restaurant that wins. We need all the publicity we can get to save this place."

"There's a lot riding on this competition. Do you think I'll be oyster-shucking ready?"

"We've got two more days to whip you into shape."

"Who are the celebrities on the other teams?" I asked as I cracked open another oyster. Once you knew where to place your oyster knife, it was really just about not slicing your hand when you gave it some force.

"I'm not sure. People are keeping their celebrity team-mates under wraps."

My phone buzzed in my back pocket. I set down my knife and oyster and then reached for my cell.

Aidan had sent a video. I pressed play. It was the space next to the bar. Shelves had been built into the walls. The room was covered in sawdust, tools, and random planks of wood. Caleb was wearing a tool belt and when the camera stopped on him, he gave me a little wave.

"Aidan, say something to your wife," a female voice said from behind the camera.

Aidan's body filled the screen. He was wearing a flannel shirt, with sleeves rolled up to the elbows, and a tool belt. His dad and one of his brothers-in-law was in the background.

"Miss you, Sib," Aidan said with a grin.

The camera lens flipped around and Em's face filled the screen. She grinned and then the video ended.

I glanced at Annie as she continued shucking oysters, her eyes currently on a very stubborn oyster. "Who was the girl?" she asked.

"Wine rep," I said.

It was true, but definitely a lie by omission. But what was I going to do? Tell Annie that her ex was dating someone new? And that I liked her?

A lot.

No. None of that needed to be said before this competition. It wouldn't do well for her mindset.

"Since when are you so chummy with the bar's wine reps?" she pressed.

"Since I accused one of them of hitting on Aidan."

"Say what now?"

"Didn't I tell you that story?"

"I think I would've remembered it if you had."

I told her what had happened with Aria. I'd successfully diverted Annie's attention. It had worked this time, but when she inevitably found out about Em and Caleb, would she explode, or wish them well?

Annie was working at the restaurant until 9 p.m., so Jasper and I were on our own. After heating up some potato leek soup and peppering it heavily, I sat at the kitchen table and went for my phone. I called Aidan, but he didn't answer. He was so busy with the expansion that I got brief phone calls in the morning and before bed. He had apologized profusely, but I understood. We both knew it was going to be like that for a while. I'd be glad when he came up here for the oyster-shucking festival and we could spend some time together.

Sighing, I shot off a text to Stacy asking how she was getting settled in Las Vegas. She'd left right before I'd come to Montauk and we hadn't had a proper goodbye. Because all of her connections were in New York, she'd do the two-city living thing for a while, so I'd definitely still get to see her—just not on a regular basis. Joe was going to go on a European tour in the fall and she was going with him. She was trying to streamline her life.

I couldn't believe a twenty-five-year-old social influencer had to streamline her life, but there you had it.

The potato leek soup went down easy and it was delicious, but it wasn't enough to satisfy me for the long-term. I'd eat again in an hour or so.

I got onto my computer, and made the mistake of going down the social-media rabbit hole. I found pictures of us on our honeymoon, and then even further back of us on a beach together. I was wearing a bikini. My hair was frizzy and I was pale and nearly blinding to the eye, but I was skinny.

Was.

Forty-five minutes after the end of her shift, Annie walked into a shit storm. I was still sitting at my computer, yelling at the screen, tears streaming down my cheeks, clutching a jar of peanut butter like a madwoman. Jasper got up from sleeping beneath the kitchen table and walked over to Annie to hide behind her legs.

"Uh, Sibby? I think you're terrifying your dog."

I blubbered and wailed and then shoved a spoonful of peanut butter into my mouth.

Annie set her keys down on the front hallway table. Her chef jacket was stained with marinara and when she came closer, I immediately smelled the oil they used to fry shrimp in, reminding me of the glory days waitressing at Antonio's.

She inched closer, carefully, so as not to spook the feral pregnant woman. "What happened? When I left, you were totally fine."

I looked at her and she flinched. I must've looked like an insane lunatic. Maybe it was the wailing and peanut-butter clutching that had been a clue.

"Pithurs," I said with peanut butter thickly coating my mouth.

"Pictures? Are you stalking an ex-boyfriend or something?" she asked in confusion. "Because that's the only thing I can think of that would make you—give me that peanut butter."

I held the jar closer to my chest. "Not on your lifhtlh."

"Sibby," she said in a very patient tone of voice one would use on a child—or an angry traveler at the airport. "Give Annie the jar of peanut butter."

"No!" I yelled as I smacked the last of the peanut butter from the roof of my mouth. "And stop talking about yourself in the third person. It's weird."

"You want to talk about weird? You're crying into a jar of peanut butter and looking at old photos of your ex-boyfriend—"

"Who said I was looking at my ex-boyfriend?"

She blinked. "Then what the hell is going on?"

"Old pictures of me. Skinny me."

Annie gently coerced me to let go of the jar. "Peanut butter doesn't give you love."

"Neither does Aidan." I sniffed pathetically, wiping the tears from my cheeks. Thank goodness I never bothered with mascara because I definitely would've had raccoon eyes.

"Aidan loves you," Annie said.

"Of course he loves me," I said.

"But you just said he doesn't."

"No, I said he doesn't give me love."

"Wait, do you mean sex? He doesn't give you sex?"

"Would you want to have sex with me when I look like this?" I demanded. A chunk of peanut butter fell from my chin and landed in my lap.

Before closing the jar of peanut butter, Annie grabbed a spoon from the silverware drawer and dipped it in. "You drive a woman to binge, you know that?"

"*I* don't even want to have sex with me now that I look like this."

"Where the hell are the Oreos?" she muttered. "Peanut butter just isn't doing the trick. I need cookies to live through this conversation."

She pulled open all the cabinets, but couldn't find them. I saw the corner of the package on top of the fridge and told her.

Annie ripped into them. She sat down in the chair across from me. Her chef pants had a squid pattern. They were cute, and I thought about getting a pair and wearing them instead of sweats.

"Why did you start looking at photos of yourself before you were pregnant?" she demanded. "That's playing Russian roulette with your emotions."

"You know how it is. You click on one photo and then all of a sudden it spirals and you start evaluating your life choices and wondering if your boobs will ever bounce back."

"That's why they invented plastic surgery."

"Gross." I bit my lip and paused for a moment. "I've kinda been spurning Aidan's sexual advances…"

She pinched the bridge of her nose. "Why?"

"Because I'm uncomfortable in my body. There's just

so much *more* of me now. The thirty-five pounds I gained is creeping closer to forty, and there are rolls in places. I have a double chin."

"Only when you take selfies, but that's because you hold the phone at the wrong angle."

"Don't lie to me. I know I have a double chin. I look like I belong on some cake-mix box you find in the off-brand section."

"Why the off-brand section?"

"Because I'm not good enough to be a brand."

Annie slowly stood up. "I need to shower the restaurant off of me."

"You're leaving me? When I'm emotionally needy?"

"This is out of my realm. This is a job for your husband."

"The one I won't have sex with…"

"That's between you and Aidan. You need to call him. I don't know how to handle this."

"He won't pick up his phone!" I yelled. "Because he works all the time and I can never get ahold of him."

"Don't you guys have a code for emergencies?"

"Yes."

"This is an emergency. You're not getting what you need. I can't help you get what you need. Ergo, emergency. Call your husband. Tell him to fix this."

"Fix *what*?"

"Fix *you*. Because whatever he's doing or not doing, you're emotionally distraught—"

"I'm pregnant!"

"Same thing." She handed me my phone. "Call him. Please."

## Chapter 20

---

Kreplach: [krep-laKH]

1. Yiddish for little dumplings. Typically filled with ground meat or cheese, and served in soup.

2. Okay, so not all of our food sucks.

I was barnacled to Aidan, not caring that everyone at the train station could see our demonstrative exchange of affection.

"Sibby," Aidan muttered, trying to move his lips away from mine.

"What?"

"Stop eating my face in public."

"But I missed your face."

He whispered in my ear, "Did you? This is new."

"What can I say? Absence makes the pregnant woman crazier."

"Does that mean you'll finally let me—"

"Oh look, a seagull. Montauk is actually really gorgeous. There's a lighthouse we should go see."

Aidan threw me an amused smile. He leaned over and sniffed me. "What's that smell? Peanut butter?"

I sighed and shrugged.

Aidan's shoulders lurched with laughter. "God, I really missed you."

"So you're not mad at me for calling you in a blind panic and pulling the SOS card?"

"You had me really worried. The SOS is for 'I'm dying', 'I'm in labor', or 'aliens have invaded the planet, meet at our *rendezvous* spot.'"

"It felt like an emergency," I said softly. "And I was freaking Annie out."

He wrapped me in a hug. "I know. I just got really worried. I thought something was wrong with the babies."

"I'm sorry about that. I didn't mean—"

"Can we stop with the apologizing?" he asked. "I'm glad you called when you needed me. Sometimes I feel…"

"What?"

"Like you don't really need me. Like you've got all this handled."

"What cave have you been living in? I feel like I'm always just seconds away from falling apart."

"I don't know. You just haven't really been the same since the bed bugs and the move."

We headed in the direction of our car. The parking lot was almost empty. No one had lingered at the train station.

"I feel like this pregnancy has been going on forever.

Nothing is how I thought it would be." I used the clicker to unlock the doors. "Do you want to drive?"

"Sure. Just tell me the address and I'll put it into my phone." He placed his suitcase in the back and then climbed into the driver's side. He took a moment to adjust the mirrors and his seat.

"Shrimp legs," he teased.

I made a noise and buckled myself in. "It's harder than I thought it would be. You working as much as you are."

He sighed. "Yeah. I know."

"But can I really ask you to pull back? To not be there to see your dreams come to fruition? That's not fair."

"The timing sucks."

We'd been over it a million times and yet it wasn't getting any easier. It was actually getting harder. But I couldn't expect Aidan to spend every waking moment with me just to ease my own inadequacy. And that was the true crux of it.

I hadn't gotten my writer mojo back. Friends kept leaving the city. My routine, just when I thought I'd gotten into the rhythm of it, would upend. I'd been in prime nesting mode and yanked from the comfort of it. Uprooted, only to have to do it all over again.

"I think I'm angry," I said finally. "And I didn't realize it until just now."

"Angry at me?"

I looked out the window. "Not at you. Resentful, maybe."

"Why do you always wait to get me into a car before unleashing your feelings?"

"I don't know."

"I wish you'd let me back in," he said as he turned down the street to Annie's uncle's house.

"I'm trying. It's just—every time I gain another pound

or I get heartburn, I get upset because I can't do anything about those things."

"The gaining weight, maybe not. The heartburn? Maybe you don't eat Tabasco sauce with everything."

"Really?" I looked at him in exasperation.

He grinned, but it slipped. "How can I be there for you, Sibby? You don't let me touch you, and when we do have a random date night together, we sit in silence, thinking about our own things. Tell me what to do and I'll do it. I don't want you unhappy or resentful or—"

"Yowsa!" I pressed a hand to my lower stomach.

"Someone kick you?"

I shook my head. "No. That was something else. I think it was a Braxton Hicks." I let out a slow breath. Thankfully, the cramp eased.

"Are you okay? Do I need to take you to the hospital?"

I looked at him. His blue eyes were wide with worry. "You're terrified too!" I yelled.

"Well, yeah, I'm terrified. I'm constantly terrified."

"Why don't we talk about this more?" I demanded.

"Because you get afraid, and then I have to be the one to calm you down and hold you up. If I'm afraid, then who's there for you?"

"We've managed to keep a dog alive."

"But the plants are dead."

"Plants are stupid," I stated.

"Plants give you oxygen. If everyone had our brown thumbs, we'd all die from carbon dioxide poisoning."

"Now who's the one who's spiraling?"

"Guilty." He pulled in the driveway and parked. "What do we do, Sibby?"

"Why are you asking me? You're Mr. Prepared Guy."

"Yeah, I'm good at keeping you warm and fed and comfortable, but what do I *do?* Aside from work all the time and telling you when you have peanut butter in your hair."

"I have peanut butter in my hair?" My hands flew to my head.

"Pretty sure, yes." He unbuckled his seat belt and leaned over, pushing my hands out of the way. "You'll never be able to get it—crap, you got it all over the seat. Hold on, where are those wipes?"

I lifted the center console, pulled out a packet of wet wipes, and let Aidan clean me and the car.

"This is what happens when you fall asleep with the jar of peanut butter next to your face."

"You fell asleep with a jar of peanut butter next to your face?"

"Annie put it away, but I waited for her to go to sleep before creeping into the kitchen to get into it again. Never come between a pregnant woman and her peanut butter," I said. "Are we ever going to be *us* again?"

"We've changed, Sibby. Our lives have changed. We're not the same as when we met."

"I'm still a klutz, and you're still the best guy I know."

He kissed me. "That's not what I meant."

"I know." I sighed. "I think that's why I freaked out so badly when I saw that picture of me in a bikini. I'm not that person anymore. I don't have that body anymore. And even if my body does go back most of the way, I'll be forever different. We'll be forever different."

"We'll be parents. Not like we can give the babies back."

"I don't want to. But in preparing for Agamemnon and Troy—"

"Hard pass on those names."

I ignored him. "We've been forgetting each other. Can we stop that?"

"Miss you, Sib."

"Miss you, Aidan."

"Crikey!" I muttered. "Do you know who that is?"

Annie didn't look up from the fryer. "Who?"

"Cliff Dalton, the country star!"

"You know country stars?"

"No. I know Reality TV, and that guy was a finalist last year on *Sing for the Stars*. He totally should've won."

"You're not going to go fangirl all over him, are you?" Aidan asked from the corner of the tent.

"No, I'm not going to go fangirl all over him." I looked at Annie. "How was my acting?"

"Rotten." She laughed.

We were in the process of setting up the Mother Shucker booth. Annie and I were in our green T-shirts. Her uncle and cousin would arrive in thirty minutes or so with the van and bring all the food that we'd spent the last three days preparing. Shrimp cocktail, bacon-wrapped scallops, mini lobster rolls, and mini crab cakes.

"Do you guys need me?" Aidan asked. "Or can Jasper and I wander?"

"Wander," Annie and I said at the same time.

"Aye, aye, captains." He kissed me gently, looked into my eyes, and smiled.

I grinned back.

The day before, when Aidan and I had gotten back to Annie's, we'd grabbed Jasper and taken him for a walk on the beach. We had laughed and held hands. That night, Annie had set up a romantic dinner for two on the patio of her uncle's home. She had crashed in the main house, and so Aidan and I had total privacy to reconnect. It was awkward and funny, and we laughed a lot. We stayed up late just talking, something we hadn't done since we'd first started dating.

Annie handed me a twelve-gallon plastic container. "Will you make the Michelada mix?" She pointed to the recipe notecard on the table.

"Okay," I said. "What is a Michelada anyway?"

"A Bloody Mary, but instead of vodka it's with beer."

"Gross."

"It's actually really good."

"I'll take your word for it."

I opened the cans of tomato juice as I read over the recipe.

"You and Aidan seem to be all twitterpated," she commented. "Glad to see he talked you down. How did he get you to stop scarfing peanut butter?"

"He hugged me with his penis."

"Thanks for the visual."

Luckily the only people at the festival this early were those with booths, setting up, so no one was there to overhear our girl talk. The day was bright and clear, and only a tad crisp. I knew as soon as we started moving around, I'd get hot. I was running warmer these days, anyway.

Annie's Uncle Robert and her cousin Wells arrived with their big, white van. They opened the back doors and started to unload all the food we'd be serving.

As I was moving the twelve-gallon plastic bin to the edge of the table to make room for the trays of scallops, the Michelada mix swished and splashed and covered the front of my shirt, dousing me in tomato and oyster juice.

"Gah!" I reached for a spare rag and quickly tried to blot my shirt.

Total fail.

"What happened to you?" Annie demanded, holding a tray of mini lobster rolls.

"Michelada mix. In my bra. And in my shoes, I think."

"Damn, you really spilled most of that on yourself, didn't you?"

"Yes."

"How?"

I raised my hand and waved. "Um, hi."

"I think we have a spare shirt in the back of the van. Hold on a second." She set the tray of lobster rolls down. I looked longingly at the lobster rolls. Just a few more months and then I was going to have a shellfish, soft cheese, and wine-palooza.

"You look like you want to make love to that tray of lobster rolls," someone said.

I turned around and gaped. "What are you doing here?"

The famous actor I'd once spilled wine on way back in the day when I was a waitress at Antonio's was standing at the Mother Shucker booth.

He looked *amazing*. And that made sense because he had earned his millions off of his great looks. I could tell that he was still really fit, despite the fact that for his last movie role he'd dropped sixty pounds to play a heroin addict.

"I have a house here, but don't tell anyone."

"Secret is safe with me," I assured him.

"Had a little mishap, did you?"

I sighed. "Yup. I got pregnant by accident."

"Congratulations on your accident?" He let out a laugh. "But I was referring to the ginormous wet splotch on your shirt."

"Oh." I blushed. "That. Yes. Sorry. I've kinda lost my filter."

He continued to grin. "Is your husband here?"

"Yeah, he's somewhere around here walking our dog. Are you here as a bystander?"

"I'm shucking with the Cod Hoppers." He opened his jacket to reveal a blue T-shirt with the name emblazoned across it.

"What restaurant is that?"

"Mulligan's."

Uncle Robert's arch nemesis.

"How did they get you?"

"They asked."

"We're rivals," I teased. "And I'm a badass Mother Shucker—you better watch out."

"I'm terrified."

"Sibby, here's a spare—oh my." Annie came to a full stop and her eyes widened.

I grinned.

"Oh my God. Do you know who you are?" she gushed at Famous Actor.

He held out his hand. "I do. And you are?"

"An idiot," she muttered, taking his hand and coming out of her starstruck stupor.

"He's shucking for the Cod Hoppers," I explained.

"Mulligan's got a real celebrity?" Annie asked.

"Hey! You said you wanted me because *I* was a celebrity." I took the shirt from Annie's hand.

"You are," she said in a placating tone. "But not really."

"You're not helping my ego."

Annie rolled her eyes. "Do you mind if I get a photo of you two in your shirts and post to social?"

"I'm okay with it," Famous Actor said.

"Me too. Let me just change into a fresh shirt really fast." I climbed into the back of the van that was now empty of all the catering trays and changed.

Famous actor was talking to Uncle Robert and laughing. They both shook hands and wished each other luck.

"That's nice that you guys are acting like buds," I said to Uncle Robert.

He grinned. "I had to size up the competition. We're going to crush the Cod Hoppers. Excuse me, I need to speak to the festival organizer for a second."

"Sibby!" Annie called. "I have to use your phone to take the photo."

"Where's yours?" I asked as I reached into my back pocket to grab my cell to hand her.

"I don't remember."

She waved us together. Famous Actor was a good sport, smiling as he posed with me.

"Okay, now one where you look like mortal enemies. Pick up the oyster knives…"

"No," Famous Actor and I said at the same time.

"I'm clumsy," I stated.

"She's clumsy," Famous Actor repeated.

"You guys are no fun," Annie said.

"Thanks for that photo op. Are you okay if we post it? You're not afraid of people descending upon you for your autograph, are you?" I asked.

He shook his head. "Nah. Things are fairly mellow in Montauk this time of year. It's not prime tourist season, so a lot of the people who are here are locals and I've shown my face enough downtown that no one freaks out when they see me anymore."

"Sibby, I'm texting myself this photo and I'll post on Instagram," Annie said, her fingers flying across the screen. "Just as soon as I find my phone."

I looked at her over my shoulder. "I thought you were still off social?"

"I'll get back on it for this." She gave me my phone.

"Annie!" Cousin Wells called from the van.

"That's my cue." She looked at Famous Actor, hearts in her eyes. "Loved your last movie, but that won't stop us from crushing you." She flounced off to join her cousin.

"You guys certainly know how to trash talk," Famous Actor said.

"There's not a lot to do in Montauk. We have to cultivate certain skills, you know?"

Annie, Uncle Robert, Cousin Wells, and I stood at the long folding table. It was covered in newspaper and we were armed with our shucking knives and competitive spirits.

Uncle Robert was baring his teeth at the three other tables. Cousin Wells was doing the same. Annie rolled her shoulders and cracked her neck, getting in the zone.

I waved to Famous Actor, who waved back.

"He's the enemy," Annie commanded. "The hot, hot enemy—focus, Sibby, focus. This is for the trophy. *For the glory*."

"Wow, you people take this shit really seriously," I commented, reaching into my back pocket with the intention of sending a text to Aidan.

He'd come back to the booth after Famous Actor had left, but then he'd gone off again when the booths opened for business. No doubt he was full of seafood and beer.

I was insanely jealous.

Turned out my husband had already sent me a good-luck text.

"Turn your phone off," Annie snapped. "No distractions!"

"Remind me to never agree to anything you ask me to do, ever again," I groused. "You are intolerably competitive."

A familiar-looking face approached the table. He was holding a clear plastic cup full of beer and his lips curved into a huge smile.

"Mills!" Annie yelled in excitement. She darted around the table to run to him. I watched her hug him tightly. He leaned down and kissed her lips.

Whoa.

They were like, totally a thing.

She grasped his hand and dragged him closer. Uncle Robert and Cousin Wells greeted him with an air of distraction. Father and son were committed to this moment and nothing, not even Annie's new boyfriend, was going to derail their concentration.

"The competition is just about to start," Annie said. "Sibby, where's Aidan?"

"I'm not sure. If you let me text him, I can find out for you."

Annie rolled her eyes and said to Mills, "You can sit with Aidan, Sibby's husband."

"It's nice to see you again, Sibby," Mills said pleasantly.

"You too."

By mutual unspoken agreement we didn't discuss the tablecloth—okay fine, table—I'd set on fire.

It made me like him, since he was clearly polite enough to ignore my amazing ability of destroying things.

While Annie was sucking face with Mills, I pulled out my phone and texted Aidan. He replied back almost immediately.

"He's in the bleachers, high up, right-hand side," I said, tucking my phone back into my pocket.

Mills removed his lips from my best friend and said, "Great."

"He's got a tan-and-white dog with him."

"I love dogs," Mills said.

Dammit. Now I really liked him.

"Good luck," he called with a wave.

As he sauntered off, I caught Annie watching his retreating form.

"Nice butt," I commented.

"Right? Solid ten."

"You didn't tell me he was coming."

"I didn't?" She blinked blue eyes at me, pretending to look innocent. "Huh, must've slipped my mind."

"Annie, Sibby, get your heads in the game," Uncle Robert barked.

"The photo I posted of you and Famous Actor is blowing up on Instagram," she said.

I hadn't checked social, so I took her word for it.

"I want to see how many likes we have," she said.

"You just told me to get off my phone, you hypocrite!" I laughed. "Are you sure you want to go back down that rabbit hole? You were doing so well not being tethered to social."

She didn't answer me. She just stood there, staring at her screen, her face suddenly paling.

"What?" I asked.

"Nothing," she muttered, shoving her cell in her pocket.

I frowned, but chose not to push it.

Dylan, the writer from *Oyster Life Magazine* came to wish us good luck. Annie smiled and conversed with the journalist, but she seemed off. Like she was distracted.

As discreetly as I could, I pulled out my phone. My screen was lit up with notifications, but the one that stood out was Caleb's handle.

I assumed Annie had seen that he'd liked our photo. Nothing threw you for a loop more than when your ex liked your post. You didn't know how to take it; you didn't know what it meant.

"Sibby, this is Dylan," Annie said, finally introducing us.

"Hi," Dylan said with a huge grin. "I love your Instagram feed."

"Thank you." I beamed. "And thanks so much for coming."

"Have you ever shucked an oyster before this event?"

I nodded. "Yes. I started learning two days ago." I tried to keep one eye on Annie, but I also wanted to give Dylan all my attention. She was the one writing about Uncle Robert's restaurant, after all.

"Well, good luck," she said. "Annie, I'll find you after the competition, okay?"

"Yeah, we'll be back at our restaurant's booth," Annie said.

Aunt Carolyn was manning the booth with a waitress from the restaurant. The booths didn't close down during the competition, which only lasted twenty minutes.

The sun was warm on my back and I removed my jacket and put it under the table. There were four, thirty-two ounce mason jars, one for each of us to fill. As we loaded them up with shucked oysters, volunteers working the competition would come by and replace them with empty ones. Twenty minutes of oyster shucking was going to be exhausting—this was purely a sprint, not a marathon.

I stood next to Annie, towel in one hand, oyster knife in the other. My heart was beating with adrenaline. Two volunteers, wearing the oyster festival T-shirts, came by and dumped a huge bucket of fresh oysters onto our table.

Someone blew a horn.

We sprang into action.

Uncle Robert and Cousin Wells's mason jars filled up quickly. Annie was holding her own, but I wasn't nearly as fast. Maybe I was more concerned about not slicing my palm with the wicked sharp oyster knife, or maybe my head wasn't in the game because I was thinking about Annie's head—or more specifically, her heart.

"Why didn't you tell me you were friends with Caleb's new girlfriend?" she blurted out.

Yikes.

This wasn't going to go over well.

"Do you think we can talk about this later?" I demanded, my eyes focusing on a very stubborn oyster that refused to open.

"Yeah, Annie!" Cousin Wells yelled. "Focus!"

"I can't focus," she groused.

"You should've never looked at Instagram before the competition," I chastised.

"You're friends with Caleb's new girlfriend," she accused.

"How do you even know that?"

"When I saw that Caleb had liked my photo, I stupidly

clicked on his profile. I saw a photo of them together. She was tagged. Then I went to her profile and it showed that you follow her."

"Following doesn't mean friends," I evaded.

"Damn rotten liar!" Annie yelled.

"Annie!" Uncle Robert shouted. "Get back to shucking! We're behind!"

Annie grabbed another oyster and began shucking like a fiend.

"Fine, I'm friends with her," I admitted. "There, are you happy?"

"Why didn't you tell me?"

"Because look at how you're reacting."

"This is my reaction to finding out that you *lied* to me."

"Oh, please. This is your reaction to finding out that Caleb has a new girlfriend."

"I already knew that, smart ass. You're not the only one who stalks social media late at night in the privacy of their own bedroom."

"I thought you had taken a social media hiatus."

"I had a moment of weakness—about a month ago, I thought I was ready. Turns out, I wasn't."

"You've known a month? Damn it, Annie."

"Will you two freakin' focus?" Cousin Wells shrieked like a banshee.

Uncle Robert and Cousin Wells were totally carrying us, but I refused to be the weak link. As I reached for another oyster, I felt a sharp contraction low in my belly.

I dropped my knife and clutched my middle.

"Sibby! What's wrong?" Annie demanded.

"Pain—it's fine. It's just Braxton Hicks contractions."

"Are you sure—son of a bitch!"

I looked over to see that Annie had sliced her palm with her oyster knife.

I felt another cramp.

"Shit, I don't know if these are contractions," I said in fear.

Her hand was bleeding furiously. She grabbed a clean rag and pressed it to her wound.

Uncle Robert and Cousin Wells threw down their oyster knives and immediately came to our aid.

"Where's your phone?" Cousin Wells demanded.

"Back pocket—I'll get it," I said, trying to breathe through the cramping in my stomach.

"Fuck that," Cousin Wells said. "Don't move."

"Just don't grab my ass."

"Only you could make a joke right now," Annie said. Her lips were pale and she looked like she was about to fall over. She hadn't lost a lot of blood, but she must've been in considerable pain.

"We're out!" Uncle Robert called to the judges. "We need an ambulance. Now!"

Someone brought two chairs, and Annie and I collapsed into them as people started to gather around. A horn blew in the background and I heard someone shout, "Time Out!"

"Are you in labor?" she asked.

Panic gripped my throat and started squeezing. "It's too early. They're not ready to come out." The pain in my belly wasn't letting up, though.

The Cod Hoppers all stopped and their leader said, "Oh my God, she's giving birth!"

"I'm not giving birth!" I snapped at him and then leaned over, trying to take deep breaths.

I heard sirens in the distance and then I saw Aidan making his way through the crowd that had gathered around. Most of the festival-goers were fairly useless, choosing to take videos of me wincing and glaring and overall trying to remain calm. Annie was next to me, slumped into the chair with the towel pressed to her wound.

"You guys really know how to make a scene," Aidan said, crouching down next to me. He put his hand on my knee.

I looked at him. He was trying to smile, to ease my worry, but he wasn't doing a good job of hiding his own.

"Where's Jasper?" I wheezed as another cramp shuddered through my lower abdomen.

"I gave him to Mills to give to Annie's aunt."

"You gave our son to a stranger?"

"He's not a stranger," Annie said. "He's my boyfriend."

"Oh, jeez, Annie. Now is not the time," I muttered.

"Your boyfriend will meet us at the hospital." Aidan wasn't at all fazed by Annie's admittance. Then again, all his focus was on me and my uterus.

Another contraction assaulted me and I moaned in agony. Now I was sure these weren't Braxton Hicks, but preterm labor.

I'd seen Grey's Anatomy. I'd passed college biology. I'd gone through my birthing class and come out with a certificate.

I was basically a doctor.

"Close your knees," Annie suggested.

"What good will that do?"

"I don't know? Keep them in there longer?" She gripped my hand in solidarity and Aidan clasped the other.

And then we waited for the ambulance to arrive.

## Chapter 21

Matzah Ball Soup: [mah-tzah ball soop]

1. Balls of rolled matzah cooked in schmaltz, and served in a chicken soup broth.

2. I wanna tongue those balls.

3. You're a perv.

"Bed rest?" I gasped. "I have to be on bed rest for the remainder of my pregnancy?"

The doctor, an older man with white hair and a furrowed brow, who reminded me of a wizard, nodded. "Yes. Twins come early, usually, but we need to minimize *how* early."

"But how? That's almost my entire last trimester of sitting around. I've already gained forty pounds," I wailed.

Not only was I going to gain more weight, but I was pretty sure my sanity was going to take a hard knock.

"I'm sorry, Mrs. Kincaid, but I've been practicing medicine for thirty years and I insist that you rest." He looked at me pointedly.

"Okay," I said with a deep breath and a nod. "Okay."

I fiddled with the hospital bracelet. I had an IV, and something that had stopped the contractions was dripping into my arm.

"Just relax now. I'll have a nurse come check in on you in a little bit."

"Thanks, doctor," Aidan said from the chair by my bed.

The doctor closed the door to the room and Aidan and I were alone.

"What are we going to do?" I demanded.

"What you're going to do is rest, and not worry about anything except keeping Agamemnon and Murgatroyd safe and warm."

My eyes misted. "You called them Agamemnon and Murgatroyd. Does that mean you're finally giving in to those names?"

"It means I'll do anything not to upset you." His hand reached out to grasp mine. "This really scared me, Sib."

"I'm sorry."

"No, I mean—it's not your fault. It's just, wow."

"Don't freak out on me," I warned him. "Because one of us has to hold it all together, and I don't know if I have the reserves to do that right now."

There was a knock on the door, followed by Annie entering the room. Mills trailed behind her, looking hesitant, but I waved them both in.

"How's the hand?" I asked.

She held up her bandaged palm. "I'll live. How's your vagina?"

"Still intact."

Mills looked at Aidan. "Are they always like this?"

Aidan nodded. "Yup."

I was suddenly inexplicably sad. If Caleb had been here, he would've made a joke. But he wasn't here. He was in Manhattan with Em.

Everything was different now.

"What did the doc say?" Annie asked.

"Bed rest. For the rest of my pregnancy." I cradled my belly in my hands. "I don't know what I'm going to do. There's no way that I can—"

"I think we have to call your mother," Aidan said.

"I thought the doctor said to keep my stress to a minimum," I told him.

"Should we go?" Mills whispered to Annie.

"No," she replied.

"But this doesn't concern us."

"Annie and Sibby are a package deal," Aidan told him. "So you might as well stay."

Mills looked uncomfortable, but he was going to have to get over that if he was going to be one of us. I didn't even know if he was going to be one of us. Only time would tell.

"Sibby, we have to ask for help," Aidan said.

"I know, but my mother…and she has her own business to run now."

"You don't think she'd drop everything to help you? Face it, Sib, we don't have any other option."

"I'll do it," Annie voiced.

I looked at her. "No. Your life is in Montauk."

She shook her head. "I think—" She looked at Mills. "I'm ready to come back to the city."

"I can't ask you to take care of me while I'm on bed rest," I stated.

"You're not asking. I'm volunteering."

"This goes beyond the best-friend clause. You know that, right?"

She smiled slightly. "Yeah."

"She can crash in the nursery," Aidan said. "We do have that spare room. It would take care of her not having to find a sublet immediately."

"You sure?" I asked her.

"Yeah." She laughed. "My uncle and aunt are driving me insane anyway and with this hand, I'm not gonna be shucking oysters for a while."

Mills moved away from the corner of the room and wrapped Annie in a hug. "I'm game for whatever gets you back into the city."

"My uterus. Bringing people together," I muttered. "Thank you. I can't tell you what this means—thank you."

Annie moved out from underneath Mills's arm and came over to hug me. She whispered in my ear, "It'll be just like old times."

"Except neither of us are drinking. And we're more financially stable," I whispered back.

"Crap, I better look for a job," she said with a grin.

"You know you're not paying rent, right?"

"Sibby—"

"No. Not happening."

"If you're sure."

"I'm sure." I looked at Aidan and he nodded vigorously.

"Yes, we're sure." He got up and hugged her. "Thank you. God, thank you so much."

"What he's really saying is thank you because this means my mother won't be forced to stay with us for weeks on end."

"I love your mother," Aidan protested.

"So do I. But from a distance."

Annie looked at Mills. "You wanna help me pack?"

"If it gets you back to the city sooner, I'm all about it."

The two of them departed, hand in hand.

"Guess that's that," I said.

"He's a good dude. I like him," Aidan said. "He reminds me of Caleb actually."

"So she's just dating a different version of the one that got away?"

"Let's not go down this road."

"Okay. You're gonna have to tell Caleb."

"I will."

"How is all of this going to work?"

"No idea."

"Easy," Aidan said, taking my hand and helping me out of the car.

Annie was in the driver's seat, the hazard lights flashing. We hadn't been able to find a permanent parking spot in front of our apartment, and there was no way Aidan was having me walk any more than necessary.

We got into the apartment and it was still new enough that coming home didn't feel like home.

"I've got a little surprise for you, but I can't have you freaking out, okay?" Aidan said.

"Okay."

He led me to the nursery and pushed open the door. My mouth dropped open in awe. "What did you do in here?" I marveled. The room was one giant mural. The far wall was light blue with clouds, a rainbow, and a herd of wild horses. As the scene moved to another wall, it became nighttime, complete with stars and tracings of the most-known constellations.

"I didn't do it. Nat did. She flew up the day before I left for Montauk and finished two days ago."

I looked at him. "You guys did this for me?"

He nodded and smiled. "What do you think?"

"I think it's perfect."

The front door shut and a moment later, Jasper's nose opened the door and he came in.

"Wow, this looks even better than the pictures," Annie said.

"You knew?" I asked, turning slowly.

Annie grinned. "Yup. Nat, Aidan, and I all brainstormed about what we thought this room should look like. I hope you like it."

"You guys," I whined and then started to cry.

"Oh, this cry-fest is all you," Annie commented to Aidan. "I'm gonna go grab my suitcases and call Mills, let him know we got here okay." She left the nursery and a moment later I heard the front door close again.

"Let's get you onto the couch," Aidan said.

"One more minute, I need to stare at this room some more." The baby furniture from Aidan's uncle complemented the room perfectly. It was truly a space I'd want to be in—it wasn't just functional, it was beautiful.

Once I was settled on the couch, Aidan brought me my phone, laptop, the remote, and three books on all things baby.

"You shouldn't have to move for a while now," Aidan said with a wry grin.

I made a face. "I kinda have to pee."

"Sibby, why didn't you go before you got settled?"

"I didn't have to go then," I defended. "Besides, I don't need your help going to the bathroom."

"You need my help getting up off the couch," he reminded me, taking my arms and gently pulling me to a stand.

"Fine, but I can waddle to the bathroom by myself."

Bed rest was totally going to suck.

The next night, Aidan walked into the apartment, carrying bags of takeout. He stopped in the kitchen to set the bags down on the counter, his mouth ajar.

"What did I just walk into?" he asked.

I hastily muted the TV. "Nothing."

"He caught us," Annie stated with a sigh. "Might as well admit it."

"We're singing show tunes," I said, hiding my head in shame.

"Before that Sibby made me watch a Sandra Bullock rom-com on Netflix. My brain is totally mush."

"You're off duty," he said. "I've got her now."

"You both act like I'm torturing you."

They exchanged a glance as Annie grabbed her cell and keys from the coffee table.

"Shut up," I muttered.

"We didn't say anything," Annie said in amusement. She looked at Aidan. "What time do you have to be out of here tomorrow morning?"

"Nine-ish?"

"Cool, I'll be back before then to relieve you. Sibby— no more show tunes without me."

I grinned.

She left and it was just Aidan, Jasper, me, and some bangin' Thai food.

"Did you guys have a good day?" Aidan asked as he brought me a plate.

"Yeah, it was nice. I love having her here. Is that terrible?"

"It would only be terrible if you pretended you needed to be on bed rest to get her back to the city." He looked at me. "You didn't pay the doctor off, did you?"

"Nope. You didn't kiss me hello."

Aidan leaned over and brushed his lips across mine. "Hello."

"How was your day?" I asked.

"Good."

"That's it? That's all I get?"

"I had to have the talk with Caleb."

"About where babies come from?"

"About Annie staying with us."

"Ah. How'd that go?" I asked.

"He's bummed that he can't just come over whenever he wants, but he understands."

I arched an eyebrow and shoveled in a bite of Pad Thai. "They're both being very adult about this."

"They *are* adults. I'm impressed by the strides Annie has made in only a few months."

"Yeah, I just hope her coming back to the city doesn't derail all her growth. You know, like how people who get out of prison find their old crowd, and shit goes south again?"

Aidan waved his chopsticks at me. "She wouldn't have come if she didn't think she could handle it. But enough about them. What did you do today?"

"From the confines of this couch?"

"Yes."

"I called Nat and talked to her for two hours, and thanked her for the mural. I ordered her a bouquet of orchids that should arrive at her house in a few days. Stacy called me and we talked about Vegas, and all the industry parties she's been going to, and the connections she's making. She's doing well, it seems. So that's good. Um, I called Zeb and told him that he and Terry have to come over soon for a hangout."

"So you called everyone?"

"Yep. Not a lot else to do."

I'd talked to my parents and told them about being on bed rest. I'd learned my lesson—my life was on social media, and I knew it would've only been a matter of time before my mother saw the video on the oyster-festival Instagram profile.

Because that was my life.

But I was an adult now and I was learning to cut things off at the pass.

"Mrs. Nowacki is coming over tomorrow. I think she's

really lonely now that we've moved out of the building," I said.

"It's good she's within walking distance. I'm glad we have people here."

"Takes a village, right?"

## Chapter 22

Bialye: [be-al-ee]

1. A flat bagel-like bread roll that is baked instead of boiled, leaving a depression in the middle instead of a hole.

2. Depression? Sounds pretty Jewish to me.

Two weeks later, Annie paused the movie on the TV and looked at me. "We need purpose."

"I have half a bag of Goldfish cracker dust on my face and I'm pregnant. I've got purpose."

"Aidan is going to kill me. I'm supposed to ensure that you eat a healthy, balanced diet."

"Goldfish crackers are fish, therefore it's protein, and therefore it's paleo."

"Yeah, I'm pretty sure that's not how that works." She sighed. "It's almost May, the weather has turned, and it feels like spring. I'm antsy. I need something to do."

"Make dinner tonight. That'll give you something to do."

In exchange for room and board, Annie had been cooking. Which had been friggin' awesome because she was a professional chef.

"Aren't you bored?" she asked, ignoring my quip about dinner. Though she shouldn't have ignored it because I was hungry. Eating had become my new hobby.

Don't judge, but I'd had to start wearing Aidan's sweats. Ugh.

"I guess I'm bored," I admitted.

"I mean there are only so many old movies we can watch."

"Speak for yourself."

"My brain is atrophying."

"Then read my baby books—then your mind will stay active."

"And terrified." She peered at me. "When are you going to write another book?"

"We weren't talking about me, we were talking about you."

"You have all this time now where you literally can't leave the apartment. Why don't you write?"

"Oh yeah, I'll just write another book." I glared at her. "You think it's that easy?"

"Jeez, Sibby, that's not what I meant and you know it."

I paused. "What is it you want, Annie? I mean, really want?"

She waited a minute before answering, deep in

thought. "I loved working in my uncle's kitchen. I love the rush of orders and timing everything perfectly. But it wasn't mine, you know? I want my own restaurant. Do everything from the ground up."

"Opening a restaurant in Manhattan is financial suicide," I commented. "You know how hard it is, how much time it takes, how much money it takes."

"I know." Her eyes were misty. "But I want to do it anyway." She exhaled a shaky breath. "Dylan came through for me. Her contact at *The New York Times* raved about the food at our booth."

"Well, of course it was a rave. You are a stellar chef. Was Uncle Robert pissed about the Dylan thing?"

"No. He was awesome about it. Totally charming when he talked to her. But he—ah—is selling the restaurant."

"I don't think I heard you correctly. After all the crap you went through trying to get him to listen to you about the menu changes and the dining room update—I thought he was just about to come around to those ideas. Now he's selling the place?"

"He realized he wasn't happy." She smiled sadly. "And that he and my aunt fight all the time."

"I thought that was foreplay."

"It was unhealthy. My cousin Wells has no head for the restaurant business, and I think Uncle Robert realized it was a losing battle."

"Then why didn't you move up there permanently and take over? He would've let you."

"I love this city and I want to be here. I also want to build something on my own. My vision. No one else's. I don't want to try and save a sinking ship."

"You really want to do this?" I asked her.

She nodded.

"It's going to take everything you've got and then

some," I warned her. "Half the time I forget what Aidan even looks like since he's gone so much."

"You do not."

"Well, no. I could never forget how hot my husband is." I grinned, but then it fell. "You're in a new relationship. It's going to strain it."

"Yes, I know. I care about Mills, but I have my dreams too, and I've had them for a long time. The time is now, Sibby. I'm only getting older and therefore more tired. In five years, who knows if I'll even have the energy to open a restaurant." She chuckled. "I've never been so clear-headed. I want this. And I'm going for it."

"Then I'm behind you one-hundred percent."

Later the next morning I was dozing on the couch with a copy of *Cleaning Up The Upchuck, A Guide to Twins* across my chest when the buzzer sounded. I came to and immediately wiped the drool off my mouth. My head was foggy and I felt like I'd been hit with a tranquilizer dart. If you looked up the definition of *lump* in the dictionary, you'd find a picture of me with one side of my hair sticking out, pillow creases on my cheeks, wearing a man's T-shirt with yesterday's ice cream chocolate-sauce stain on it.

Annie was already up and answering the door when I finally registered what was going on.

"Mrs. Nowacki?" I asked. The woman visited every

morning, and, God love her, she always brought me something baked that was poppy seed and a little something for Aidan too since she figured out I wasn't into sharing my hoard.

Seriously, when did I become the creature that ate and slept? I put the word sloth to shame.

Annie pushed the intercom button. "Who is it?"

"I've got a package for Sibby Goldstein." I heard a male voice through the intercom say.

Annie buzzed the delivery guy in. "He's got a *package*." It was one of Annie's biggest dreams for a cute delivery guy to answer the door, who turned out to be a stripper. Anything was possible, but I hoped for my sake this guy wasn't a stripper, because I wasn't supposed to get excited, or move, or generally do anything except become one with the couch and try not to drool too much during naps.

"Ah, is Ms. Goldstein available?" I heard him ask.

"I can sign for the package," Annie said.

"It's not that kind of package."

"Who are you?" she demanded as her defense mechanisms started to engage.

"I'm Noreen Richards's personal assistant."

"Shut up," Annie said. "Really?"

"Yup."

She immediately moved back to let him in. He was a cute, skinny guy with glasses and he was wearing a pair of dark jeans and a blue button-down. Jasper went to investigate, but quickly realized there was no treat in it for him, so he went to his dog bed and collapsed onto it.

"I would get up, but I'm supposed to be on bed rest. Doctor's orders," I explained, immediately trying to fix my hair. I quickly threw it up into a messy bun, using the hair tie that always hung out on my wrist. I reached for my glasses that were resting on the coffee table, and then discreetly pulled the blanket up my body to cover my stained shirt.

"Bed rest, that kind of sucks," he said.

"You have no idea." I was in a bemused state. What was Noreen Richards's assistant doing here?

Apparently, he read the confusion on my face because he handed me a manila envelope. "She wanted me to hand deliver this to you."

"Um, that's really nice, but how did you know where I lived?"

"Her agent called your agent."

"Oh." I let out a breath of relief. "Thank you."

He moved to the door.

"Do you want something to drink?" I called after him.

"Nah, I'm good." With a wave he left.

Annie shut the door and then came over to the couch. "Well, are you going to make me wait? What's in the envelope?"

"I'm guessing a book." I shook the packet. "Feels like a book."

"Books are good. You like books. Open it."

"Do you mind? I kind of want some privacy."

"Writers," she muttered. "Fine. No problem. I'll take Jasper out. Sound good? Come here, Jasper! Wanna go outside? Wanna go for a walk?"

When Annie said the *W* word, he stretched and then trotted to her. I waited until the front door shut before turning my attention back to the envelope.

I'd been reading Noreen Richards since I was a teenager. She had the career every author dreamed about. Huge book advances, movie and TV deals, and multiple homes she could afford to travel to when she pleased. I'd read that the previous year, she'd moved to Ireland with her husband and dog. And it was pretty clear she'd just bounce right back to the States whenever she felt like it.

Maybe one day, I would be like Noreen Richards.

I opened the envelope and pulled out a paperback book titled *And Then She Ran*. It was in pristine condition, but it wasn't a title of hers that I recognized. I opened the book and found a *To Sibby, Love Noreen Richards* on the title page. There was no way she'd have her personal assistant hand deliver this book with a run-of-the-mill autograph. This was Noreen Frickin' Richards. I'd steal her grocery list and frame it if I could.

I turned the envelope upside down and a piece of paper fell out.

"Jackpot."

The paper was thick, cream, heavy stationary. I gulped as I began to read a personal note from my idol.

*Dear Sibby,*

*May I call you Sibby? Ms. Goldstein sounds too formal. When our paths eventually cross one day (and they will), I expect you to call me Noreen.*

*There.*

*Now that we're on a first-name basis, let me explain what I've sent to you and why.*

*The book in your hands was the seventh book of my career. I'm going to assume that you're not familiar with it. Most people aren't. My publisher had only allotted one-hundred thousand copies for circulation because they didn't believe in the success of this book.*

*This is a classic case of art versus money, and sometimes the two do not intersect.*

*In this case, my publisher was correct. The book, as they say, "flopped". It never picked up any steam, the critics ripped me to shreds, and I got a lot of letters saying—this was back in the day when readers had to send actual snail mail if they wanted to tell you how much they hated your work—how disappointed they were in the story, that this didn't feel like a* Noreen Richards *book.*

*I was fortunate enough to find success early in my career. It was a time when people were willing to take a chance on an unknown. My agent was young and hungry. I was young and hungry. We talked for hours—days—weeks, about* And Then She Ran. *We knew it was a risk. I believed in the book and my agent believed in me.*

*It sold, but with a meager advance. My publisher was very hesitant.* And Then She Ran *wasn't like anything I'd given them before. It was off-brand. It was women's fiction and there was a romantic theme running through it, but that wasn't the true focus. Not really. The heroine was a tough cookie. She was unlikable. Which, as authors, we know it's easier for readers to forgive a jerk of a hero than a witch of a heroine. Not that Isobel is a witch, by any means, but she's not for everyone. She's not easily palatable.*

*Am I making sense? I think I'm making sense. I'm on deadline and I'm sleep-deprived. But you understand that too.*

*I read your newest book. I loved it from the first page to the last. I reread it the moment I finished it. I'm not telling you this to inflate your ego; I'm telling this to revive your soul. I've been where you've been. I've written books that don't have mainstream appeal, and I wrote them anyway. Those books are for me.*

*Not every book is going to hit a list. Not every book will be loved the same. That's okay. Keep writing, Sibby. Don't give up because you wrote a book for you and the world doesn't care.*

*Always write for you first; the rest will fall into place.*

*With deep affection,*
   *Noreen*

## Chapter 23

Pickled herring: [pikeld herING]

1. Small, fatty fish native to the Atlantic that have been cured with salt, and then preserved in a dressing that usually contains vinegar, sugar, and salt.

2. It'll put hair on your ass.

I had Noreen's letter framed, and I hung it in my office. Even though I didn't spend time in there yet, I knew I'd want to get back there as soon as I could. She'd said everything I needed to hear, from someone who'd lived it.

It was one thing to have your husband and best friend support and love you and attempt to talk you through the demoralizing process of writing a book and having it panned by critics, but it was quite another to have another writer—an icon, no less—tell you to keep going.

My book flop would be the first of many. And that somehow made me smile, because it meant I was ready to get back to it. I was ready to keep going without the fear of failure. I would fail. Many times. And I would celebrate those failures and learn from them.

I opened up a new document, my fingers itching to type.

I didn't even have a story in mind, but I had words that wanted to come out. I purged and released, creating for the first time in months.

Spring came and I continued to write. I wrote until I had a rough draft.

Most of it would probably end up being deleted, but at least I had something to work with. When there was nothing else to do but sit on the couch and write, the writing somehow got done.

As soon as Annie had decided that she wanted to open her own restaurant, she'd hit the ground running. A friend from culinary school put her in touch with an architect who would not only design the space, but had deep pockets and had decided to become an angel investor. Annie needed the money and a contract was signed to get the ball rolling.

I visited the obstetrician constantly, and Aidan went with me as often as he could. He'd been able to pull back just a little bit at the bar, and would take even more time off after the babies were born. It was the home stretch of many things, all happening at once.

When I'd made it to thirty-six weeks, the doctor deemed I was far enough along in my pregnancy that I could start moving around again. Twins usually came early, and I wouldn't make it to forty weeks. If they came now, they'd be early, but still healthy.

Which also meant that Aidan and I could get naked with each other. We'd been griping and sniping at each other—something that always happened when we went too long without being intimate. So, as soon as the doctor said I no longer had to restrict my movements, I'd let out a *yippee* so loud that people in the waiting room had heard me.

"Date night?" I asked eagerly, walking hand-in-hand out of the doctor's office into the warm air.

He grinned. "Yes. And then fun times afterward."

"Afterward?" I repeated. "That's happening the moment we get home."

"But Annie's there." He pressed the down button for the elevator.

"Then we kick her out. And then you can shuck me all night long."

"You're neither an oyster nor an ear of corn."

"How do I shuck thee? Let me count the ways." I grinned. "It might be time to kick her out because I'm officially off bed rest which means I don't need to be waited on like a fat, lazy sultan."

"But you handled it with such charm and grace," he quipped.

Today was the first day that I'd actually put on something aside from sweats. I was wearing a maxi dress and my hair was in pigtails to combat the heat and humidity. But even hot, humid air seemed like the best thing ever when you'd been breathing apartment air for weeks.

We got down to the sidewalk and hailed a cab. Once we got home, we took Jasper for a walk.

"God, it feels so good to be outside. I was beginning to think I was becoming a mole person."

"Or at least an agoraphobic writer," he teased.

"Nah, that's too cliché. Though I do think I need a quirk. I'm thinking of getting a monocle and a top hat. Thoughts?"

"Well, you wear glasses, so wouldn't a monocle make it really hard to see out of one eye?"

"Point."

"And the top hat? Are you planning to wear it in public?"

"Just around the house."

"Then I say go for it."

When we got home from our walk, Annie was already in the apartment, taking a plate of leftovers out of the microwave. She'd made meatloaf and potatoes the night before. Maybe I wouldn't let her leave. Maybe I'd chain her to the stove instead. Whip her when she failed to cook.

"Sibby?" she prompted.

"Huh?" My eyes were still glued to the plate of food. She sighed and passed it to me.

"You love me," I said as I questioned whether I should even bother with a fork.

"What did the doctor say?" she asked.

"She's officially off bed rest," Aidan commented.

"Yay!" She jumped over to me and gave me a hug. "That means I can leave!"

I looked at Aidan. "You can't let her leave. Who's going to cook?"

"You have four months of frozen food in your freezer," she said with an amused grin. "But you're not allowed to eat it until the twins come."

"Probably for the best," Aidan stated. "The rate Sibby devours food—"

"Watch it."

"—is utterly inspiring," he finished quickly.

"I'm going to miss hanging out all the time, though," Annie said, heading back to the fridge to find something else to eat.

"Then find an apartment close by," I suggested. "That way we never have to be parted from one another ever again. But there's no rush."

"Let's just play it by ear, shall we?" she said. "Because, no offense, I'm not going to want to live here when you have two newborns. Free rent or not."

"Yeah, I don't blame you. I'm not even going to want to live here when we have two newborns…"

I mock-glared at Aidan who only grinned wider.

"Uh oh, you guys are doing that thing where you make everyone else around you uncomfortable because you want to have sex with each other, but don't know how to kick other people out. Well, so long, friends. Happy humping."

"You're weird," I said with a laugh.

"I'll stay at Mills's tonight, so you guys can do weird married-couple things in every room in the house."

She skipped out of the apartment and the door hadn't even fully shut before Aidan was dragging me to the bedroom.

"You. Are. A. Beast." Aidan panted. "I can't keep up with you."

"What's it like, getting all old and stuff?" I joked as I

dragged a hand down his awesome chest. He had just the right amount of chest hair to be manly without looking like he was wearing a sweater all the time.

He grinned. "Pretty frickin' fantastic."

"I know, right?"

Aidan placed a hand on the mountain of my belly. I felt like Vesuvius ready to blow. "Anything yet?"

"Did you really think that your penis had magical powers to jump-start me into labor?"

"Uh, well, *yeah*. Plus the doctor said intercourse was a good way to get things going."

"Ready for me to be done being pregnant?"

"Am I an ass if I said yes?"

"No. You're being truthful. And I'm ready for this to be over too. I feel like I've been pregnant a gazillion years. I'm ready to meet the *bébés*."

"Oh, so we're French now?"

"Yup." I smiled. "Let's go to Veritas. I haven't seen the place since the renovation has been completed."

"You've seen photos and videos."

"Not the same."

"That's true."

We got dressed and it took close to an hour because we kept stopping to kiss and hug.

"I feel like I have you back," Aidan said when he locked up the apartment.

"I know. I'm feeling more like myself too."

"Think it's because you were able to be creative again?"

"Probably," I admitted. "My world isn't right when I don't write."

"Boom, look what you did there," he said with a laugh. "I admit I wasn't sure how to help you, except be there for you, you know?"

"Yeah. You're good like that."

He clasped my hand in his and we enjoyed the sunshine as we walked to his bar. We stopped in at the new store section of Veritas so I could run my hand over the handmade wooden shelves. There was no sawdust or lingering tools. Everything was up-to-date and met city codes, and all we needed was product to sell. Inventory was already coming in, but most of the shelves were still empty.

"I'm so proud of you guys," I said to him. "You really did it."

"We haven't done it yet," he corrected.

"You did the heavy lifting."

"No, that comes when the inventory comes."

I rolled my eyes. "Will you just let me compliment you?" I asked in exasperation.

"Okay. Go ahead."

I wrapped my arms around him and kissed his bearded chin. "I love you, and I'm so glad you did this."

"Even though it took time away from you?"

"Yes."

He let out a sigh and brushed a kiss across my forehead. "Is it too early for chicken wings?"

"No. Lead the way."

"What do you say to having Caleb and Em meet up at our place in a few hours? Annie has plans tonight so we're in the clear to have them over."

I nodded. "I love that idea."

Though I'd seen both of them in random in between times when Annie wasn't at the apartment, it felt like I was sneaking around behind my best friend's back. Caleb and Em had understood my wanting to keep the peace and my being absent for a while, but it would be good to see and catch up with them.

One of our favorite bars had twenty-five cent wings

during happy hour and we'd been going there forever. They had the best bleu cheese dressing in the history of the world, and I was salivating in anticipation about when I could eat it again. I'd ask for a straw after the twins were born and drink it by the pint glass.

"Spicy or really spicy?" Aidan asked with a grin as we slid into an open booth.

"Really spicy."

We held hands across the table, talking about what type of vacation we could take once we were able to leave the babies with our parents. It was nice to converse with each other about what we wanted and not focus solely on the twins. I knew once they arrived, that would be *all* we talked about.

The wings came and we devoured them like ravenous beasts. Our first round was gone in ten minutes and then we threw in another order for a dozen more.

Once we were finally finished, I ripped open a wet wipe to clean my hands. "You'd think we've never eaten before, based on what just happened."

"I blame the aerobic workout."

I batted my eyelashes at him. "You mean playing basketball with Caleb tuckered you out? Surely, it wasn't little ol' me who did that…"

He laughed and just because I could, I tossed my dirty wet wipe at him which he caught. Balling it up, he put it in the basket over the chicken-wing carcasses.

We paid the bill and then walked down by the pier. Aidan and I parked it on a bench and watched the water taxis. We would've waited for the sunset, but that would have put us out too late, and Em and Caleb were due at our place at any moment.

"We should get home so we can let Jasper out," Aidan said, standing. He reached his hand down and I grasped it.

My eyes momentarily strayed to a family with two children. A boy of about three and a toddler on the mother's hip.

"That looks nice," I said with a smile.

Aidan glanced at the family and he smiled, too. "That will be us. In about eighteen months."

"You're a fun dose of reality, you know that?" I said with a laugh. "Come on, let's go see our pup."

## Chapter 24

Kasha Varnishkes: [Ka-sh-ah Var-ni-sh-kehs]

1. Buckwheat with bowtie noodles.
2. I don't even know what buckwheat is.

"You look amazing," Em said as she stepped into the apartment.

I frowned. "What lens are you looking through?"

She laughed. "I'm serious, you look great."

"I think it's because I'm upright, showered, and finally in a dress."

"Don't forget that you put on makeup, too!" Aidan

called out as he took a six-pack of beer from Caleb and set it down on the counter.

"Really? Makeup?" Caleb peered at me. "Oh yeah, you've got that goopy stuff on your eyelashes."

"It's called mascara," Em said with a laugh and a swat to his arm.

"Since when did you become so girly?" Caleb asked.

"Since I became friends with a YouTube makeup influencer and she has more samples than she knows what to do with."

They chuckled.

"We brought brownies," Caleb stated.

"And vanilla ice cream," Em added as she set the grocery-store bag down onto the counter.

"I love you both so hard," I said. "Though to be fair, my price for love is really low these days."

I grabbed bowls and spoons, and then let Aidan do the honors of serving. "Go sit down, Sibby," he said.

He didn't have to tell me twice. My ankles were swollen and I'd moved more in one day than I had in weeks.

"So everything is good?" Em asked as she sat down on the couch next to me.

"Things are good. Doctor cleared me to be up and about. I'm ready to be done with pregnancy. Aidan is ready. I think the world is ready. But how about you guys? What's new with you?"

"Meeting his parents in a few weeks," she said, blushing. "I'm kind of nervous."

"Don't be. They're going to love you."

The guys joined us and Aidan handed me a bowlful of brownie sundae. He'd even added a banana.

"You're a true hero, Aidan Kincaid," I said with a grin.

"Yeah, just hold onto those sentiments when you're squeezing my sons' heads out of you."

"Oh God, seriously?" Caleb moaned, dropping his spoon into his bowl with a clatter. "Do we need such a visual representation?"

"Yeah," I added. "And I really don't want anyone thinking about my—"

The front door opened and Annie tromped through the doorway. "You guys aren't going to believe what—oh. Shit."

She came to a grinding halt as she looked at Caleb and then at Em, and then back to Caleb.

"What are you doing here?" I asked quickly. "I thought you had plans."

"I did," she said, backing away toward the door, looking for an escape. But Jasper came running up to her, and Annie's back hit the wall of the closed door, effectively sealing her inside our apartment.

With her ex.

And her ex's new girlfriend.

"Awkward," I blurted out.

Four pairs of eyes looked at me. Aidan was the only one struggling not to laugh.

"I'm gonna go," Annie said quickly. "Get back to whatever you were doing."

"No, you should stay," Em said.

It was our turn to stare at her like she'd grown another head.

"Come on, we're all adults," Em went on. "And Annie is Sibby's best friend, so it's not like we're not going to see each other in the future, right?"

If any other woman recommended this as a grand idea, I would've thought they had ulterior motives, but Em was a legitimately nice person.

But I glanced at Caleb who was looking down at the ground and frowning. He clearly wasn't okay with his new girlfriend being in the same room as the old one. Not to mention, this was the first time Annie and Caleb had been in the same room since Annie's move out of the city.

Annie told Jasper to get down and then she slowly walked toward the living room and came to sit by me. I shoved my bowl at her and she wasted no time taking a big, stress-relieving bite.

"Congratulations on the bar expansion," she said to Caleb.

"Thanks," he muttered.

"You've been staying with Aidan and Sibby, right?" Em asked.

Annie nodded. "Yeah."

"She's been a huge help," I said, grasping her hand and giving it a squeeze.

Caleb got up from his chair and went to the kitchen. He looked like he was about to grab another beer, but instead, he went for a bottle of vodka.

Oh, boy.

This wasn't a good idea at all.

"Em, I need your help," he called to her.

Em hopped up and immediately went to him.

"I'm so sorry," Annie whispered to me as soon as Caleb and Em were occupied, clearing the way for us to have a discussion about how to get her out of there.

"You didn't know. But what made you come back here? I thought you were crashing with Mills."

She made a face. "The dingus asked me to move in with him."

"Yikes."

"Why is that bad?" Aidan asked.

Annie looked at him. "Because we, like, *just* started dating."

"Yeah so? When you know you know," Aidan said.

"She doesn't know, that's the point," I said.

From the kitchen we all heard, "Why are you so bent out of shape?"

Em had spoken loud enough to draw all of our attention.

"Will you keep it down?" Caleb asked.

"No, I will not." She crossed her arms over her chest. "I will not give up a night of hanging out with Aidan and Sibby just because your ex is here."

"I think Em has been drinking," I said to Aidan.

He nodded. "Yeah, they were at Veritas earlier."

"She held it together so well," I said with a sigh.

"I guess I pushed her over the edge," Annie said. "I'm going to go."

"Go? Go where?" I demanded.

"Anywhere but here." She got up and went to grab her purse.

"You don't leave," Caleb yelled at Annie. "We're leaving."

"I'm *not* leaving!" Em defended. "We're staying! We can all stay!"

"Aidan," I said softly.

"Hold on, Sibby. This is about to blow up. Man, this is better and cheaper than pay-per-view."

"*Aidan.*"

"Yeah?" he asked, finally looking at me.

"I just had a contraction."

## Chapter 25

Maror: [mah-roar]

1. Horseradish.

2. This is what we use to prevent ourselves from tasting gefilte fish.

"I hope you choke on an overly hot Hot Pocket!" I screamed at Aidan as I gripped his hand.

"Inventive, Sib." Aidan grimaced as I squeezed his fingers, trying to inflict pain.

Another contraction assaulted me. I yelled and cursed. Sweat-drenched hair stuck to my face and neck. I'd been in labor for eighteen hours and I wasn't sure I'd be able to do it much longer.

I should've gotten the epidural.

But nooooo....

I had decided to be a warrior.

Warriors were dumb. I *hated* warriors.

Tears leaked out of the corners of my eyes as exhaustion gripped every part of my body.

"Push!" the doctor called. "Give me a big push now."

I pushed.

"I can see the head," the doctor said.

Aidan immediately went to look between my legs. "Oh. My. God."

"What? What's wrong?" I cried.

"Nothing," he said, his face slack with shock. "I just can't believe you're about to give birth to our—oh, man! It looks like a *Braveheart* battle scene down there!"

I would've laughed if I hadn't been in so much pain. But then I tuned everything out except for the doctor, who continued telling me to push. There was a rush of endorphins that relieved a bit of pain and I clamped down hard.

A few moments later I heard the beautiful sound of my baby crying.

"Congratulations," the doctor said, holding up a goo-covered infant. "You have a son."

I let out a laugh of pure relief, and then started to cry. The doctor handed the baby off to a nurse who immediately took him to get cleaned up and checked out. My heart protested, already wanting to hold him close and never let go.

Round two.

Twenty minutes later, the doctor was telling me to give one final push.

Baby boy number two was born, and I smiled at Aidan

as best I could through the fatigue. Aidan brushed a kiss to my forehead and I felt his tears fall across my skin.

"Congratulations!" the doctor said. The corners of his eyes were creased and he was smiling behind his mask. "You have a daughter."

I blinked tired eyes, his words not sinking in right away. "Daughter?" I croaked. "Did you say *daughter*?"

"Daughter," the doctor confirmed as the nurse took the baby.

"But we were told we'd have two boys," Aidan protested.

"Yeah," I said in bemusement. "We ordered two boys."

The doctor let out a chuckle. "It happens all the time with twins. One baby hides behind the other, so you can't always get a good read on a sonogram. Parts get confused, and so here we are."

Aidan looked at me in disbelief.

An hour later, it was just the four of us resting in the room. I cradled both babies in my arms. One wore a blue cap, the other pink. My gaze kept bouncing between the two of them, afraid that while I was staring at one, the other would do something I'd miss.

"Well, Sib Vicious," he teased. "We have two children."

"Yes, we do."

"They need names."

"Agamemnon doesn't really work without Murga-troyd," I commented, staring down at our daughter. "I don't think it's fair to name a girl Murgatroyd."

"I don't think it's fair to name a boy that, either." He grinned, chuckling softly.

"Not the way to win," I teased.

He sat on the end of the hospital bed, looking exhausted but happy. He'd been such a champ. He was there for me for every moment of labor, rubbing my back, trying to distract me in between contractions. He was the best husband I could've ever hoped for.

I dreamily stared at him for a moment.

"What?" he asked, his hand going to his chin. "Do I have something on my face?"

"No. You look perfect. I just—I really love you."

"I really love you, too." He smiled and then said, "So, I had an idea. What if I name one and you name one?"

"I like it."

"Each of us gets veto power though—you can damage a kid for life if you screw up their name too much."

"How many vetoes?"

"Two. Each."

I nodded. "Okay. But who names which one?"

"Rock, paper, scissors, obviously."

"How am I supposed to use my hands? My arms are kind of full."

"Just say your answer aloud, okay?"

"Yes, okay," I agreed.

"First round is to see who names our daughter…"

One, two, three—

I said *rock* just as he laid his hand down flat.

Aidan had won.

"I was thinking Sophia Edith. But we'll call her Sophie."

"Sophia Edith Kincaid. Sophie Kincaid." I nodded, my eyes misting. "I love it. I really do."

"And our son? What are we naming him?" Aidan's own eyes looked a little watery.

I thought for a moment and then I said, "Oliver. Oliver Philip."

"Yes." Aidan peered down at our son. "He looks like an Oliver."

My eyes began to close, but then shot open. "Uh oh."

"What's wrong?" Aidan asked, his voice already sounding panicky.

"One, or maybe both of your children just peed on me."

Aidan started to laugh.

"Be quiet. It's not funny."

That only made him laugh harder. "*Sibby Does Motherhood.*"

I sighed. "Who's going to read that book?"

Aidan leaned over and kissed my lips before looking down at our babies. "This is about to get so good."

# A Quick Guide To Yiddish

*Bubbe*: Grandmother.

*Chutzpah*: Impudence.

*Gefilte Fish*: A dish of stewed or baked stuffed fish, or of fish cakes boiled in a fish or vegetable broth and usually served chilled.

*Gribenes*: Crispy chicken on goose skin cracklings with fried onions.

*Hamantaschen*: Triangular shaped cookie filled with poppy seed, fruits, or nuts.

*Kibbitz*: Chit chat.

*Kugel*: A sweet or savory noodle pudding.

*Latke*: Potato pancake.

*Mazel tov*: Congratulations.

*Mensch:* A person of integrity and honor.

*Mishpacha*: An entire family network compromising relatives by blood and marriage and sometimes including close friends.

*Tuchus*: Slang for butt or rear-end.

*Verklempt*: Overcome with emotion.

*Zayde*: Grandfather.

# Additional Works

**Writing as Samantha Garman**

The Sibby Series:
*Queen of Klutz (Book 1)*
*Sibby Slicker (Book 2)*

*From Stardust to Stardust*

**Writing as Emma Slate**

SINS Series:
*Sins of a King (Book 1)*
*Birth of a Queen (Book 2)*
*Rise of a Dynasty (Book 3)*
*Dawn of an Empire (Book 4)*

Ember Series (SINS Series Spinoff):
*Ember (Book 1)*
*Burn (Book 2)*
*Ashes (Book 3)*

Web Series:
*Web of Innocence (Book 1)*
*Web of Deception (Book 2)*

## About the Author

Samantha Garman was a waitress in Manhattan for many moons. On her last day of work she did the Chicken Dance.

It's possible there's a video of it on YouTube...

71879313R00198

Made in the USA
Columbia, SC
28 August 2019